T0288778

the
LEARNING
Curves

{ of }

VANESSA
PARTRIDGE

CLARE STRAHAN

ALLEN&UNWIN
SYDNEY · MELBOURNE · AUCKLAND · LONDON

First published by Allen & Unwin in 2018

Allen & Unwin
83 Alexander Street
Crows Nest NSW 2065
Australia
Phone: (61 2) 8425 0100
Email: info@allenandunwin.com
Web: www.allenandunwin.com

A catalogue record for this book is available from the National Library of Australia

ISBN 978 1 76029 679 7

For teaching resources, explore www.allenandunwin.com/resources/for-teachers

Cover and text design by Astred Hicks, Design Cherry
Set in 11pt/16pt Adobe Caslon Pro by Midland Typesetters, Australia
This book was printed in April 2019 by Griffin Press, part of Ovato, Australia

10 9 8 7 6 5 4 3 2

For my nieces Taya, Holly, Jacci and Em
& for my daughter, Georgia, always.

Remembering my lovely dad who, at the end,
after Mum and us, loved Nature and Music best.
John Joseph Strahan
1929–2015

I acknowledge that this book was written
on Wurundjeri and Boon Wurrung country in Victoria
and Gundungurra country in New South Wales,
and pay my respects to Elders past, present and future.

CHAPTER 1

'Our moral obligation is to strive for exemplary behaviour that reflects our earnest commitment to the highest ideals.' Mrs Bhatt gestures to the polished beams and oak-panelled walls of the assembly hall and then to the yawning, fidgeting students keen for the last half-day to be over and for summer to begin. 'We who are the lucky recipients of such bounty,' she exhorts gently, 'are honour-bound to uphold the excellent reputation of our great school, even over the break.'

When Dr Olga Skutenko nods sternly at me over her glasses, I sit up straighter. I can't help it, despite the fact that she stares like that at everybody, even Mrs Bhatt. I am doubly convinced that it *is* a 'prestigious institution' and that I *will* strive harder to be a fine representative even while on holidays. The Big O looks away and I breathe again because if she knew what *else* was rattling around my brain, I'd die and so might she.

What I *should* be doing is going over the carefully crafted speech I'm about to give explaining my model Earth and accompanying musical composition intended to portray the interplay between the planet (hydrosphere, biosphere, lithosphere) and its atmosphere (troposphere, stratosphere, mesosphere, thermosphere and exosphere) but what I *am* doing is imagining what I'd say if Darith Laurie asked me to sleep with him.

Yes. That's what I'd say. *Yes, yes, yes.*

He's got a prime spot in the front row because he won Senior Cricketer of the Year. The first three rows are reclaimed pews from the old chapel and entirely uncomfortable, yet he's perfectly relaxed. How do boys manage that particular upright slouch that seems both stillness and action? And how do they dare take up so much room with their legs? If girls sat like that we'd be accused of debauchery.

Still, Darith's legs are the perfect length of long; and his unruly hair is the perfect length of long, too, curled rebelliously against the shirt-collar of his summer uniform. No wonder he's the 'Cultural Relationships' poster boy on the school website, even if he is the only Indigenous kid on the cricket team.

He and my brother ramped up their friendship from cricket buddies to bromance at the beginning of last year. One day when Ash was unexpectedly late home, Darith and I spent the whole time looking at my *Encyclopedia of Animal Science* and talking about everything in the world. When Ash finally arrived and heard what we'd been doing, he said, 'Oh no, you poor bastard,' but Darith only smiled. 'It was kinda fun,' he said, and that's when I knew that I'd love him forever.

The pair of them are always ranting on about politics. Darith is so kind but he tore *strips* off the chaplain in front of the whole cricket team for assuming he must be a scholarship-boy. If you ask me, he's been just the bad influence Ash needs to keep his mind off how broken up he is about our parents getting divorced.

Not that anyone asks me.

Darith catches me staring and gives me a 'good one, Van' nod, almost imperceptible.

At least I'm safe to blush. The whole school is crammed in here and I'd be amazed if there was one person who'd imagine for a minute that I've been having lustful fantasies about doing it with Darith Laurie.

Including Darith Laurie.

Not that I'd ask them.

ME: Mrs Bhatt, do you think I'm a raving sex-o-maniac?

MRS BHATT: Why, yes, Vanessa. Your sensible plaits and interest in philosophy have made that perfectly clear.

Suyin, who only has a week-and-a-half left before she gets her braces off, is my favourite friend at school but even she wouldn't know.

ME: Suyin, do you know I want to have sex with Darith so badly that sometimes I touch myself just thinking about it?

SUYIN: Eeeew.

We don't talk about sex and certainly not about having it by yourself. We talk about music, phobias, interesting facts, philosophy, books we've read, and sometimes men we've seen in films. Suyin's got a crush on Ben Affleck, which I think is unnatural because he's about three thousand years old. I much prefer Felix Mendelssohn . . . who, to be fair, has been dead since 1847. Anyway, we never really talk about sex. Not about wanting to have it. Sometimes we talk about how girls *shouldn't* want to have it.

And then I feel like screaming.

ME: Suyin, do you ever feel like screaming?

SUYIN: Van, vocal cords are muscle tissue – screaming isn't good for them. I don't want to damage my larynx.

ME: Do you know what your larynx looks like if they stick a camera down your throat? A vagina. A vagina in your neck.

Suyin wants to be an opera singer but if I told her that, she'd scream.

I'm susceptible to suggestion so I probably shouldn't be thinking about screaming, or about how I'm not even sure if I've ever said 'vagina' out loud, because my name's going to get called soon and I'll have to get up there and make my award-acceptance speech and what if I blurt out *VAGINA* in front of the whole school?

I'd like to thank the school for giving me this opportunity to enter the Middle School Science competition and make a model of my VAGINA. I'm pleased and humbled to have won, especially because all the other model VAGINAS were—

'Vanessa Partridge,' calls Mrs Bhatt, leading the applause and turning to me, sitting behind her on my special chair, facing the audience. Well, I say special chair but it's exactly the same as all the other chairs except it's one of a little row on the stage. This is the only scenario where the six of us high-achieving-dorks up here are the winners and the sea of students-with-lives out there in the auditorium are, presumably, the losers. Mrs Bhatt is proud of me. 'Well done, Vanessa,' she says into the microphone.

Vanessa. It's not a name I can love. It sounds like a brand of sanitary product, if you ask me. Or a nineteenth-century heroine if you ask my father, who named me after his great-grandmother, Vanessa, who was English, poor, died of consumption, and buried in an unmarked grave.

I shake Mrs Bhatt's hand. She awards me the Perspex trophy and it's shaped like . . . well, like a vagina, or vulva, to be technical about it. 'I'd like to thank the school for, er . . . M-middle School Science Award, um, the school. All the others,' I stutter. 'Earth's eight spheres and music.' I think it's meant to be the shape of folded wings. The wings of science? Or is it hands? 'All the other entries were. Well done.' There are beads of sweat on my upper lip and Mrs Bhatt is looking peculiar. 'Thank you,' I manage.

Dr Skutenko turns away from the proceedings and I choke back tears because I am a high achiever and that was not the excellent speech Mrs Bhatt and I worked so hard on. In my rush to get back to my chair before I start crying or shout *VAGINA* and then have to kill myself, I lurch into the winning-project display. My earth-globe teeters and rolls off its stand and off the stage and when I lunge for it, my vulva-award flies out of my hands and lands at Darith's feet. A river of laughter snickers over me, swelling to a flood as, mortified, I twist away, trip over the microphone cord and flash my giant school-regulation underpants to everyone in the hall.

Darith hands the globe up to Mrs Bhatt. 'Don't cry, Van,' he says. I'm pretty sure he's suppressing laughter too but his smile is so kind, I sniff back the sobs and almost laugh myself. He hands me the trophy. 'Careful with that,' he says.

Mrs Bhatt hovers. 'Thank you, that's very considerate. Now both of you, back to your seats.'

Suyin pats me on the back, waiting patiently for order to resume so she can collect her Middle School Maths Award.

Well, I say 'order to resume' but I mean various teachers finally managing to suppress the chaos. Thank God it's the last day. No one will remember my undies by next year. Surely.

I wipe my face with the tissues Mrs Bhatt stuffed into my hand and sneak a grateful peek at Darith but he's leaning over the back of his pew talking to the Year Eleven girl behind him. I comfort myself by silently reciting lesser-known definitions – like that the tip of the middle finger is called a 'dactylion', and then the categories of finials, but that leads to remembering I wanted to be a haberdasher when I was little and that the other day *I told Darith that.*

This is why I'm destined never to have sex with anyone, ever. Not that Darith was surprised to hear me say something so stupid and random, as if I were answering a question he'd never asked. He's known me a long time. I was ten and working in my vegetable patch in my secret garden when Ash first brought him home from cricket practice.

I say secret garden but I mean the sandpit.

'I like your overalls,' he'd said.

'That's just my little sister. Ignore her.'

Ash could be so dismissive, even at twelve.

I'd have done anything my big brother told me to when I was ten, like that time I picked my nose and wiped the snot on Darith's arm. I groan and stuff my face into the tissues to think of the ninety-seven thousand other anti-alluring things I've done over the five years that Darith and I have known each other.

When I look up, Ash is squinting at me as if he can't figure out what species I am. I surreptitiously flip him the dactylion and shake my award as if to say 'you're one of these, mate' – but now I'm thinking of its *other* name. Why is the swear word for female genitalia the insult of all insults, the most offensive thing we can possibly imagine saying? My only satisfaction is the brief confusion that crosses my brother's face before he looks away in disdain.

Suyin's award is also shaped like a vulva but she doesn't seem to notice and her acceptance speech goes off without a hitch.

My mother insisted on the 'ordinary family holiday' every summer and even though we spent last Christmas in divorce-court-hell, it looks like this year Dad's going to cherish the flame, probably just to annoy her. They spent a lot of time (and money) with the lawyers over who got the beach house and Dad won, so we're heading down there today.

I make a beeline for the parents' lounge to show Dad my award (he can't possibly know what I think it looks like) and apologise for my less-than-perfect speech (before anyone else does) but he only nods at it and says, 'Well done,' and Rochelle puts it on the bench, not even in the display cabinet, and they turn back to the real business of the afternoon: Ash sitting at the dining table like an interview candidate.

He's been photographed at a rally with his *FREE PALESTINE* T-shirt and a raised fist and someone with 'Ashton's best interests at heart' has brought it to Dad's attention.

My brother seems disconcertingly cool, given the circumstances. 'Where did you get this?' he says, as if our father were the one under scrutiny.

Dad brushes him off with a wave. 'I hardly think that's the point.'

'I think it's *exactly* the point.' Again that calm voice, as though he, Ash, were the adult.

Dad's face pulses red. 'Who's this guy?' He points at something on the iPad.

Ash leans back and crosses his feet at the ankles. 'How should I know? It's a rally. There were hundreds of people there.'

A strange stillness comes to my father's face, mirrored by Ash, staring at his shoes. 'He followed you home.'

Ash looks up. 'How do you know?' He tips forwards with his accusation. 'Are you spying on me?'

'We're just watching out for you. There are—' Dad swallows. 'Business concerns.'

'Dirty business.'

'What the hell's that supposed to—'

'Look,' Ash cuts him off. 'What's your actual problem?'

'A beeline isn't only a straight line,' I blurt into their strained faces because a) that's the kind of thing I pipe up with when things become brittle enough to snap and b) words snag in my brain and I wonder about them a lot, something only Mrs Bhatt seems to understand. 'Bee-lining is bee hunting, too,' I add, by way of explanation.

A blank space opens around me, as if everyone's suddenly three steps away.

'Let's go on holiday,' Rochelle suggests cheerily into the apparent confusion, shooing us along to pack with one hand and sliding the other up my father's back. 'There's no real harm done, Simon.'

Distracted, Dad puts his arm around her. Ash pushes back from the table to fume off to his room.

'They're hunting the honey, really,' I say. 'But you can't get honey without bees.'

Dad kisses Rochelle's fingertips. 'I'm worried about the boy,' he says.

Dad kept us and the new nanny, and gave Mum a lot of money and the dog. The 'new family' are staying on in the house until it sells: me, Ash, Dad and Rochelle – who's only ten years older than Ashton and not the nanny anymore. She bounced into the family fifteen months before her self-described 'fairytale romance' with Dad became public. I think the rationale for hiring a 'young person' was because we were a bit old for a nanny when Nanny retired. A turn of events of which I still don't approve; I mean, how can people be allowed to 'retire' from our family? But it is true that what we kids needed was more of a nanny/housekeeper/personal assistant. When it comes to that side of things, Rochelle hasn't been a great loss. When it comes to the stepmother side of things, she hasn't been a great win, either.

Mum took it well, when Dad announced his intentions towards Rochelle. That's what he called it: his 'intentions' and they were, apparently, *towards* her which, naturally, also meant *away* from my mother.

Well, I say Mum took it well but what I mean is neither of them would move out and Dad insisted Rochelle stay too, so we spent over a year living like actors in some kind of torturous *Brady Bunch* episode where Mr Brady was sleeping in the guest bedroom with a much younger and sexier version of Alice and Mrs Brady took up drinking and listening to Lucinda Williams's 'Joy' at full volume in the middle of the night, which was, no offence to Lucinda Williams, not joyous.

One night, Ash and I couldn't stand Mum stumbling about and crying any longer but when we tried to make her go to bed, she wouldn't and snarled, 'Don't call me Mum ever again. Call me Marion,' at us over her vodka, which might not have been so bad if her name wasn't Fiona.

The day the newlyweds got back from their honeymoon was the day Marion-Mum finally moved out. Dad said, 'Vanessa's come to terms with it, and you will too, Fiona. You wait and see.' He looked straight at me and said, 'Haven't you, Nessie?' as if he was the most misunderstood little boy in the world and the only thing between him and utter despair was me saying I was on his side so I lied and said, 'Of course I have, Dad,' and he smiled and said, 'That's my girl,' but Mum winced as if I'd punched her. She turned away from us, gathered up the last of her bits and pieces, gave us a general wave and headed out the door. She didn't say anything except, 'Come on,' to the dog, but Roger Federer didn't want to go and she had to drag him by the collar and shove him into the back of the car.

I haven't seen either of them since. For nine weeks and three days it's been just a text message every morning that says:

Hi Nessie, thkng of u, luv x Mum

And one every night that says:

Xxx

The same ones, every day, no matter what I write back – not even when I tell her it's 'thnkng' not 'thkng' and that either way there's no good reason to leave out the vowels.

I'm hoping it's because of her general uselessness with technology. She's made knowing nothing about it into an art form, part of her dinner party performance (we all had one: Ash's was being a chip-off-the-old-super-sporty-block, mine playing the cello). 'Technology is your father's thing,' Mum would say, which is true. He's made his fortune from it.

We call it a family holiday but Dad will be entertaining at the house: business people, international 'friends'. Dad's always working these days: holding meetings, clinching deals, or whatever it is that he does, but he still has time to make sure I've been practising. It's the highlight of his year, he says, when we play for his friends and associates. I don't mind being trotted out every New Year's Eve to play the cello (by myself, since Ashton deliberately smashed his violin last year and they haven't been able to beg, bribe or bully him into picking up the new one) but it is annoying not to be allowed to stay and enjoy the party. This year the song choice is mine. I wanted to play Mendelssohn's Opus 109 – the song without words he wrote for the legendary Lisa Cristiani back in 1845 when a girl cellist was a rare thing – but I can only play the beginning and the end with any certainty, so I'll probably play Saint-Saëns *The Swan*, which is also hard but I don't care about it quite as much.

Dad texts me:

You'll have to do your own packing. Luggage in the car by five-thirty.

A few minutes later, he sends another one telling me to hurry up.

He hasn't replaced Rochelle yet because there hasn't been a nanny/housekeeper/personal assistant that she approves of, or 'of whom she approves' to get technical about it (which Rochelle wouldn't). Ash and I have started to notice all the things that Rochelle the housekeeper used to do that Rochelle the stepmother has 'no intention of ever doing again' that we never noticed Rochelle the house-keeper doing in the first place and subsequently, things have become pretty chaotic down our end of the house. God help the removalists when the time comes, that's all I can say. Luckily, it'll have a good clean while we're gone: the annual 'dose of salts'. Unless Marion's cancelled the cleaners.

She might have, out of spite.

It's refreshing to be in charge of my own suitcase for once but I can't think what Mum'd want me to pack. Without her here to supervise, it's like she's more here than ever. I jot that down in my *Book of Observations* for Philosophy Club: *Absence is presence.*

The red-poppies-on-chartreuse suitcase lies open but empty on my bed like an invitation. I curl up in it, cocooned by its stiff sides and the smell of lavender bags, and stare out the window.

Dear Marion, did you always want to leave us or is it something that came over you quickly, like a rash?

Vanessa, darling, I didn't always want to leave you but I couldn't resist the opportunity to spoil things for your father.

I say Dad kept us but in actual fact, it wasn't in the newly-weds' plan for Mum to take the money and run – without the children. The only good thing about my father ending up stuck with us was Rochelle's bewilderment at this unfortunate turn of events. Mind you, she's not the only one.

I told Ash I felt like a leppy, the week after Mum left and Dad announced she'd dropped the dog off with her sister in Sydney and gone overseas, renting some one-bedroom apartment in Paris. Aunty Sue reckons she doesn't know the exact address. I guess Mum wants to make sure Dad doesn't ship us over there. 'Your mother's gone to "find herself",' Dad said in a shell-shocked way, as if he didn't quite believe it himself.

'A leper?' Ash said accusingly, as if that were the last straw. 'You feel like a leper?'

'No, not a leper – why would I feel like a leper?'

Honestly, at times he could be ridiculous. I wasn't a leper; it wasn't *my* fault our parents' marriage had broken up. If it was anybody's fault, it was Ash's: quitting orchestra *and* tennis, letting his drinking buddies trash the house and then nearly getting arrested with Darith Laurie for graffing at the school.

'It's what they call an orphaned calf in America. Let me show you,' I explained, with a patience he could have been grateful for if you ask me, but he had no time for the *Cowboy Dictionary of Cattle Terms* and later, when I thought about it, I did feel a bit like a leper.

Why did you take Roger, Mum?

Well, your father loves that dog.

It's true, Dad does love the dog – named after his number one hero. He texts me again: we're leaving in ten minutes. I rouse myself out of the suitcase (it's harder to get out than it was to get in) and dig through the clothes in my drawers and on my floordrobe but there's not one alluring thing. Darith Laurie is coming on holidays with us and I possess not one alluring thing.

I take stock of myself in the mirrored wall of my walk-in wardrobe. I say I don't have one alluring thing but I *do* have my breasts which are somewhat alluring, even if I do say so myself. It's as if all of a sudden they went berserk. My friends all got theirs before me and we talked about them on and off – embarrassing conversations with tape-measure-wielding shop attendants, things like that – but I was still an A-cup then and thought the whole thing would pass me by. But no. Now they're bigger than Rochelle's.

My hair is brown, like Mum's. Not bottle-blonde like Rochelle's, or the girls Ash dates. I can't see what he sees in them. Well, when I say I can't see what he sees in them, I mean they are thin and pretty and hang on his every word without contributing too many of their own. These things may well be contributing factors to what, indeed, he sees in them.

I am not thin. Not in the way *they* are thin. I've tried starving myself but I couldn't do it. Food: I love it too much. The girls at Ash's recent spate of 'motherless son' and 'goodbye housie' parties are martyrs; I've always felt it a service to put them out of their misery by eating their share of the food before Ash finds me and sends me to bed.

I suppose my breasts could be alluring if I wore something other than neck-to-knee sacks. My mother had firm ideas about what a girl of my age should wear and it's true, I did love those cheesy clothes when I was a kid. Mum loved to see me 'dressed sensibly' so much that I turned thirteen, then fourteen, then fifteen but my clothes stayed twelve. I suppose I let them. Fashion seems another country altogether, where most of my peers have gone to live; a land of brands and reputations. I haven't wanted to put in the effort. I've had other fish to fry, like debating whether we even exist at all. Suyin's convinced Plato is trying to tell us that we're all holograms.

But even an utter absence of flair becomes a style in the end. My long undyed plaits, baggy uniform and hairy legs have become my 'look' as surely as Rachel Emerson's thigh-gap and super-bronze fake tan have become hers. I guess

I'm lucky *my* look has never landed me in hospital, despite the fact that Ash repeatedly suggests I need a psychiatrist.

I pull my uniform against my body and reveal the softness of my belly, the pudding swell of my shoulders. Maybe if I were angular and spare, Darith might notice I was a woman? I slide my hand across my collarbones, wishing it was his.

'Vain, or what?'

I drop myself like a hot potato. How long has Ash been watching me stare at my own reflection? 'Creep,' I say.

He bows, as if I've offered him a compliment. I step closer to the mirror and fossick near my hairline, squeezing a blackhead. My brother, undeterred, leans on the wall. 'So, what's going on?'

I flush, as if Ash can somehow beam into my secret thoughts. We were close enough, when we were little, for me to think it possible. United, probably, under the onslaught that was our parents 'carving out a future in the world of business and culture'.

'Influence is everything,' Dad likes to say. 'Influence is everything.'

Ash used to lead the way on our adventures, when he still wanted to take me on adventures, that is: armed with a stick, commanding me and the dog, warning us to look out for snakes. But Roger's in Sydney now, a hostage to my parents' cagamosis and Ash dried up a few years ago, shrunk away from me as if I were contagious.

He jiggles a leg. 'Well?'

'Cagamosis means unhappy marriage,' I say, to check if

he is indeed reading my mind. His look of incomprehension confirms he isn't. A mercy, given the lascivious state of my thoughts these days, and nights, with Darith practically living with us.

'You haven't even got changed.' He pushes himself off the wall and away from me. 'Are you nearly ready to go?'

'Yes.'

'Good, because Louise is loading up and I don't want to get stuck sitting in the car with *them* waiting for *you*.'

Dad's personal assistant and golf caddy is one of the family; like the good PA she is, Louise 'gets on with things'. She's never seemed particularly pleased or particularly angry, and the only time I've ever seen her cry is when David Bowie died. But she's made no secret that she isn't happy about the betrayal of Fiona and the birth of Marion. 'Your mother dedicated her life to your father,' she said to me, tearily, at Dad and Rochelle's wedding, after one too many of the boutique pale ales she'd commissioned for the event. 'She worshipped the ground he walked on.'

Short and pear-shaped but strong as an ox, I bet she's chucking his stuff in the back of the car like an airport baggage handler in economy, as Dad might joke – if it were someone else's luggage. If Louise damages his Alfred Dunhills, there'll be trouble.

'You won't get stuck with them,' I tell Ash.

He swings away. 'Hurry up.'

I shovel a few books, my old teddy, a hairbrush and all the clean underwear I can find into the suitcase and chuck in my favourite PJs for tonight – the top says *Good Grief* and Snoopy is fighting the Red Baron on the bottoms – arm-sweep everything on my bathroom vanity into the matching toiletries bag, clip and lock.

I could have brought a friend, too, but even when we were younger my friends from school didn't quite gel with my friends at the beach and, as I explained to Dad, I hang out with Suyin all year but I only get Kelsey for the holidays. He said it was all right as long as I promised to keep up my cello practice (no one practises more than Suyin). 'She does her old man proud,' he told Rochelle when we were discussing it, his arm around my shoulder for a squeeze. Rochelle practically rubbed her face on him like a cat and purred, 'Not so old,' which completely missed the point if you ask me.

I text Dad that I'm ready. Me and Darith sitting next to each other in the back of the Range Rover all the way to the beach. Oh my hat, I'm beyond ready.

With all the tension in the car, the drive down isn't as much fun as I'd hoped, even sitting in the middle with Darith's leg knocking into mine. I had also underestimated the dampening effect of wearing my school uniform while on holidays. 'Want to listen to the surf report?' Dad calls back over his seat. 'Looking forward to some waves?'

Given that I've never been invited to go surfing with my father, I presume this invitation is not for me but Ash doesn't answer. Darith glances at him, then me, then out the window.

'I mean the podcast from this morning,' Dad elaborates encouragingly.

The awful silence stretches further than I can bear. 'That's a good idea, Dad,' I say.

'Yes,' chirps Rochelle. 'Put on the surf report.'

I jot down *distraction is cowardice* in my *Book of Observations* for Philosophy Club. I say Philosophy Club but I mean me, Suyin and Martin.

Ash grabs the *Book of Observations* out of my hands but Darith grabs it off *him* and hands it back to me, so now it's a holy book and I have to restrain myself from kissing it, and him.

'Thanks,' I manage.

'You're such a little suck,' says Ash.

I reckon I know the moment my brother started to hate our father: a blip of impending chaos embedded on my childhood radar. Years before Rochelle, my mother threw her drink in the face of a woman called Barbara at one of our parents' parties. Our father shook Mum by her arm in front of a room full of guests. Barbara was holding her hands in front of her mouth and looking down at her dress as if that patch of wet was the most shocking thing in the universe. Dad put his hand on the small of Barbara's back and said to her, 'I'm so sorry about this,' and then to Mum, 'Go upstairs. You're embarrassing yourself.'

'I want to go to the toilet,' I said, putting my eight-year-old hand in Ash's ten-year-old grip. He pulled me through the chastened throng, all eyes on the scene between our parents, yet somehow averted, to canapés, champagne glasses, the floor. It was only a moment, I guess, in retrospect, but it's crystallised in my memory like a slow-motion scene from a movie watched through tuxedoed legs and a lady's swinging black-sequined handbag. Ash stopped dragging me when our mother reached out a trembling hand and placed it on Dad's lapel. It was a quiet gesture, and so nervous, and Ash squeezed my hand a little tighter. In my memory we held our breaths, willing Dad to put his hand over Mum's, pat it kindly, say he was sorry, tell her everything would be all right – tell us, too, but he pushed her hand away. 'For God's sake, Fiona,' he said. 'You're delusional.'

And that was when I wet my pants.

For God's sake. What does it even mean?

Ash was different with Dad after that. Maybe no one else noticed because he wasn't disobedient or wilful – that didn't happen until he was fifteen and decided our father was the corporate devil – but *before* that time Ash's voice had buzzed with pride when he talked about our dad, a pride I'd felt too. *After*, there was a flatness to it. A scorn.

I say maybe no one else noticed but the fact is, Dad did, but 'doesn't know what has gotten into the boy'.

To make it up to my father, I've worked hard to excel at school, made a fuss of everything he's given me (even when I got extra cello lessons for Christmas the same year Ash got to pilot a helicopter) and not yelled at him about Rochelle or Mum (though I couldn't help crying when Mum drove off with the dog), but despite the fact I'm apparently his 'number one girl', a number one *girl* is never enough. Nothing I do makes his face light up the way it does when he gets one tiny spark of affection from Ash; one shared joke, even accidental on Ash's part, or the unavoidable camaraderie of sharing the corporate box at the footy.

But the fact is, our father is a digamist and Ash won't forgive him for it.

'What the F is a digamist?' Ash asked when I shared this observation.

'Someone who divorces and marries again.'

'Dickheadamist, more like it.'

And we laughed, which was nice, because up until then we'd mostly been crying.

'Did you make that up, Van?'

'No, it's a real word.'

'Fair enough but never say it again.' And he patted me on the head a little too hard and I hated him all over again.

We've been able to see the sea for a while and at last we turn into the entrance of the property. Only a few kilometres and we'll be at the house built by Mum's great-grandfather, Albert, who raced cars and spent time in America and France and fell in love with all things art nouveau, which means curves and flowers and a longing for beauty. Mum says that in 1911, when it was built out here in the boon-docks, Shearwater was considered a 'folly', but has stood the test of time. And it's beautiful, still, even if the upkeep is outrageous because of the salt and wind; long outlasting Pa-Albert who died at forty-three having never quite recovered from the injuries he received as an officer in the 'Great War'.

With its render graduating from orange to yellow, the house rises like the sun at the end of the drive on the far side of a roundabout planted with roses in various shades of red. Kelsey and I used to play in the rose garden when we were littler and lower to the ground. We were the Rose Queens and ruled over the Kingdom of the Ladybird People. Our palace was the memorial garden seat with its embossed plaque engraved with Pa-Albert's name and dates and embraced by the long hair of two beautiful women all twined about with flowers, aka the Rose Queens, aka Kelsey and me.

The closer we get to the house, the more swamped I am by my surprise plan to buy an entirely new wardrobe while I'm here. What if Dad's happy for me to spend the holiday alternating between my school uniform and my one pair of pyjamas? What if he totally loses his mind?

'Oh, Simon, it's gorgeous,' says Rochelle and I remember that she hasn't been here before – summer used to be her time off, when she was staff, a tradition left over from Nanny who always went home to her sister's for Christmas.

No escaping us now, Rochelle.

She reaches out and strokes the back of my father's head and a devil perches on my shoulder to whisper *convince her to take us shopping as a bonding thing.* Rochelle's made quite a few disparaging remarks about my wardrobe (and floordrobe, for that matter) so she might like to put Dad's money where her mouth is. It could be our girly secret and he wouldn't ever have to know about the empty suitcase. She's an expert at secrets.

Despite the fact that my father is now holding Rochelle's hand on his lap and they're laughing together like creeps, driving through the stunted bush and tall gums in the dusky light and glimpsing the house up ahead feels good. I'm glad to be back here. Darith and Ash loosen up and start fake-punching each other across me.

Shearwater has it all – the bush, the beach, a pool – even its own caravan park.

When I say its own caravan park, I mean that the Lepskis have leased forty acres of the property for their caravan park since not long after Shearwater was built, because Great-great-grandpa Lepski saved Pa-Albert's life in the war. This was a good thing but not just for my great-great-grandfather: Kelsey Lepski is probably the best friend I have.

I say probably but I mean definitely.

When we tumble into the foyer and dump our gear on the black polished-concrete floor, the place seems empty and the electricity is off. Darith says, 'Woah,' and trots halfway up the grand spiral staircase with its beautiful wrought-iron balustrade that tells the story of Orpheus and Eurydice in illustrated panels, and leads to a landing that overlooks the foyer. As the bride dies, that particular Greek myth seems especially tragic considering Shearwater is used for weddings the rest of the year.

The upstairs consists of two 'wings' accessed from the landing and a couple of hallways. We kids have the Red wing with its movie lounge and music room; Mum and Dad have the Turquoise, which has the huge master bedroom that's used as the bridal suite. Well, when I say wing, I mean half-a-dozen ensuite bedrooms, not our own kitchen staff or anything. And when I say Mum and Dad, I guess now I mean Dad and Rochelle. Louise stays downstairs in the original staff accommodation, close to the kitchen, laundry, reception area and formal dining room.

Only the chef and a skeleton staff stay on over the summer to keep everything ticking along. But nobody emerges to greet us and tell us what's for dinner.

I suspect this may be Marion's doing. I still can't believe she let Dad have Shearwater in the settlement but when I asked her about it she said, 'We should never have sold him Sue's share. Your father's gone mad.' I changed the subject to her precious Melbourne Symphony Orchestra so she'd stop crying without finding out what Dad going 'mad' meant, beyond the obvious fact that the pair of them had started treating each other like hostile strangers, which did seem like madness considering they'd been married for twenty-five years.

'I'll call Louise,' says Dad, his hand sliding around Rochelle to cup her hip. 'And while she's sorting things out, we'll go for a wander along the beachfront and then out for dinner. Vanessa, put on something respectable.'

A heaviness takes me over. I'm a person made of play-dough, barely upright. 'I can't.'

Dad withdraws his encircling arm. 'Can't what?'

I may have made a terrible mistake. I love my father but he has what one might call a 'short fuse'. The boys flop onto a foyer couch to watch.

'Can't get changed,' I confess. 'Unless you consider pyjamas respectable, which in essence they are, but not when you're going out for dinner. Besides,' I add, as chirpily as possible under the circumstances, 'I'd rather find Kelsey and could probably stay for dinner with the Lepskis.'

Ash sits forwards and asks, 'Didn't you bring any clothes?' the same way I might ask the ranger a question about the migration patterns of mutton-birds, a subject for which I have more than a passing curiosity.

'I'm looking forward to seeing the mutton-birds this year, Dad,' I say.

My father stands to attention, nods at my suitcase and folds his arms. 'Open it.'

'Well, you see—'

'Open it.'

Rochelle puts her hand on his arm. 'Simon—'

'Go upstairs and get changed, Rochelle.'

Ash and I exchange a look: he may as well have called her Fiona. But Rochelle isn't Fiona. 'I'm happy with what I'm wearing,' she says firmly.

'*I* like what you're wearing,' I pipe up. 'And, well ...' I unzip my suitcase and flip open the lid. 'I'm hoping you'll take me shopping because I've outgrown my clothes.'

Ash and Darith snort with laughter. I'd forgotten my 'empty' suitcase would be scattered with 'sensible' cotton undies, not to mention Ted doing bear yoga draped with one of my stupid flesh-coloured bras. I slam it shut, sure my face is a beacon, but I think the plan is actually going well.

Rochelle claps her hands. 'I'd love to.'

But Dad growls, 'For God's sake, Vanessa, I expect more from you than this nonsense,' and the weirdest sense of shame washes over me. All I need now is to wet myself.

Ash lurches to his feet. 'We're out of here. We'll walk down and get fish and chips and see you back here later.'

Darith stands too, hands in his pockets. 'You coming, Van?'

Dad may look like an active volcano but I don't care: my heart is full of stars. Ash swings in next to me and says, 'Can Vanessa come with us? We won't be late,' and the stars flame up, like sparklers. Ash is going to save me. It's been a while since he asked our father for anything other than cash.

'I don't think so, Ashton.' Dad pulls out his wallet and hands him a fifty, then adds another twenty. 'You boys be back by ten-thirty.'

I say I don't care that my dad looks like an active human volcano but what I really mean is, I'm scared.

'It's okay, Van,' says Darith. 'We'll bring you back something.' He squares up. 'If that's all right with you, Simon?'

'Yes,' says Rochelle. 'That's all right with us.'

There's a tectonic rumble at that but Dad's got his eyes on me. 'What's all this?' he says as the boys sidle out.

'I need new clothes. That's all.'

'You have plenty of clothes. I've seen you wearing them.'

'It's not that big a deal, is it?' I don't see how it is. A little sneaky, I suppose. 'It's not like I'm asking for a helicopter,' I joke.

Dad doesn't laugh. 'There have been a lot of sacrifices, Vanessa,' he says, 'to give you and your brother every advantage in life but you've never struck me as *spoiled*.'

As if being spoiled is some sort of crime.

I feel a rumble of my own. 'You gave Rochelle money to buy a whole new wardrobe *and* accessories.'

Rochelle smooths her white Carolina Herrera miniskirt. 'That is true, darling.'

'Is *she* spoiled?'

Rochelle stalks away from my accusing finger, clicking on her phone torch and huffing about finding a bathroom.

'Your— Rochelle and I have been through a difficult time. We deserve some happiness without you trying to hijack our first summer holiday as man and wife.'

'*You've* had a difficult time?' I hiss, steam from the crater. 'What? Your honeymoon in America? And why should *she* get to spend Mum's money?'

Dad's face is thunder. 'What did you say?' He catches me by the arm but I can't stop. It's as if something inside me has come unhinged. 'Mum says you robbed her blind, diddling Shearwater out of her. And it's *husband* and wife, husband and wife – we're not in the Dark Ages.'

Move over Vesuvius. My father yanks my arm and I stumble. 'Who the *hell* do you think you are, speaking to me like that?'

I'm Marion's daughter.

'Sorry, Dad,' I whisper.

'Sorry won't cut it, Vanessa . . .'

While he's yelling at me about my 'insufferable disrespect' Dad looks exactly like he used to when he yelled at Mum. If he ever shouted at me, it's now long past the time Mum would have slipped in between us. I'd believed Ash when he said she was chickenshit for not standing up to him, for letting him rage on at her, but now I get it: my father never rails like this at *Ash* and Mum was the bravest woman alive.

How could she leave us?

'. . . and your academic achievements won't get you far if you can't learn to appreciate what you have.' He takes a breath and steps back, letting go of my arm, leaving the red imprint of his fingers. He brushes me off like a dismissed staff member. 'As far as I'm concerned, you can spend the whole holiday in your school uniform.'

High achievers don't take criticism well but they do vow to try harder in the future, which is what I do now in a repetitive, sobbing sort of way.

When I say I don't take criticism well, I mean that when the dust has settled and they've gone out for dinner and left me on the couch with a candle and no phone, so I can think about my behaviour, I consider killing myself.

But I don't know how.

I comfort myself by listing as many categories of rock as I can remember. I've given up on sedimentary and started on metamorphic by the time the boys get back. The fish and chips are cold and my pineapple fritter has congealed. Still, it's funny how it doesn't take long before a bit of company can restore a person's will to live.

This is the worst holiday ever.

After a breakfast as frosty as Rochelle's pearl nail polish, Dad still won't let me go out with the boys or down to Kelsey's. The only thing that makes it bearable is that Louise arrives, dressed in her so-called 'holiday attire' – suit shorts, a short-sleeved shirt, and white knee high socks with sandals; no tie at least – to hand over Guilhermina, my cello, fresh from the luthier.

Happy as I am to see them both, the thought of playing my cello makes me feel tired, as if I were suddenly back at school crapping myself about exams.

But I do love the Mendelssohn and will have to practise the Saint-Saëns if I'm not going to be a complete failure at the New Year's Eve party, and I'm keen to keep working on the opening movement of Elgar's Cello Concerto in E minor. I want to play everything Jacqueline du Pré played, even if I'll never be half as good as she was. Dr Skutenko says I don't have the emotional maturity to pull off the Elgar (or the Mendelssohn, or *The Swan* for that matter) but I say she doesn't have the emotional maturity to cope with me playing anything she hasn't instructed me to play. Anyway, with a mind like mine, Dad says I'm better off studying to be a research scientist, or a linguist; Louise reckons there's more money in creative accountancy.

I trundle the cello down to reception, a big, elegant, airy room next to the kitchen that opens out to a sheltered patio overlooking the pool. The view always takes my breath away and the ocean thunders in the distance. 'Come on, my dear old nemesis,' I whisper, lifting Guilhermina from her coffin.

It feels good to have her between my thighs again.

By the next day, Dad seems to have forgotten about making sure my life is a misery, disappearing with Rochelle to meet guests who are flying in by helicopter and only available for the afternoon. He's certainly forgotten to say goodbye.

It doesn't matter how often I've been here, or the other beaches I've visited, walking the clifftop path that links Shearwater to the Oceanview Camping Park brings a fresh sense of wonder, as if the air has never been breathed and the ocean never before witnessed; only by me, for the first time in all creation. The scrub is a patchwork of textures; miniature rolling hills of salt-resistant succulents dominated by *Carpobrotus rossii* with its plump, diamond-shaped leaves – how on earth did it come to be called pigface? Tufts of coastal grasses rise up like wild muppet hairdos. The vista seems only varieties of green but shy flowers peep here and there: yellow, purple, white, pink-striped. 'It's what beauty is,' I say aloud, parroting my mother, my words snatched by the wind and winged out to sea.

Kelsey's parents have run Oceanview – generally known as the 'funny little caravan park' by everyone except them – all my life. Everyone calls them Mr and Mrs Lepski, too – even Mr and Mrs Lepski call each other that. They say it keeps an 'air of respectability about the place'.

The park draws nearer and the path becomes populated by old people with dogs on leads or beach-paraphernalia-laden parents who look like they wish they could put their kids on leads. The lookout rail is rough and sun-warm under my trailing fingers, the ocean a murky blue below. Not the aqua and serene ultramarine of more tropical waters: cobalt in places, green in others, choppy and untamed. The horror of my bungled speech and Dad's fingerprint bruises slough off with the wind, fresh and tangy with salt. Mum's voice echoes across my memory. 'A restorative,' she says.

Used to say.

The weight of her absence is a boulder on my chest, pushing me to the side of the path with a thud, everything smeared by the tears it's pushed out of me. Something tickles my arm and I jump out of my skin but it's not a spider, it's a yellow daisy nodding on its long stalk. I've landed in a whole patch of them.

The caravan park is just the same as it ever was: slightly lopsided and scruffy around the edges; the weatherboard office with the kiosk around the back; the concrete shower blocks with the toilets that smell of bleach and brine and defy any sane person to enter without thongs on, though people do. The permanent sites that line the main road have tiny fenced-off gardens and along the clifftop, cabins squat against the wind. Campers, caravans and tents fill most of the sites, hooked up to electricity on poles, several with dogs on chains that bark as I wander past on my way to the 'communal entertainment and barbecue area' – a big trampoline, several totem-tennis poles and a shed with darts, ping-pong tables and a television on the wall that, unless something radical has happened, only plays DVDs.

Ever since I was little, spending time with Kelsey's family has been like visiting another planet where everyone lives on top of each other and has to rinse their own dishes and stack them beside the sink, sort their own washing and 'contribute to the general tidiness' as well as *share a toilet and bathroom* – guests included! Kel and her three brothers are worked like slaves in that household. But seeing her again is like putting on slippers: instant comfort, even after missing last year. She doesn't hesitate, jumping on me with hugs and kisses, dragging me to the trampoline, accepting my daisy-chain gift as if it were a delicate golden crown.

'Crikey,' she says, examining me. 'You grew bigger boobs.'

'So did you.'

Kelsey is tiny. She may be part elf; seahorse-delicate, though last time I was here she wrestled two of her brothers into crying submission over whose turn it was to choose the movie (it was the littlest one, Coop's). She pulls her sleeveless flannelette shirt back tight over her chest. 'Hardly.'

I adjust my bra-strap. 'I'm beginning to understand why

Mum used to pull her bra out from under her top and fling it across the room as if it were a viper.'

Kel plucks at Snoopy. 'So, you wear PJs as clothes now? Is it some hipster thing? Are you a hipster now, Van?'

'I didn't pack any clothes. On purpose.'

She bounces to one elbow, losing her crown, and I explain my grand plan.

'An ambush,' she says, approvingly.

'A failed ambush,' I correct her.

'My dad would be furious too. I'd have to wear hand-me-ups from Harry.' She shivers with horror at the thought.

I refrain from suggesting that she already appears to be wearing hand-me-ups from her brother and we flop onto the tramp. Sea air makes me breathe deep. 'Do you ever wish you were adopted?'

She sits up, resettles her daisy crown, blows her bubble as big as it can go, expertly sucks it back in and chews furiously. 'Nup.' She spits her gum at the bin but it misses and lands with a little puff in the dust.

'Why's it so dry?' I ask.

'Dunno. Probably climate change.' Kel crashes back on the trampoline and the crown disappears through the springs. We bob gently. 'Who wishes they were adopted?' she says. 'Your parents might be divorced but they're still rich rich rich. Your house is massive and your school has its own leisure centre. You don't even know what you're talking about.'

A ribbon of annoyance flutters over me. 'I think I might be adopted, that's all.' What possible difference could it make if you lived in a mansion or a caravan park? And what did having a pool at school have to do with anything? Maybe I should have brought Suyin after all.

'Thinking and wishing aren't the same,' Kelsey says. 'Do you think it, or wish it?'

I roll away from her and stare through the treetops. 'Do you think it'll rain?'

'Think or wish?'

'Wish.'

'Yes, I wish it would rain.'

'Not the whole time.'

Kelsey shudders an exaggerated shudder. 'No, caravan park people go stir-crazy when it rains for too long.'

A pre-pubescent rabble on pushbikes rowdies past and Harry throws his crushed drink can at us. Kel hurls it back as hard as she can but they're already gone. 'I wish Harrison was adopted,' she says. 'Then maybe I could return him.'

'I don't think it works like that.' I shuck up the leg of my PJs to scratch a sandfly bite – already. 'He's all right. Better than *my* brother.'

'You want him? You can have him.' Kel pops a fresh pellet of gum in her mouth. 'I've got spares.'

'Let's swap.'

'Deal!' She rolls over, squirming dramatically. 'I've been thinking a lot about kissing lately. Wouldn't mind a crack at Ashton Partridge.'

'Ew.' I roll closer, conspiratorially. 'I don't know why you'd even look at him while Darith's around.'

'Your brother is *waaay* better looking than anyone called Darith.'

I make what I hope is the most disgusted face in the universe. 'No, he's not.'

'You're his sister. You're not meant to want to stick your tongue down his throat.'

'Kelsey!'

Kel squawks with laughter and almost chokes on her gum. She spits it out, this time making the bin.

'And anyway,' I roll onto my back, 'you haven't met Darith.' A thought surges through me, stirring up the butterflies in my science award. 'They're digging a bike track obstacle course thingy, over at our place.' I fold and unfold the waxy square of Kel's discarded bubble gum wrapper. 'They'll probably have their shirts off.'

She sits up, cross-legged. 'We could be paparazzi!'

The wrapper flutters from my hand like one of my butterflies, the thought lifting me and putting my stomach muscles to the test. 'Really?'

She snorts. 'You're not serious? What do you want to do – stalk them?'

'Nah.' I fall back, hard, hoping the tramp will bounce the embarrassment out of me. Why am I more debauched than everyone else?

'It must be weird,' she says, 'to have people secretly photographing you in your undies or whatever and then posting it on the internet.'

'They want the publicity, don't they?'

'What about that girl who got drugged and dragged around to parties by those horrible boys?'

'I wasn't thinking of drugging Darith *or* putting pictures of him in his undies on the internet.'

'Have you done any drugs?' She picks at a jagged toenail. 'Some guy outside the supermarket asked me if I wanted some meth the other day.'

'Did you call the cops?'

'Nah, I ran off.'

'You should tell your mum.'

'She's got enough to worry about.' Kelsey flicks the corner of toenail away. 'There's a posse of weirdos camping in the bush behind the caravan park.'

'Are they allowed?'

'Yeah, they've got some sort of permit but Mum reckons it's Sodom and Gomorrah down there.'

'What *is* Gomorrah?'

'I'm not sure, but I think it involves bongs.'

Mrs Lepski chooses that moment to stick her head out of the office door and holler, 'Lunch!' When she sees me, she steps out to wave. 'You're back! We missed you last summer.' She looks exactly the same as she always does in her thongs, black leggings and coloured top, like a cheerful emu.

'Hi, Mrs Lepski!' I wave back.

'Plenty of food if you want to stay, Van.'

'Thanks, but I'd better get back.'

Kel slides off the trampoline. 'Aren't you coming?'

'I don't want Dad to find out I'm not there.'

She lurches forwards to give me a hug. 'Oh yeah. Good plan.'

∽◯

I mean to make a beeline back to the house but the honey is out on the tracks and I find myself climbing a tree to hide and watch the boys, imagining the muscles rippling under Darith's skin like in the movies. I rack my brains for a movie where muscles ripple under skin. Darith is working hard, shovelling dirt, and while I know his muscles aren't exactly undulating under the skin, the non-existent movie-image rises up in my mind nevertheless and I blush with the power of it.

Ash drops his shovel, stretches and sees me through the branches. He shouts, 'What the actual—?'

Darith shakes his curls. 'Ash – chill.'

I shrink against the trunk. It's as if all my strange thoughts are printed in the air for anyone to read. Ash slugs water from a drink bottle and wipes his forearm across his mouth before offering it to Darith. 'What do you want?'

How can I explain what I want? To be allowed to stay here, to watch Darith, to pretend he wants me to watch him. I hear Kel, disdainful, saying, 'He's not an *object*.' Then her laughter. 'Now the Bieber: *he's* an object!'

But I don't just love Darith's body – body: the word itself a quiver even with my brother staring bloody murder at me and my desires splattered like mud against the sky – I love his mind, his soul. He's the only boy in the world who even uses the word 'soul'. He told me Australia won't find its soul until it reckons with Black history. You'd think since colonisation that Black history and White history would be the same history but that doesn't take into account history being written by the victors. I tried to tell him what Plato said about tyrants but he was late for cricket practice.

Body and soul: that's how they describe great romances, isn't it? Cathy loved Heathcliff, body and soul.

But she betrayed him.

'What's wrong with you?' Ash shakes his head. 'Are you deaf, or insane?'

I had been deaf, my ears filled with the drama of swelling music, of dark-clad lovers running in slow motion towards each other over the moors.

'Get yourself some help. Or some friends. Or something.' He picks up his shovel. 'Every time I turn around, you pop up looking like you've just run a marathon. What's wrong with you?'

Darith screws on the lid and drops the water bottle on the grass. 'She's just climbing a tree.'

'*Hiding* up a tree and *spying*.' Ash's shovel bites into the earth. 'Go on, piss off.'

I don't need to be told twice. Arrows of mortification rain down on me. I'm already running, making for the old cubby Dad built for us years ago in the bush not far from the house. It's not like we didn't have plenty of places to play already but we loved it, hidden away enough to have a certain magnetism and close enough that we could be summoned with a shout. Ash hasn't wanted to go there for ages. I think he's forgotten it exists. The wooden door has warped and I have to shove hard to push inside; it's good to be able to jam it behind me.

Safe.

Where do tears come from? I used to think we had a magic lake inside us like the one the sword Excalibur is thrown into in Alfred Lord Tennyson's poem 'Morte d'Arthur', which is hard to read but wonderful to listen to. Mum was good at that sort of thing – reading poetry out loud to us and getting all dramatic with the verbs.

> *Then quickly rose Sir Bedivere, and ran,*
> *And, leaping down the ridges lightly, plunged*
> *Among the bulrush-beds and clutch'd the sword*
> *And strongly wheel'd, and threw it . . .*

It's strange to think that Mum's not in the country. Mum's in France, Dad's in . . . Rochelle. Yuck. Better to picture Arthur floating off with the three queens to the island of Avalon, and just as sad. I curl up and chant:

> *Then saw they how there hove a dusky barge*
> *Dark as a funeral scarf from stem to stern,*
> *Beneath them; and descending they were ware*
> *That all the decks were dense with stately forms*
> *Black-stoled, black-hooded, like a dream – by these*
> *Three Queens with crowns of gold – and from them rose*
> *A cry that shiver'd to the tingling stars,*
> *And, as it were one voice, an agony*
> *Of lamentation, like the wind, that shrills*

All night in a waste land, where no one comes,
Or hath come, since the making of the world.

Weeping, I place myself in the barge and drift away, leaving poor Sir Bedivere on the shore, but floating and looking back in my agony of lamentation, I see it's not Sir Bedivere after all, that was a mistake – it's Darith. He calls to me, *Vanessa*, my name romantic, the dreamy vowels wafting over the water. I throw myself from the barge (the water's warm) and swim effortlessly to shore and Darith wades in to meet me, to sweep me up and carry me back to the shallows where we lay down and he slides his hand inside my underpants.

'Van?'

I jerk to attention, cracking my head hard against the cubby roof. 'Ow, crap,' I say.

The real Darith is giving the door a shove. 'You all right?'

'Yes.'

He stops shoving. 'Can I come in?'

Embarrassment rolls over me. 'No.'

'Hey, I …' He trails off. A flock of cockies rampage overhead like a raucous aerial bikie gang. 'Well,' he says into the weird silence the birds leave in their wake, punctuated by random squawks like the screams of the dying. 'I guess I'll see you then.' There's a rustling and the sound of Darith's thongs flip-flopping into the distance.

And on the mere the wailing died away.

Dad isn't too worried about where I've been when I finally slouch back to the house. I'm hungry and Louise has rounded up our chef and the part-time locals who run errands and wash the dishes. Dad's not the only one keen to see what's for dinner.

I say he doesn't seem too worried but I mean he doesn't even ask. I'm not surprised: my PJs are hideously grubby, especially the seat of my shorts. Hardly an incentive to be gallivanting about in public.

Ash corners me outside my bedroom. 'Where've you been hiding all day?' He juts out an arm to hinder me ducking up the hall. 'How come you've started following me around?'

'Following you around?'

'Yeah. Spying on me.'

'Spying on *you*?'

'Are you going to repeat everything I say?'

The lifting pressure bubbles across me like the surface of a cooking pancake and I feel like crying with relief. My secret's safe. But there's a sour note of disappointment, too. Darith is as far as ever from knowing how I feel about him. What if I hadn't run away but strode across and thrown the shovel from his hands to launch myself into his arms, Darith shocked but secretly ready for me all along? Or flung open the cubby door—

'Are you even listening to me?'

Ash comes back into focus and seems almost hurt. 'I'm hungry,' I say. 'And Sharif's cooking. Can't we just go down for dinner?'

'No one's called us, yet.' He slides down the wall, settling in for a chat.

I'm suspicious but slide down too. 'Where's Darith?'

'On the phone to his parents. Why?'

'No reason.'

We haven't sat in the hallway off the landing, our knees a tunnel, for ages. Ages and ages. Probably since before Rochelle. I don't know what to say. My brother is more than a taller, broader version of who he used to be; he's like another person. Ashton is 'exceptionally bright' apparently and probably *is* good looking if you're not his sister, with his Jareth the Goblin King cheekbones. He sails through school with minimum effort and doesn't give a flying fart if he gets a B; I have to knuckle down and study if I don't want to disappoint Dad. It makes me sick. I drop my knees away, ready to get up and go see what's happening with the food.

Ash knocks his shoulder against mine. 'So, *did* Dad tell you to spy on me?'

'No. I think you may be suffering from paranoid delusions. Why would he?'

Ash rubs the back of his head against the wall. 'Cos he's a prick.'

I settle back. 'What have you done?'

'Nothing.'

'Then why do you think he'd ask me to spy on you?' I wriggle to relieve my numb butt, pushing my lower back against the wall, reluctant now to break the connection.

'To see who I'm hanging out with.'

'Why – what's the big deal?'

'Did he?'

'How many times do you want me to say no?'

He looks at me sidelong. 'Do you promise?'

'Ash—'

'Swear it, on Roger's life.'

'I swear!' I look at *him* sidelong. 'Who *are* you hanging out with?'

He jiggles his foot, sizing me up. 'Do you know what they're saying?'

I swat away the prickling of panic. The old cubby is miles from the road. No one could have seen me this afternoon, could they? 'No.'

'Dad's some kind of property fat cat now.'

'So?'

'He's going to build a casino.'

'So what?'

'Here – on our beachfront.'

'He can't – there are conservation laws. And why would he want to?'

'Money. And rich men make their own laws – especially now that the US have chucked democracy out the window.'

'Our beachfront is heritage protected,' I say. 'I did an assignment on it.'

'Yeah, but apparently a bunch of federal government boffins have been lobbying the minister for local government to have it reclassified. They have vested interests and that's illegal.'

The way he says 'boffins' makes him slightly less annoying. 'And this is what they told you in town?'

'They told me some company Dad's working for called Champion has already surveyed Shearwater for a casino development.'

'No way.'

'Yes way.'

'Who is this "they"?'

'They're called the Foxhole Resistance. I met one of them at a rally and when he found out who I was, he told me about it.'

'And you believe him?'

He shrugs. 'Yeah.'

'Ash, everyone knows you shouldn't believe weirdo-strangers that you meet at rallies.'

'Everybody does *not* know that.'

'Why Foxhole?'

A waft of smug floats over him. 'Don't you get it?'

I'm sure it helps to stare fixedly while the brain clicks and whirs.

'What's another word for foxhole? Earth,' he says, hardly giving me a chance. 'Get it?'

It's true I am swayed by the wordplay but foxes are also tricksy and untrustworthy. Dad would never turn Shearwater into a gambling den. I cross my arms. 'This casino thing hasn't got anything to do with us.'

Ash puts his foot against the wall like mine. We have the same toes, except his are so much bigger. And hairier. 'They're camping here, behind Oceanview—'

'Gomorrah!'

He gives me his WTF look. 'I think they want me to help them find out shit about Dad.'

'What shit? And how?'

'Not sure. They found me on Facebook and have invited me to a Foxhole meeting, down in town here.'

'Everyone *definitely* knows you shouldn't meet up with weirdo-strangers who contact you on Facebook!'

'It's in a cafe in the middle of the day – I'll be fine.'

'I could *ask* him about Champion,' I offer. 'Maybe *they*'ve got it wrong?'

He swivels towards me and crosses his legs. 'Please don't do that.'

'Why not?'

'Van, could you just not?'

I look down at his hand on my arm. It must be two years since we've been this close. Rochelle calls, 'Dinner,' up the stairs.

'Promise you won't say anything?'

'Take me with you to the meeting. Then I promise.'

Dad yells, 'For God's sake!' and we get up.

Darith emerges from his bedroom and just when I think I'm going to die, he jostles me cheerily with his shoulder and we follow Ash down the staircase. When we hit the family table in the dining room and take our seats he says, 'In your Snoopy pyjamas up a tree. You're a classic.'

Ash lifts a cloche and good smells waft forth. 'Classic dork,' he says.

'Nothing wrong with being a swot,' chimes in my father,

encouragingly, as if he's doing me a favour. 'If you gave your studies the same attention as your sister does, who knows what you could make of yourself.'

'It would be nice to give Ashton some inspiration, and reward Vanessa's hard work,' says Rochelle, breezily, giving me the quickest of winks as if we're old friends even though when she was the nanny she told me I was the most annoying kid she'd ever met. 'So perhaps it's time for that bit of shopping. After all, it's nearly Christmas.'

Despite my utter mortification at the anti-allure bandying of 'swot' and 'dork' and having to suppress the desire to yell out *CASINO!* I can't help but admire Rochelle.

'We'll go tomorrow,' she says, as if it's all settled.

෮◯

The boys head out after dinner but when I come down for a drink of milk before bed, I hear them in reception, Darith tinkering around on Pa-Albert's baby grand piano.

'Model O,' Ash tells him. 'They reckon the old man had Steinway commission the artwork when he built the house – that's why it's all flowers and birds.'

'Beautiful sound.'

'Yeah, Mum used to play it.'

By the time I pad back up the staircase, they're gone, just the ghosts of our trio left in the room; Mum on piano, me on cello, Ash on violin, playing 'easy' songs for Dad. I trail my fingers over Eurydice weeping and wonder if my father ever did look back.

CHAPTER 2

Rochelle has certainly taken the shopping bit between her teeth and spends the morning impressing me with her skills at the old online purchase. Now we're heading out into the real world. She lends me a stretchy tube-skirt (none of her shorts will fit over my thighs) and a pair of thongs and sends me to borrow a T-shirt from my brother.

You'd think I was asking him for the One Ring.

Darith swings into the doorway to supervise. 'Just give her the smallest one.'

Even the smallest one is big on me – a green number with *REVISOR* stamped on it, a relic of Ash's ill-fated rock band. 'That's a collector's item,' he warns me.

Darith says, 'The glory days,' and they break into the lyrics of the band's signature tune.

Revisor
Never look back
Revisor
Stay on track
Revisor Revisor Revisor

It's remarkable that someone who could play other people's music on the violin quite beautifully could also be so terrible at making their own music with a guitar. Thank God that turned out to be Revisor's only tune. 'Your one hit blunder,' I say. 'Please stop.'

Ash brushes me off. 'You philistine.'

I waddle down the hall and overhear him snort, 'Remember when Karen Armshaw took her top off?' and Darith say, 'The highlight of your career.'

When I get to the car, Rochelle purses her lips. 'Oh, dear,' she says. 'It's quite the emergency.'

Shopping with my supposed stepmother is nothing like shopping with Mum. Rochelle's enthusiastic, for a start. But maybe my mother loves shopping now she lives in Paris. That's what people do there, isn't it? Shop. Or have torrid affairs with artistic types while drinking absinthe and playing melancholy piano in romantically seedy cafes. Or dance the cancan. Husbandless, childless, dogless.

I wonder if she's lonely.

It's hard to imagine Mum without Dad. She always seemed like ... part of him. Maybe that's why she can't communicate with me, because Dad always spoke for her and now she's lost her voice? Or maybe she hates me.

Still, shopping with Rochelle is fun.

Well, I say fun but I mean negotiating the lunatic fringe of Christmas shoppers stickily devouring ice-creams while bad-temperedly swatting their offspring up and down the footpaths. And enduring Rochelle's excruciating dissection of my body shape, its faults and potential assets: a SWOT analysis. A laughing, bantering family with several generations intermingling wander past and I consider asking them to kidnap me. 'That chest of yours is magnificent,' Rochelle says in a businesslike tone, confirming my most optimistic suspicions and raising the embarrassed eyebrows of a passing grandfather. 'Which is good,' she qualifies, 'because you're a little heavy around the hips.'

It's like being an eclair, airy pastry pumped full of whipped cream, and then dropped – splat, fat globules everywhere. Rochelle, on the other hand, does not possess a fat globule. She's pulling out clothes for me to try on that my mother would never have considered in a thousand million years. Short things. Tight things. Things that show my cleavage and ... my shape.

So far we've found nothing for me but several dresses for Rochelle.

'Not the bare midriff thing,' she says, appraising me in a halter-neck that turns my boobs into mountains. 'You've got to make the best of your assets but there's no point accentuating your flaws.' She makes the 'get it off' hand signal. 'Every woman has them, Vanessa. It's how life is.'

That gives me a start. My mother has never, ever, inferred that I am a 'woman'. I sidle to the safety of a rack of more sensible-looking jeans. 'What are yours?' I ask.

She laughs. 'Now that would be telling.'

I don't want to have flaws and if I have to have flaws, I want them to be as well-hidden as Rochelle's. I try to picture my mother's body but I can't: all I see is her head stuck on a storybook cut-out of a cancan dancer.

Rochelle herds me into Beachside Hair and Beauty. 'Come on,' she says. 'I've booked you in.'

My hairdresser's name is Nora and she's tall and blonde and fake-tanned, which does not strike me as reassuring, but when she sits me in the chair at the mirror her massive eyelashes frame the kindest eyes I've seen since I last looked at Mrs Bhatt. 'So,' she says, her eyes flickering over my outfit, 'what were you thinking of?' She nimbly unplaits and lifts my hair, letting it drop from her fingers. 'You've got beautiful hair,' she adds. 'Lovely and natural.'

I look from her to my reflection and back again. 'What would you do?'

'Well,' she considers, 'it depends. I'm guessing you'll want to keep it simple—'

'What about a fringe?' Rochelle suggests. 'Or a bob?' Her face lights up. 'Or foils?'

Nora *hmmms*. 'It's already a lovely colour. And I think a bit of shaping will bring out its natural highlights.' She looks at me. 'You don't want to go for too big a change all at once – it can be . . . upsetting.'

'I don't want to dye it.'

Rochelle shrugs.

'So.' Nora squares me up in the mirror. 'How about we take off an inch or two? To just past your shoulders.' She lifts my hair again. 'And take some of this weight out. It's been beautifully cut straight along the back here, but a few long layers will give it some shape. Maybe we could even try a side-part – what do you think? We can always flip it back if you don't like it.'

'Yes,' I say, Darith-worthy butterflies fluttering around inside me. 'Let's do that.'

She winks at me and addresses Rochelle. 'Can we get you a tea or coffee while you wait? Though, I'd have to say it's worth wandering up to Beanz Meanz – they make a great cappuccino. Vanessa will be all right with us, won't you?'

'Are you sure?' Rochelle asks my reflection.

'Hundred per cent,' I say.

Nora lifts my hair to fasten the cape that now hides Ash's precious T-shirt. 'We'll be done in about an hour.'

'An hour,' Rochelle repeats. For a minute I think she's going to try to give me a kiss but then she waves.

'Not your mum,' Nora says when Rochelle's gone.

'No. My dad's new wife.'

'Right.' She nods down at my legs. 'Do you want me to book you in with Tahlia for a wax?'

I consider my reflection. *In for a penny, in for a pound*, as Nanny used to say.

∾

I am in an agony of lamentation.

'I've never heard anyone make *that* noise before,' says Tahlia, smiling, ripping a few more hairs out by their roots.

∾

If you weighed the mountain of hair I'm leaving behind to be thrown away by Nora and Tahlia, I suppose it would only be a few grams but I feel lighter all over and perhaps it's shallow, but my legs look like they belong to a completely other human being and I calculate that the new human being is fifty-eight per cent more alluring than the old one.

I say fifty-eight per cent but I mean one hundred.

'I love my hair,' I tell Nora and give her a hug.

'I'll go one night and look out for those shearwaters,' she promises. 'You've got me curious now.'

Rochelle drags herself away from the product display to usher me out the door. 'Right, let's go and find you some bathers.' When we hit the street she looks me up and down, sagely. 'You may well be better served by a really flattering one-piece.'

I'd pictured myself in a Darith-luring bikini and done a bit of googling on the evolution of this revolutionary garment so I'm disappointed at her lack of enthusiasm and the implied repulsiveness of my stomach.

I say I'm a bit disappointed but what I mean is that I cry and not even on purpose.

Dad agreed to a 'few essentials' and likely won't notice our online purchases when they arrive by mail but when we get back to Shearwater, we've still managed to accrue a stagger-worthy number of shiny bags from the local boutiques. Rochelle's feeling nervous; I can tell. Her shoulders flip back and her chest becomes even more pert. This is an acceptable term for describing a woman's breasts

(I found out at Elite Swimwear), but no one will ever describe mine that way.

Puddingish, maybe?

Darith, here, hold one of these. What do you think, pudding or pert?

Like a firm blancmange, Van—

'—Van?'

Darith's actual face swims into view.

'Yes?' I croak. On top of everything else, the Enid Blyton-ness of the word 'blancmange' has me halfway up the Faraway Tree. I hope it's the Land of Get-What-You-Want.

'Hello, anybody in there?' Darith says, and waves. 'Do. You. Want. A. Hand?'

Now, apparently, I'm the deaf old Saucepan Man. Like a complete nincompoop, I drag up a bag-weighted arm and return the wave.

Rochelle saves the day by unloading as much stuff as she can onto him. 'What a darling. Get these into Van's room before Simon finishes his meeting.'

I hesitate, glad and sad that my hands are too full to easily give her a hug. 'Go on,' she says. 'It was my pleasure.' My foot is on the first stair when she adds, 'I do love your father, you know.'

∞

Darith lurches the bags onto the bed as if they're heavy and with a partial somersault settles himself, back to the wall. I flop on a chair, clumsily disentangling myself from ribbon and reinforced paper and the thrill of having him in my bedroom.

'You don't have to care about Rochelle's feelings,' he says.

This seems a radical thing to say, and cruel, like spilling the f-word in front of Mrs Bhatt.

'You just don't, that's all I'm saying. She hasn't given two shits about yours.' He nods at me. 'You look ...' But instead of finishing his sentence he busies himself with the bags, poking at the tissue paper.

'Look what?' Nice? Different? Stupid?

He pulls out a soft orange top. 'This is a pretty colour. Is that why you hoodwinked your dad, because you were sick of wearing green?'

Hoodwinked. I love him, even if he is ignoring my burning question that I don't have the guts to ask twice. I take the now-favouritest-top-in-all-the-world from him and lay it reverently in a drawer. 'I did not always wear green.'

'Yeah, ya did. Bottle green, brown, blue. For some reason you always looked like you were going to a funeral. Or a farm. Anyway,' he gestures to the bags, 'now you'll be able to give Ash his precious T-shirt back.'

'Where is he?'

'On the phone.'

'Who to?'

'Some girl he met at the beach.'

'Already?'

'What can I say? We're irresistible.'

'We?' And I snort. I actually *snort*. Just as well Suyin isn't here or I'd most certainly become hysterical. Even Darith is laughing. But it's true: he *is* irresistible. I sit next to him. The bed is soft and I roll slightly, my thigh against his thigh.

A seriousness drifts over us. Darith's grin disappears and he looks small, as if his force field of cool has been turned off. His long fingers touch the stone of my amethyst ring, my own slightly freckled hands clasped in my lap like a Class Six monitor.

'That's pretty, too,' he says and the sky turns over and the universe is new.

His neck is ropey but fine. I'm close enough to see the individual curls packed blackly on his scalp, each one sculptured and the whole thing a ridiculous mess. What would it be like to put my fingers in it? They'd get caught. He turns his head to look at me, close enough for me to feel a puff of his minty breath. His face is ideal beauty, like a Gustave Moreau painting of Saint Sebastian. A holy angel, but full of suffering, somehow, as if the angel has already fallen.

I'd be embarrassed by my breathing, loud in my own ears, if Darith's breathing wasn't loud, too. Maybe I really am up the Faraway Tree? He touches the long curve of hair that newly frames my face.

Rochelle's accusatory voice strikes like a reflex hammer. 'Vanessa!' We jerk, clunking foreheads; Darith says, 'Christ,' and I say, 'Sorry,' even though he may have given me concussion. He springs to his feet while I plunge face first into the shopping.

Rochelle steps in, hands on her hips. 'What's going on in here?'

'Nothing,' says Darith, rubbing his head.

I sit up, tentatively exploring the contours of the swelling above my left eye.

He sidesteps away. 'We were just talking.'

'I have an egg,' I say, appealing to Rochelle with a plaintive moan but she is not diverted by my imminent death. Her eyes are narrowed and trained on Darith. 'Did you try to kiss her?'

Darith recoils even further as if the very suggestion were repulsive. 'Of course not!' Now he's the one who glares accusingly. 'That would be . . . gross. She's Ash's little sister!'

Each word is the bite of an axe and my heart is chopped to pieces. 'Doesn't anyone care that I have a haematoma and may die?' I sob.

Rochelle's attention rivets onto me. 'Did he?'

'No.' I clench my teeth to stop the tears. 'And can you please shut up and get out of my room? I have a headache.'

Rochelle almost stamps a foot. 'I can't believe you're being so rude to me after everything I've done for you today.' She seems even more annoyed when my brother swings by to lounge briefly in the doorway, nod breezily at her, glance around my room, say, 'You having a party, Van?' and disappear again, calling, 'Come on,' to Darith.

Darith slips past Rochelle. 'See ya down the beach,' he calls back and then I overhear him say, 'Is she gonna be there?' and Ash reply, 'Yep, and I told her to bring her friends,' and then they're gone.

Rochelle still has her fists on her hips Wonder Woman style but now there's only the two of us. If it was awkward before, it's positively painful now. 'Do you need an aspirin?' she says.

'Yes.' I flop back, sniff loudly and rub the tears from my face. 'And I think you should call an ambulance.'

Her voice softens. 'What were you two really doing?'

I stare at the ceiling cornice. 'We were just talking. I don't know why you're being so weird about it.'

She pulls the turquoise dress from one of the bags, rubs the fabric between her fingers and drops it back in. 'Hmm, okay. Well, we're flying to Sydney for your father's meeting with, wait for it: Richard Marks. *The* Richard Marks! And then VIP seats for the *Viva Las Vegas Spectacular* at The Marksman casino.' She punctuates this with jazz hands. 'We're just about to drive out to the airport. Home tomorrow.' She points at me in a nanny-like way. 'Staff's in and dinner for you lot is at seven.' She swans off but reappears a second later. 'And don't forget to practise for the party: your father is keen to impress.'

I heave myself up to examine my forehead, which appears to be growing a horn, pucker up and whisper, 'Gross.'

Kelsey swerves in, pulling up short at the dishevelled splendour on my bed. 'Are you kissing yourself?' she says. 'Your hair!' She squints at me then nods. 'I love it.' She peeks in a bag, 'Wowza!' and throws herself on the bed. 'Was that *the* Rochelle I nearly knocked down the stairs?'

'Yep.'

'Do you think it's weird that she looks like your mum?'

I turn my back on the mirror. 'She does not.'

'You don't think so?' Kelsey pulls out a dress and stands up to shove me along and check it out. 'I mean, she's younger and everything, but you know,' she swishes the dress a little, which seems somehow unnatural coming from Kelsey, 'the bun and everything.'

'Nup.' But now I can only see Rochelle's head on the cancan dancer and I still don't even know what my mother's body looks like. 'Maybe I'm becoming athazagoraphobic,' I murmur.

Kelsey's face goes blank. 'A-wha?'

'Pathologically afraid of forgetting.' I lump onto the bed. It seems too hard to add the bit about being forgotten.

'Riiiight.' She lumps next to me. 'Is that what you're so sad about? Because, frankly, it's not *that* likely that you're going to forget about your mother and if you do, you can't be bothered by what you've forgotten unless you remember that you've forgotten it, in which case, it's no longer forgotten, right? I mean, something forgotten is only waiting to be remembered, and it's immediately unforgotten the minute it *is* remembered, or if it's truly forgotten, it's the same as if it never existed, and therefore truly forgotten things can't bother us, ever.' She takes a breath. 'You should write that down in your observations book. Mind you, if it *is* a phobia, no amount of sense is going to do you one jot of good.'

One jot. I give her a squeeze. 'Will do.' I pull out the book and write, *Where do forgotten memories go—?* It occurs to me to clarify, but my head hurts.

'So ... what's up?' Kelsey's eyes flash. 'Are you missing your old clothes?' She laughs cheekily before opening a shoebox to gasp, 'Real ones!' at my Crocs.

Don't ask me why, but Kelsey nearly always wears cheap fake Crocs and not only as slippers, either.

'No. Okay.' I grab her hands to give the revelation the gravitas it deserves. 'I'm ninety-five per cent sure Darith was going to kiss me just now but,' Kelsey squeals and I have to shush her, 'then stupid Rochelle comes in at exactly the wrong time and asks him flat out if he was trying to kiss me—'

'Nooo!' Kelsey stops spasming and sits, suddenly serious. 'But ... only ninety-five per cent? And what's with the lump?'

I waver. It all seems entirely improbable and I'm beginning to believe I must have made it up. 'Make it sixty-five per cent.'

'Sixty-five?'

'Fifty.'

'Hang on—'

'He said kissing me would be gross.'

Her outrage is comforting. 'Why?'

'Because I'm just Ash's little sister.'

She considers this. 'Then why mention ninety-five?'

'We were this close.' I lean towards her until our lips are nearly touching. We breathe. For a moment I wonder what it would be like to kiss Kelsey. We sit back. 'And when Rochelle came in, he accidentally smacked me in the head.'

Kel touches her lips with a finger, almost a caress, then fossicks in a bag, looking a bit embarrassed when it's a bra she pulls out. She shakes it off admirably, dropping the bra and sitting cross-legged. 'Let me get this right. He tried to kiss you, smacked you in the head, said you were gross and threw you under the bus as merely the little sister.'

I nod, feeling the tear-ache at the back of my throat.

Her brow wrinkles and she tries to lift an eyebrow but they both arch up. 'And this is the "nicest guy in the world"?'

I sigh myself into a prone position.

She lies next to me in sympathy. 'He was probably trying to avoid being killed by your parents. Or your brother. I mean,' she points at my chest, 'what about those?'

'I think my egg's going down,' I say, mollified, exploring with tentative fingers.

'Well, quick, show me your bathers. I've got to go soon to pick up Coop from his friend's.'

When I put on my new bikini in the shop, I'd already tried on about fifteen styles. It had been a relief to find something that didn't make Rochelle and the shop lady exchange looks and go searching for another pair; and Rochelle said aqua suits my colouring. But trying it on now, I don't think I can wear it out in public. I feel a pang of longing for my red-and-white polka dot one-piece with the boyleg that's at home in my bedroom in the bottom left-hand drawer. Maybe I'll ask Louise to go back and get it.

'Perf.' Kelsey makes me do a twirl. 'Have you trimmed your pubes?'

'I can't see any pubes,' I say, lifting a leg and poking my butt at the mirror.

'Everyone does it.'

ME: Suyin, do you trim your pubes?

SUYIN: Trim them? I shave them right off.

ME: No, I can't believe that!

SUYIN: You're right. I wax them off!

The thought of that makes me blanch with horror. I shake Suyin away. 'What would I trim them with?'

'I dunno. Scissors?'

'Don't you do it?'

'Nah.' She gives a wiggle. 'Board shorts: the best.'

She gently bumps me along and models the Crocs for the mirror. 'They're so comfy.'

A hot prickling creeps over me. I mean, I haven't even worn them yet. It's not my fault her mum hardly ever buys her new stuff. And besides, she's much smaller than me – they're a size too big for her. Probably.

'You can have those,' I say. 'For keeps.'

Did my face light up like that when Rochelle bought me any of these things?

Kelsey has to pick up Cooper but she walks down to the Oceanview beachfront with me for moral support and leaves me at the top of the stairs. Hugging her old thongs, she skips off down the track calling back, 'Little sister, my arse,' and shocking an elderly beachgoer who says, 'Charming!'

'Sorry, Mrs B,' she says.

Below, the sand and shallows are littered with holiday-makers. Mum used to complain about how we had a whole surf beach to ourselves at Shearwater but she still couldn't drag us away from the lure of the sheltered cove. Darith and Ash have gathered a coterie of older kids on towels spread in a loose fan from the water, punctuated by a miniature forest of water bottles poked into the sand. Above, an arcus cloud hangs in the blue, a giant roll of textured magnificence stretched over the ocean. It's breathtaking. Salt-fresh wind whips my hair, hinting at the cold front, and pulls at my towel as I negotiate the trek down. In the water or in the air, salt makes you lighter.

According to my research, back in the old days, not that long after the bikini was invented, an actress called Ursula Andress rose out of the surf wearing one in a James Bond movie and ever since, that's been the benchmark for women rising out of the water in a bikini, although, like most legends, the origins are forgotten now. I say rising out of the water in a bikini but I mean doing anything at all in a bikini. A special casualness is required, as if the bikini-wearer has forgotten the fact that they're wearing less fabric than your average knickers and bra (certainly less than *my* average knickers and bra). No, not forgotten the fact: *transcended* it.

Like netball, special casualness is not an area in which I am a high achiever but no one ever got anywhere without trying. I make it down the many wooden steps without a stumble but am almost thrown off my game when my thongs flick hot sand in small fountain-sprays up the back of my legs. Nevertheless, I billow out my towel as if I belong there and sit – more heavily than I would have liked, but I've done it. I've arrived.

Laying on my back makes my stomach look flattest but Darith is in the water and I can't see him from that position so I lever myself up onto my elbows. Be still my beating heart, the breasts have worked! Darith beckons me. 'Come on in,' he calls winsomely from the water.

I rise up in my best Ursula Andress mode and, guessing it's better not to reach behind and unwedge my wedgie but brazen it out and pretend I don't *know* or *care* that my bather bottoms are slightly tucked in between my bum cheeks, I jog, nonchalantly, to the water. One of the Indigenous girls who was a towel behind me on the beach jogs nonchalantly too, right past me, like some kind of teenaged Cathy Freeman-esque goddess.

Darith smiles at her and says, 'Nadia,' in a way that leaves no doubt that it's Nadia he's called into the gently lapping water, not me. So *this* is why the bikini was named after a nuclear bomb site. I silently cry out to the Spirit of Ursula to sustain me, make a sharp left and continue jogging, as if this is what I was doing all along, going for a nice jog up the beach. Jog, crikey, no – a run! A nice revitalising run up the beach. I arc away from Nadia at speed, away from Darith, away from the great crushing disappointment that is the universe, and along the beach, negotiating toddlers, child sandcastle-builders, sun-bronzed senior citizens, and pale hairy men who call out,

'Smile, love,' and, 'Run over here, sweetheart,' and, 'Look at those tits!' until they're set upon by a raucous group of middle-aged women who leave off their hysterical wrestling with a pop-up beach-shelter to tell them to 'shut their sexist traps'. The shoreline at last curves out of sight behind dunes where, breath rasping, chest heaving and nauseous with exertion, I collapse in physical exhaustion. Out of the wind, the sun beats down hot upon me.

Well, I say in physical exhaustion but I also mean in tears.

If there's anything worse than collapsing into the black hole of humiliation, it's having a witness. Tim Bickford is sitting on a sand dune wearing ridiculously long board shorts and looking down at me from behind his glasses – the invisible kind that don't have any frames but still glint in the sun. Tim's family stay in the same 'rustic' cabin at Oceanview every summer and Kelsey and I agree he's the most annoying boy that was ever born. The kind who throws sand in your lemonade as a way of 'joining in' or deconstructs your stuff to see how it works but then hands you back the pieces without anyone ever being one jot closer to knowing how it works.

'What's up?' he says.

My heart is broken, Tim, and I think I've partially wrenched my boobs off by running along the beach in a bikini. What's up with you?

'Nothing,' I say, wishing I had a hanky.

'Do you want a tissue?'

I nod. Damn it, I do.

Tim slithers down the dune. He's twice as tall as he used to be; his once-chubby legs have stretched thin, with knobbly knees. And there's something terribly wrong about his board shorts and it's not only because they have many pockets and one for carrying tissues. 'Mum made them,' he says with a shrug, settling next to me. 'I'm glad I bumped into you.' He's digging sand with his feet and patting it down with his strangely long toes. He must have spent last Christmas holidays on the rack.

'Why's that?' Funny, how when I talk to Tim, I sometimes hear myself sounding like Ash. I clear my throat. 'I mean, hi Tim, nice to see you.' After all, maybe Tim likes me? Maybe he feels the same way about me that I feel about Darith – well, without the lustful fantasising bit. Ew. Maybe that's why he's sitting here next to me being my friend even though the last time we saw each other I assaulted him with my ice-cream because no matter how much we asked him not to, he wouldn't stop insisting Kel and I watch his terrible pop-up magic shows.

'Do you still do magic tricks?' I ask.

He shakes his head in a way that makes me think there's now a permanent snow cone smear between him and his creativity. He pushes his glasses up his nose. 'Are you still friends with Kelsey?'

'Yeah, of course.'

'Tell her . . . ' He jumps to his feet, sprinkling me generously with sand. 'Ask her if she'll hook up with me.'

And he's off, running up the sand dune and away and against the glare of rejection loom Darith and Nadia, complementary shadows against the sun. 'Are you all right?' Darith asks. 'You ran off like . . . well, I dunno what.'

Like a Bond-girl FAIL, Darith, that's what I ran off like.

I wave to where Tim disappeared. 'I had to meet Tim and didn't want to be late.'

Nadia shades her eyes even though the sun is behind her. It's probably the blinding glow from my red face. 'Is he your boyfriend?'

No, Nadia, DARITH is my boyfriend – he just doesn't know it yet and clearly neither do you.

'Yes,' I say.

An excruciating cover-up stretches out before me involving Tim Bickford, who chooses that moment to bob up at the base of a distant sand dune high enough that he has to grab onto grass tufts to pull himself up. He scrambles theatrically, loses his grip and disappears helplessly back down the slope. It's more than I can cope with.

'No,' I say.

They exchange a look that suggests to me that they're suggesting wordlessly to each other that I'm one strange kid.

'It's complicated,' I manage, grumpily, adjusting my bikini top which seems to be wanting to flash the curve of my boobs to the world. 'I'm going home.' I slouch off in the mulligrubs, not even hesitating to unwedgie my wedgie.

'Aren't you going to grab your stuff?' Darith calls.

I slouch around in yet another rethink-your-idiocy curve and follow them back to my towel. If nothing else, I'm grateful for a drink of water.

Darith hovers, hesitant. 'We're going for an ice-cream,' he says. 'Want one?'

I swat angrily in his general direction.

'That's a no, I'm guessing,' he says and Nadia laughs. Darith shows me his palms and says, 'Come on, Van, I'm—' but I jump up and away from them, running down to dive into water that's rough and cold and cleansing and perfect except that it nearly rips my flimsy top off.

I catch Rochelle on her way to the kitchen. 'Can we go shopping again tomorrow? I think I want a one-piece after all. Maybe that one with the sleeves and shorts.'

'I'd rather not.' She tilts her head and squints at me. 'What's happened to you, Vanessa? Are you all right?' She puts a comforting hand on my arm. 'Did someone say you were fat?'

I run off, up the staircase.

'Ignore them!' she calls after me. 'You've got the body of a goddess!'

I flop my body-of-a-goddess onto a couch, turn on the TV and disappear into *Labyrinth*. Just when it finishes, Ash brings up dinner. He hands me mine and crashes at the other end of the couch.

'No Darith?' I say as disinterestedly as possible, flipping to a new movie.

'Gone with Nadia for a walk on the beach.'

My determination not to cry stretches between us like mozzarella. Ash shovels the food in and asks, 'What are we watching?' with his mouth full, almost bursting with glee at his own grossness. If he's done it to cheer me up, it's worked.

I match his food shovelling and say, '*Agora*,' through it. He laughs and I practically snort cauliflower au gratin out my nose.

He tosses me a discarded beach-towel. 'Ug, I remember this. Why are we watching it again?'

I wipe my face. 'Hypatia of Alexandria never gets old.'

We empty our plates. 'She does, you know,' he says and pushes up off the couch.

'Don't leave your dirty dishes!' I yell, but he's gone.

He pokes his head back in. 'Meeting's at that new cafe where the old cafe used to be – tomorrow at ten.'

'Your plate!'

But he's really gone this time and I'm left alone to see superlative mathematician and cosmologist, poor Hypatia, stoned to death by fanatic misogynists and contemplate Darith and Nadia's romantic evening stroll along the beach. It also occurs to me that since Mum's abandoned her post and I'd rather eat boiled snot than ask Rochelle for money, I hope Louise knows what I'm giving Ashton and Dad for Christmas.

CHAPTER 3

The infamous cafe used to be called The Owl and the Pussycat and serve delicious Devonshire tea if you didn't mind fighting your way through the tasselled cushions, quilt displays and crocheted doilies. Now it's called No Sign and fitted out with nothing but reclaimed school chairs, driftwood sculptures, bare unpolished wood sanded back to within an inch of its life and no actual sign. There's a green rubber thong hanging from the ceiling on a piece of string and a few plump succulents sit in scrubbed tins of various sizes.

Darith goes for a patronising head-pat as I make my way past but I duck and the clasp of his ridiculous 1980s stainless steel watch gets caught in my hair. 'Don't you brush it?' he says. I can't retort because I've just seen his bicep undulate under his skin and even though my nose was practically in his armpit he smelled nice, like lemon-grass soap.

Of course, he's invited Nadia to the meeting. I can't work her out. She's quiet, pretty much *shy*, but she wears fake eyelashes and fingernails. Her skin is flawless. I bet she never goes blotchy when she gets nervous. She's suctioned onto Darith like a limpet on a rock, a giant squid on a submarine, a leech on a pulsing vein.

I'd do anything to be her.

I say meeting but I mean a bunch of bearded men and sharp-faced women all with tattoos and buns who are apparently disinterested in everything. I've drunk my (delicious) coconut milk iced chocolate out of an old jar and eaten my faux scrambled eggs on kale sourdough served on a lump of wood, been comforted by the fact that the new owners have kept the runcible spoons and am itching to get down to the beach with Kelsey. It's hot and still and I want to wear my swishy-thing-that-goes-over-your-bathers that arrived in the mail. I look to the ocean; the shearwaters are out there somewhere, riding the wind. Pretty graceful for birds nicknamed after sheep.

Darith untangles himself to slip off to the loo and Nadia smiles uncertainly at me over her apple and celery juice. 'Hello,' she says.

I should act like a normal human being and say hello back but, no. I babble, 'Hungry mutton-birds sometimes fall out of the sky,' instead and mime a cartoon bird dropping dead from the sky which I realise too late is a) slightly threatening, and b) makes it seem like I don't care about the fact, which I do – desperately.

Nadia falters but then rallies. 'I like your dress,' she says and I'm chuffed until her eyes flicker over me and she adds, 'It's very flattering.'

My body is fine – I'm the right weight for my height according to Paula from Beach Horizon Boutique. At the top end, perhaps, but officially not overweight. Doesn't anyone understand science? Am I going to have to spend the rest of my life being compared to the super thin who, statistically, are more susceptible to anaemia and the flu?

'Are you a girl who needs flattering?'

I look up, stunned that someone I don't know has spoken to me. And he's not even a person: he's a fairy king, fey, as if held to the earth by dew-sparkled cobwebs and butterfly wings. I'm enchanted, even if he does wear a somewhat grubby silk rainbow scarf and there are sticks and bits of wool in his blond dreadlocks.

The most terrifying woman I've ever seen – dark-brown dreadlocks high on her otherwise shaved head and a tattoo of a tiger snake winding up from her collarbone to behind her ear – answers, 'I didn't think it *was* flattery,' on my behalf. It's thirty-four point seven degrees but she's wearing pale-green velvet pants, raggedy at the calf, and strange leather shoes that seem both sturdy yet a thousand years old. Her singlet looks like an old man's but also perfectly feminine on her, even when she salutes someone across the table and reveals an unshaven armpit. Perhaps it's because her bra is showing and it's dainty, a pale apricot colour. She looks down at me with Amy Winehouse eyes and says, 'Do you feel complimented, kid?'

'My BMI is twenty-four,' I say.

Yep, that's what I say.

She laughs, says, 'Good for you,' and holds out her hand saying, 'Marlene,' in a way that asks me to give her my name as well as my handshake. I'm tempted to pretend my name is Suyin, even though Suyin says everyone in China's named Suyin, or Lydia; because either of those are so much better than being named after a sanitary product, even an imaginary one.

Marlene raises her eyebrows at me. 'Are you okay?'

'Van,' I blurt out. 'It's Van.'

Ash is dying of embarrassment, elbows on the table, head cradled and one eye covered by a despairing hand. He leans towards Darith. 'I knew this was a mistake.'

'Ah, the sister,' says Marlene and the beards and sharp eyes swing to me. Marlene nods over to the fairy king. 'Say hello, Bodhi.'

He bows to me, and says, 'Nice BMI,' and there's something in the way he smiles at me that makes me tingle.

Luckily the focus shifts quickly – everything about the meeting changes when these newcomers sit down. A fine mist of conspiracy descends. There's talk of gambling and its human cost, of property development and its accompanying environmental degradation. The guy next to Nadia says, 'Always was, always will be Aboriginal land,' and the whole group turn to her and Darith.

'Word,' says Bodhi, solemnly.

Nadia blinks like she's been asked the million-dollar question and doesn't know the answer, but Darith looks back at the sweep of expectant faces with the same expression he gave Rochelle when she said it was 'incredible' that he played cricket not footy. Ash tips back in his chair, looking amused and laughs when Darith says, 'Congratulations.'

Bodhi says, 'What for?'

'Noticing.'

The wait staff rescue us by sliding a board piled high with chopped up cornbread across the table and clunking a bowl of olive oil at either end.

I'm not sure what I was expecting from this meeting but I suppose Ash knows what's going on. Then I look at his stupid sporty face and I'm just as sure he hasn't got a clue. I square my shoulders and turn to Marlene but she's not looking at me and she's far too intimidating to interrupt. Everybody seems busy paying attention to her, or the yellow bread, or each other, except my brother, whom I'm ignoring, and I wouldn't dare *breathe* in Bodhi's direction in case I hyperventilated so I look over at Nadia who covers a yawn with her hand.

'So,' I begin, but my voice comes out as an overcharged whisper. I clear my throat. 'So, do you know what they do?'

'Who?'

I wave, meaning all of them, and Marlene looks over and says, 'Hello, there. Do you need something?'

Nadia, startled, nudges me with her wrist in a way that makes me feel like I've been offered up as some kind of sacrifice. She leans over to Darith to say, 'Can we go?'

I'm surprised out of my uncharitable thoughts about them getting up and leaving by Marlene's arm sliding across my shoulder. 'What did you want to know?' she asks.

'What are you?' I squeak, fumbling breadcrumbs into a tiny pyramid. 'Foxhole Resistance, I mean. What is it?'

'We started off as a poetry group,' she says and laughs.

73

There's a sesame seed stuck between her teeth. 'Poetry readings, hikes, lectures: trying to raise awareness of the impact of coastal erosion along here.' Her banana and chia-seed coconut smoothie arrives and she takes a mighty slug, wiping her mouth with the hem of her singlet. 'That's originally what brought us here.' She leans in and gives me a sidelong look. 'But then we heard rumours about what's happening at Shearwater and decided to investigate. It's totally corrupt, what they're doing. Someone has to stop them.' She turns to Ash. 'And that's where you come into it.'

He sizes her up. 'How?'

She sucks at the sesame seed. 'You're a bit of a computer whiz, aren't you? Or so Bodhi tells us.'

Ash shrugs but I can tell he's flattered. 'And?'

'We want you to hack Simon Partridge's computer.'

It's as if she's dunked me under water; I come up spluttering but Ash is as cool as a cucumber. 'I can't,' he says. 'I tried when Bodhi first told me all this shit – just so I could know, one way or the other. It's locked up tighter than the Pentagon – and I'd need his thumbprint to get in.'

Marlene keeps her eyes on Ashton. 'Well, try harder. See if you can find anything – anything at all related to Champion. We need evidence.'

'What do you want me to do? Chop off his thumb?'

'Figure out a way to get him to let you use it. Or record his conversations.' She nods, confidently. 'You'll think of something.'

A flush creeps up Ash's cheeks. 'How do I know you're not just a bunch of conspiracy nuts?'

'Didn't you tell Bodhi you'd stand up to your father?' Marlene spits the seed on the floor. 'Well, time to put your money where your mouth is.'

'Piss off.' Ash pulls out a fifty and throws it on the table, then adds another twenty. 'That should cover lunch. Come on, Van.'

I follow him out, hurrying to keep up. It's impossible to talk until we get to the foreshore park and he pulls up under the palms.

'Do you think Dad's doing what they're saying he's doing?' I ask, puffing.

'Maybe, I dunno.' He pushes the hair off his face. 'But screw them; they probably just want in to Dad's computer so they can rip him off.'

'Are you going to ask him about it?'

'I tried. He changed the subject like he always does if I ask him about anything real.' Ash rolls his neck. 'But realistically, the Marksman's like ... a massive hero. *He*'s not going to do anything dodgy. Is he?' He nods back towards the cafe. 'Those guys are a bunch of wankers.' He puts on his sunglasses. 'You'll have to walk home by yourself.'

'Where are you going?'

'Meeting Dana at the pub.'

'Who's she?'

'Nadia's cousin Ellen's best friend,' he calculates as if he's doing maths.

'But you're underage.'

'I've been there heaps of times.'

'Can't I come, then?'

'No.'

'Why not?'

'Because you're fifteen.'

'Plenty of kids go to the pub when they're fifteen. You did.'

'Yeah, and got kicked out. Sorry Van, just because you came to that stupid meeting doesn't mean I want my little sister hanging around.'

'Why are you so horrible?'

'Why are you so annoying?' He stalks off.

I plump on the grass overlooking the foreshore and fume. I'm *not* some little kid he and Darith can just ignore whenever it suits them. It's not fair. A shadow falls and then Marlene and Bodhi are sitting on either side of me.

'Hey,' Marlene says. 'That brother of yours has got a bit of a short fuse.'

Bodhi nudges me with his elbow. 'Why don't you hang out with us?'

'And do what, exactly?' I ask.

'A bit of volunteer landcare.' Marlene cracks her knuckles. 'We're losing ground for the mutton-bird rookeries, you know.'

'That's terrible. I love shearwaters.'

'Then you might be just the girl we're looking for,' she says.

∞

I'm the newest recruit to the Foxhole Resistance and Bodhi thinks they're very lucky to have me.

This is the best holiday, ever.

∽◯

The alarm jingles in the pale dark of the pre-dawn and I force myself up to do my morning practice early so I'll be on time to meet Marlene at the cafe by seven-thirty. Technique is always boring but even scales are sublime when you're playing as the sun comes up, especially on the reception balcony at Shearwater with its view over the pool and the bush, right out to the ocean. I launch into my childhood favourite, *Ode to Joy*, serene, transported, until Ash jerks out onto his upstairs balcony to shout down, 'Shut the F up!'

Affronted, I retire to the music room to work on *The Swan*. It's not the funeral dirge I'm grinding out – it's much harder to maintain your intention when you play slowly, to keep the sound alive and sensitive. '*Andantino grazioso,*' I whisper to myself, 'slow and graceful.' I can almost hear Dr Skutenko clicking her tongue at me. Perhaps I should've chosen something less technical. I burst into *La Cucaracha* to let out the tension.

Ash opens the door. 'That your performance piece this year?'

'Yeah.'

'I'd pay to see that.'

The Norse goddess Freya pops her head in too and says, 'Hi.' This must be Nadia's cousin Ellen's best friend or whatever. I wave. I'm not scandalised: Ash has had girls sleep over before.

'Dana and I are going down for breakfast seeing as *somebody* woke us at the sparrow's fart,' he says. 'So we'll leave you to your . . . art.'

'Your violin's here.' I reach over to tap it with my bow. 'Louise brought it down.'

'Alas, poor Louise,' he says with mock regret, 'because that's not *my* violin.'

Darith appears behind them. 'What are we doing? Are you putting on one of your impromptu shows, Van?'

'They were never impromptu,' Ash corrects him.

If Nadia squashes herself into the music room doorway I shall most certainly scream. An upsweep of nausea makes me focus my attention on Guilhermina's comforting maple and ebony. I take deep breaths.

'Watch out.' Ash pushes Dana ahead of him. 'Looks like she's about to murder the Mendelssohn.'

I overhear Dana say, 'What's that?' from the landing and then, 'I didn't know you played the violin.'

Darith falls into one of the music room's stuffed armchairs.

I aim for nonchalant. 'Is Nadia here?'

'Nope.'

We stare at each other for a minute.

'Aren't you going to play *Song Without Words*?' he says.

'Nope.'

'Oh.' He seems genuinely disappointed. 'What *are* you going to play for me then?'

'Go away.'

'Have you heard the Marga, Carsten and Luca version of *1916*?'

'Only because you've played the clip of their version three thousand times.'

'I've been learning the piano part.'

'I thought you'd left orchestra?'

'You don't have to be in the orchestra to play the piano, Van.'

'Play it.'

'Okay – if you play the cello part.'

'I'd need the music.'

His face lights up. 'I'll get the iPad.'

I shrug. 'Sure, no worries.' But Darith has already dashed off.

Well, I say I shrug and say, 'Sure, no worries,' but what I mean is I squeal a desperately oppressed squeal and dance around Guilhermina before carrying her over to the keyboard to compose myself. Well, I say I compose myself but in truth, I think I'm having a panic attack.

When we begin it surprises me that Darith seems nervous too. But it doesn't take long for transposing the score to take us over, to direct our attention, to force us to listen to each other, just like the Big O is always telling us it will. We get it down pretty well, in the end. Maybe when we're back at school, Suyin could sing it with us. 'Let's go and play it on the baby grand,' I say.

'Won't your dad—'

'Who cares – it's Mum's anyway. Besides, heaps of

randoms must bang away on it when Shearwater's out for rent.'

I trundle Guil down the stairs and out to reception where the Model O sits collecting dust because the cleaners aren't coming until just before the party. Darith lifts the lid and I'm delighted anew by the birds of paradise painted on the underside. He strokes the keys and picks out a few notes.

It takes us a few tries to get into the right rhythm and when we've played it twice through, we sit quietly in its aftermath. It's such a sad song.

'You're really good at arranging, Darith,' I say, rubbing my bow shoulder.

Darith sighs. 'RIP, Lemmy.' He rouses himself. 'I'm starving. Let's go cook some eggs.'

'Oh my God, what time is it?'

He checks his watch. 'Nearly eleven-thirty.'

I race away like Alice's white rabbit, my heart full of the classical joys of Motörhead.

Marlene's heading out the cafe door when I arrive, breathless, hoping she'll invite me in for ethically sourced poached eggs on toast. 'Sorry!' I pant. 'I was playing the cello.'

This does not appear to land well as an excuse. 'You're lucky you caught me. I only popped in for my secateurs.' She sizes me up. 'Got gloves?'

'No.'

'A hat?'

I touch my head as if I'm too stupid to know without checking whether I'm wearing a hat or not. 'No.'

'And you're wearing thongs.'

'Yes.'

She holds the cafe door open and ushers me inside. 'Come on,' she says.

When I joined the Foxholers, I'd imagined taking part in renewable energy experiments that would transform the world – in a good way. Or making a noble sacrifice like Julia Hill who lived in a tree for just over two years to save it from being chopped down. Or, at the very least, feeding bottles of milk to cuddly rescued wildlife.

Not weeding.

And rubbish collection.

My stomach is groaning after missing out on the ethically sourced poached eggs on toast Marlene had *not* been inviting me in to eat. 'Don't worry,' she scoffs at me, 'there's planting, too – nothing better.'

'Awesome,' I manage.

'We've got a grant to weed out anything that's not native along this section of coast.' Marlene stretches out her arm to take in the vista. 'The invaders let their sheep graze right to the clifftops until they were barren and crumbling. Then planted kikuyu grass because it's hardy and helps with erosion – but also kills everything else that might want to grow. Birds can't burrow in it, and that's why we're losing the rookeries – as well as the damage done by residents and their bloody pets.'

I think of all the walks we've taken with Roger Federer off the lead and cringe. 'That's awful.'

'It's a huge problem. Coastal care so far has been to poison the kikuyu and let the natives reseed naturally but we've got a grant to systematically revegetate, with a focus on cultivating Victoria's floral emblem.'

'What is Victoria's floral emblem?'

'*Epacris impressa*,' she says. 'Common heath – the pink one.' She rolls her arm to show me a tattoo of a flower. 'Like that.'

She gives me a booklet called the *Guide to Australian Coastal Native Plants* and 'allocates' me to Renate, who adjusts the seventeenth-century bonnet over her grey hair, reties it under her chin, nods at me, and continues her work. Perhaps her attitude is catching because a wave of quiet purpose rolls over me while Marlene teaches me about identifying what's native and what's 'weed' in my patch, which, to be honest, is mostly kikuyu grass.

'You know a lot about plants,' I observe, presumably in case she hasn't realised that about herself.

'Yeah, I'm a bona fide plant lawyer.' Marlene laugh-sighs in a way that makes me think of a sad cello movement – not a sweeping adagio, just a drop into the minor tone, with an edge.

'She's not kidding,' Renate adds without looking up. 'That's a thing.'

I clamp my wind-threatened hat to my head with my clumsy glove-hands. 'How do you become a plant lawyer?'

'You complete a Bachelor of Agriculture slash Law degree and prepare for a lifetime's disappointment, unless you want to work for Monsanto or something.' She spits in disgust. I'm in awe. I want to spit like that – like a pirate. 'Anyhow,' she says brightly, 'thanks to our Coastcare Community grant it's all hands on deck while the money lasts.'

'What's the money for?' I ask, waving at flies.

'We're all volunteers but we've got to be fed, and have decent tools, and there's transport, and tip fees. Nurseries donate natives from time to time and we grow our own from cuttings, but propagating still costs money.' She stretches. 'Drink water; if in doubt ask Renate; and make sure you keep that hat on.' She heads back down the path calling, 'And you can have that advice for free,' over her shoulder. She laughs again, properly this time and disappears from sight.

This, and the quiet beauty of the bush sustain me for ages.

Well, I say for ages but what I mean is that ten minutes after Marlene leaves me to it, I'm bored and lonesome and my back hurts. 'Pretty hot out here,' I say.

Renate glances at me, waves away a fly and sniffs before returning to her silent beavering. She obviously didn't join Foxhole for the company.

We toil on.

In the quiet, Darith's hands roll over the piano keys to pluck away at my heartstrings. I slide the image of his hands down onto mine as I pull at the tough grass. With a shiver, I wonder about hands that laboured here long ago, the first feet that ever stood here. Well, not that long ago. I'm playing music written at the same time the settlers were arriving.

Settlers. That's what they call the Israeli families moving onto Palestinian land. Settlers.

Absence is presence.

Or is it the other way around?

Despite mocking the Foxholers for saying it, Ash has an *Always was, always will be Aboriginal land* sticker on his cricket bag and he and Darith almost got expelled last year for burning it in huge kerosene letters across the oval after they'd been to a rally to protest the closure of remote communities. But despite the popularity of the dramatic drone-photos they posted and Mrs Bhatt's subsequent assembly lecture about Recognition, I've never really thought about it being ... true.

A crow lands on a yellow banksia tree sticking up from the scrub and caws, startling me. Renate straightens up and points. 'Look,' she says. 'Eagles.' The crow hops from one bouncing branch to another and flies off.

The eagles circle out of sight and Renate bends back to work, me copying her like a little puppet.

What I *do* know to be true, suddenly, like a march fly bite to the brain, like the settling of something clammy on my skin, is that my father might be trying to sell off a chunk of coastline to an American celebrity-turned-casino-magnate and I don't even know whose country this is. I'll google it. Or maybe Bodhi will know.

As if I've summoned him, Bodhi emerges from the bush, washing over the clammy feeling with a peppermint thrill. He's like a Pan-ish god of the ancient Greek myths, something of the mischievous satyr about his pointy, handsome face, his dreadlocks, the hint of coloured beads under the neck of his collarless shirt. He should be dancing along on hooves, or at the very least bare feet, but he's wearing sturdy boots not dissimilar to the ones Marlene lent me. As he comes close there's a sharp smell about him: strange, like burnt sweat.

'Bit lonely out here,' he says, jigging his eyebrows towards Renate, who stops to take a drink of water and acknowledge him with a disapproving glare. 'Did you see the eagles?'

I *am* lonely. He's looked into my soul and seen exactly how things are. 'Yes.' My fingers curl around the handle of the wheelie bucket for something to lean on but it rolls away, and after a fleeting yet apparently entertaining dance of clumsy missteps, I land on the sandy dirt. Bodhi reaches out, saying, 'Woah!' and we laugh as he helps me up, snatching back the spilled scraps of rubbish.

Not him laughing at me.

Us laughing at me: together.

He takes his hand out of mine to blow a mozzie off his arm. It must have bitten him because he scratches, shrugs wryly, watches it buzz, then leans towards me to half-whisper, 'A Buddhist,' and his lips brush against my earlobe sending a shiver through my insides.

The rustle of the bush announces Marlene, who puts an arm around my shoulder. A plume of musky body odour wafts up from her. 'That mosquito was a Buddhist?'

she jokes, not very funnily, if you ask me, though Bodhi smiles.

He's got the nicest smile in the world. It's probably because he's a Buddhist.

ME: Hi, Suyin. I'm a Buddhist now.

SUYIN: Nietzsche will be disappointed.

'Are you a Buddhist?' I ask Marlene.

She claps viciously, wipes a tiny creature's remains on her trousers and says, 'No.'

Despite the fact that she's as far from motherly as any mother I've ever met, except maybe 'Marion', there's something protective in the way Marlene shields me, as if Bodhi were some kind of threat. I don't *think* they're together. Perhaps Marlene's jealous that Bodhi is a Buddhist and she's not? I wonder what I'd have to do to become a Buddhist. 'How do Buddhists feel about entering science competitions?' I ask Bodhi.

'Oh, the Dalai Lama is a scientist of the highest order,' he says and his non-sarcastic-taking-my-question-seriously-ness knocks me like the blow from a boisterous wind. My body's standing there with Marlene's arm draped across its shoulders but I'm whirling like a hat blown off my own head and tumbling around in the bush.

'Yeah, well,' says Marlene tiredly, breaking the spell, 'the ole Lama isn't afraid of a bit of hard work, either, so let's get on with it – it's going to be too hot soon to do anything. Isn't that right, Renate?'

Renate says, 'That's right,' but Bodhi upstages her, giving Marlene a bow, like a prince giving way to the wisdom of a queen. He winks at me. 'I'll teach you how to meditate,' he says and skips off, light on his feet despite the boots. By the time I thumb through to the camera on my phone, he's nearly gone. I make the photo larger on the screen. He looks like Mr Tumnus in Narnia. Not the movie version but not the faun from my childhood reading, either.

Marlene puts herself in front of me, like she's sizing me up again. 'You know what you're doing?'

'Oh, yep.' I lift a clump of weeds from the wheelie-bucket to prove it. A torn and trampled chip packet clinging to it gusts off. Renate nabs it with her foot and it's uncomfortably like paying homage to her when I retrieve it from under her boot.

Marlene swings her backpack on. 'I'll be back in an hour or so to see how you two are going, okay?'

'That's fine,' says Renate, bending back to her task without looking up.

Resisting the urge to follow Marlene, I bend too. Within minutes my back hurts and the sun's too hot and I could use a pair of kneepads but I don't care.

ME: Suyin! Pan is going to teach me how to meditate.

SUYIN: Why? Doesn't he know you're the founding member of 'meditate on maths'?

ME: Shh!

SUYIN: Hang on ... PAN! You do remember The Bacchae, don't you? Pan causes the women to devolve into debauchery and Agave rips her own son's head off in a frenzy.

But I'm not going to let Suyin spoil things. It's not my fault that when she got her braces Martin calculated it wouldn't be hygienic for her to kiss anyone for two years; payback for her telling him he had breath so bad he'd never kiss anyone, ever, no matter how straight his teeth were. At the time, I told them both that whoever these mythical kissers were, they'd love us for our brains ... but considering I've barely been able to string together an intelligible sentence around Bodhi, I'm not so sure about that theory.

They'd hardly recognise me if they saw me now, in this wide-brimmed hat with this dress, these woolly socks and boots, almost like an indie.

I say almost but I mean exactly.

By the time Marlene finally returns, I've drunk my water, killed two march flies, which probably means I've been kicked out of Buddhism already and, determinedly chatting to her unresponsive left shoulder, shared the biography of Jacqueline du Pré with Renate, who pretended to be uninterested but then asked several pertinent questions, all of which helped distract me from my ravening hunger.

When Marlene tells us it's too hot to keep working, it's as liberating as being excused from PE (which I am whenever Mr Velour wants to win) and I shout, 'Yes!' like a five-year-old and nearly pass out from embarrassment at how startled they are.

Renate narrows her eyes at me. 'You've only been at it two hours.'

Marlene is kind enough to smile. 'Come on. Time for a chai.'

We return to the cafe, the group regathering, but Bodhi is nowhere to be seen and I pass on the chai, which smells like old socks. 'Will we see you tomorrow morning?' Marlene asks. 'Nice and early to get a proper day's work in?'

I say, 'Oh, yeah, of course,' but frankly, I'd rather not.

Swapping my boots for thongs, it strikes me that I might have been mistaken about the source of the smell.

I race through the bush as quickly as one can race in thongs to Kelsey's to tell her that this is the best holiday ever. I say bush but coastal bush isn't really the bush; everything squat and windblown and toughened by salt.

Mick the Maintenance Guy is in the office. 'All gone to the big smoke,' he says over the top of his newspaper. 'Shopping.'

'When will they be back?'

The phone rings and he reaches for it. 'Late.'

I nick around to the kiosk for sustenance and when I ding the bell, Mick comes shuffling through to serve me, which is awkward.

Armed with snacks, I drift around looking for Ash and Darith. The bike track is abandoned and they're in none of the usual places. Eventually, I spot them in silhouette out on the rocks showing-off for a group of girls and slouch home to while away a thrilling evening watching *The Life of Birds*, stuffing junk into my face and chatting with Suyin on Facebook.

She Snapchats me her smooth, white, even, braces-less teeth. I had forgotten what Suyin looked like before the braces and now feel like I've forgotten what she looked like a week ago. I think she looks older.

You look pretty.

She writes back:

Pretty smart.

I'd Snapchat her my new haircut but I don't want it to seem like we're in some kind of competition.

She sends me a barrage of photos of food. Her family is eating their way through the Bazaruto Archipelago. In a bizarre way, I feel closer to Suyin right now than I do when I'm actually talking to her in the flesh. I venture:

Any boys?

She Snapchats me a too-close-up photo of her ten-year-old brother stuffing his face with a handful of coconut pudding.

What about you?

If we were together, I'd be totally busted because I can feel that my face has gone beetroot. Her mother would definitely contact my father if she got even a whiff of the Pan-god Bodhi and to send Suyin a photo of Darith would be taking excruciating to a whole new level.

I send a photo of Felix Mendelssohn instead.

She sends me Ben Affleck from *Going All the Way*.

I turn off David Attenborough and send a picture of him to Suyin. She Snapchats me her hands making a heart shape. Three thousand Snapchats later, we say goodnight and I feel sad.

She sends one of herself pretending to cry.

Going to some stupid island tomorrow. Two
weeks with no reception ☹.

I send one back pretending to cry too.

Absence is presence.

I ring Mum. She has to join Facebook, or Skype me,
or something. Why hasn't she rung? I'm not the one who
bloody divorced her. But she doesn't answer and I don't
leave a message. I don't even know what time it is where
she is.

I mosey out to get myself a drink of water before bed
and through the crack of the music room door spy Ash,
by himself, quietly trying to nut out the melody of *1916*
on his violin. A wave of nostalgia washes over me for the
hours we once spent playing duets, Mum tapping away,
our living metronome. I withdraw, hoping he doesn't
notice me and clam up. Dad should have listened when
Ash said he didn't want to play for his corporate cronies
anymore.

Is there something wrong with me, I wonder, reaching
for cheesecake, that I like any chance to perform?

Swinging into Oceanview the next morning means negotiating a bicycle-swarm of Lepski brothers and associated
caravan park rats. Harrison, Lachlan and Cooper Lepski;
all sun-bleached hair and elfin looks, skin brown as berries.
They seem like giants compared to when I last saw them,
especially Coop. They pull up around me in a semicircle
and look solemn. Harry, the oldest, nods, obviously the

spokesperson. 'We're sorry your mum won't be home for Christmas.'

I swallow back the sudden lump of sadness. 'It's not your fault.'

The boys exchange a look. Harry shakes his head. 'It still sucks.'

Christmas. Whatever happens, it will never be the same again. Lachie reaches out to pat me, like I'm a dog. It's nice, for a minute or two, to be encircled by appreciation-without-reservation of exactly how much it sucks.

'Kel is on kitchen duty,' pipes in Cooper at last, pushing back the fringe of his shock of hair. It doesn't seem that long ago he couldn't even talk. I say thanks and they ride off to reswarm. Harry calls, 'There's still the shindig!' over his shoulder.

Mrs Lepski meets me at the door and gives me a squeeze. 'That girl's forbidden from the beach until the dishes are done,' she warns and sweeps her hand over the unholy mess of papers strewn across their dining room table. 'I'm doing the books.'

I skip through to the kitchen. 'Your brothers are adorable.'

Kel splutters theatrically, 'Yeah, right,' and tosses me a tea towel. She appraises my hair which, after a few washes and swims, looks very different to how Nora left it. 'I like it even better,' she pronounces.

It's so quaint how none of the Lepskis' crockery matches. 'I hate how movie adaptations of books usurp the imaginations of childhood,' I say, wiping a weird plastic gizmo with Disney's Winnie the Pooh plastered over it. 'What does this do?'

'It's a watermelon dicer. What do you mean, "usurp"?'

I brandish the watermelon dicer. 'I mean they steal your characters and put their version of them in their place. Look at *The Hobbit*. I had to read the book again to get Bilbo and the dwarves *back*.'

Kelsey shudders. 'You know I hate that movie.'

'I hate it more.'

Kelsey dumps a pile of cutlery into the dishrack and gives me a withering look. 'No one hates it more than me.'

The soapy cutlery slips from my grasp and a couple of forks clatter to the lino. 'Oops.' I scoop them back in the water. 'What I hate most is how they've barely set out and Bilbo jumps out in front of an orc—'

'I know!' Kelsey is satisfactorily disgusted. 'As if he would've, and what the crikey Moses was an *orc* doing there anyway?'

'I know. So wrong.'

'But the wrongest bit was making Thorin some kind of sex object.'

We join in a bit of fake vomiting before Kel throws her rubber gloves into the empty sink and drags me into her bedroom. She drops her iPod into the dock and turns up the volume. 'Tell me everything.'

I tell her everything.

'Sooo ... it's the best holiday ever because of weeding?'

'Yes!' I twirl and fall onto her bed and Kel's tiny room is

so crammed my head smacks against the wall. 'Ow. Bodhi is going to teach me to meditate.'

Kelsey makes a face. 'Sounds awesome.' She pulls her doona over her head, squeals and says, 'There's going to be a beach party on New Year's Eve and I think Tim and I might . . . ' She emerges to jiggle her eyebrows at me.

'Do you love him?'

'No.' She flips the doona back over her. 'But I'm not sure that matters at this stage.'

'Doesn't it?'

'Does it?'

She wafts the doona up and down. 'I'm hot.'

'Hot for Tim Bickford.'

We roll about laughing at this bizarre concept. Kelsey kicks the doona to the end of the bed and lets out a sigh. 'I'm pretty sure when it comes to first pashes and stuff, liking someone is as good as loving them. Probably better.'

'So, you like Tim?'

'Well, I might this year,' she says and we laugh and laugh.

Thank God for Kelsey.

Thank God.

Thank God.

Thank God.

Not that I'm a hundred per cent convinced on the God thing, though nature is so beautiful and maths so mystical it's hard not to give some weight to the idea of intelligent design; but not just intelligence – beauty, tenderness and humour, too. And the source of music is surely divine?

I share these thoughts with Kel on the way down the beach and when we get to the stairs she says, 'This is not the time for questions of epiphany, Van.'

'Why not?'

'Tim is coming.'

Below, in the distance, Tim is, indeed, climbing over the sand dunes.

'Well, considering what you just told me,' I reason, 'this seems the perfect time for questions of epiphany.'

Framed by the patch of coast, Tim takes giant steps down a dune. His knee bends weirdly and he plunges into a sandy tumble. 'Your husband,' I remark. When we've recovered from laughing, I add, 'Are you sure you want me to come down? I could—'

'God, don't leave me alone with him.'

'I'll have to leave you alone with him at some point, if you're going to . . . you know.' I jiggle my eyebrows.

'I think I've changed my mind already.'

When we've found our place to sit, Tim presents Kelsey with wildflowers. Like him, they're crushed, bent and sandy but still, it's sweet of him. Kelsey barely glances at him but makes a little sand-mound to poke them into. 'I'll try to remember them when we go,' she says magnanimously.

The swish and sigh of the sea is quiet, the wind fresh and light. We wade in until the water hits our thighs and stand, shivering, the occasional rolling swell strong enough to lift me to my toes. Now that they've separately told me they want to hook up, Kelsey and Tim appear unable to make eye-contact, let alone converse. I guess it's time for me to leave them alone so they can tell each other and besides, I feel ill: Darith and Nadia are skipping down the stairs laughing gaily. Darith jumps from halfway up, showing off. The way he bends over and then shakes his legs out, I know he's corked himself.

'I'm gonna head back,' I say and begin wading to shore.

Kelsey wades after me, looking panic-stricken and Tim wades after her looking confused and suddenly it's as if they're both chasing me out of the water. I face them. 'What are you doing?'

Kelsey says, 'What are *you* doing?'

Tim practically crashes into her.

'I'm—' Well, I have no idea what I'm doing. I just want to stop feeling uncomfortable, be out of my skin, be *not me* for once, and free from humiliation. I fight the urge to rip my breasts off and throw them up the beach at Darith. How I wish the stupid things had never grown. I let out a desperate, gurgling cry and leap on Kel, wrestling her into a massive dunking. The water is thrillingly cold and somehow washes through me as well as over me. When we lurch to the surface, we stagger forwards and take Tim down with us, almost drowning ourselves with laughter.

We separate and float, feet poking out of the water like my dad taught me back in the days when he used to come swimming with us kids. Darith whizzes a frisbee from the shore; it grazes the top of my head. Tim splashes through the water for it and flings it to Kelsey, losing his footing and dunking himself in the process, which is hilarious.

By the time the frisbee makes it back to me, Nadia and Darith are in the water and not long after, Ash joins our loose circle with Ellen, and Dana – who's flirting with my brother in a style I can only describe as awesome because it involves grabbing him by the ankle and flipping him upside down.

Dana's not like Ashton's usual suspects. She's a bit older than him and rumour has it she drives a combi. She's blonde, it's true, but her hair is pixie-short and her tan is real. She hardly wears make-up – just a bit of zinc as lip gloss – and her eyes are ridiculously blue and clear, and seem to be holding a challenge as, in fact, do her athletic arms and legs. Together, Ash and Dana look like deities shoving each other around in the surf.

Maybe it's because her cousin's here but Nadia and Darith keep a respectful distance between them, which I can only consider a blessing.

The Lepski boys and other kids from the caravan park turn up to plant the wicket and we emerge to the hard sand. Harry declares Ash and Darith the captains and I'm so grateful when, after choosing Nadia first and zooming though the best of the boys in fierce competition with Ashton, Darith chooses me over the eleven-year-old on crutches with a broken foot.

It's Nadia who turns out to be the closet sportsperson among us, smashing out runs like a pro, fake fingernails and all. I'm the eleventh man but she's still not-out when I take the bat. I do my best, running as though the furies are after me but despite my efforts, she's forever bouncing at the crease, waiting for me so she can run again, which would be fine if it didn't mean I had to run again, too.

Ash bowls me out as soon as I face him and you'd think he'd won the Ashes. But it turns out Nadia and Ellen play women's cricket in Townsville and Ellen has a sneaky spin arm. When she bowls my brother out for a duck, it's nothing less than glorious.

It's a beautiful thing, to walk home in a clump of friends, sandy, salty and exhausted. After all that leaping about on each other, it seems quite natural (in a surreal way) that Tim and Kelsey have their heads close, nattering, bumping arms as they walk. Nadia runs ahead to Ellen and Dana, and Darith slips in beside me. 'Nice to see you laugh today,' he says.

'I'm always laughing.'

'Not lately. Anyway, I'm starving.'

'Me too. Can't wait to get back and have a shower.' I squint up the path into the sun. 'Oh my God, is that Bodhi?'

Darith squints up the path too. 'Looks like it.' He flips his towel over his shoulder. 'Do you reckon that's his real name?'

'What do you mean?'

'Who calls their kid Bodhi?'

I shrug. 'Who calls their kid Darith?' He laughs and I add, 'Or Vanessa, for that matter.'

'But, *Bodhi*? I reckon he made it up. His real name's probably . . . Craig.'

'Shh.'

'Or Nicholas.'

'Shh! He's nearly here.'

And so he is. He bows charmingly to the girls ahead.

'What a wanker,' Darith scoffs softly. I guess he's jealous of the way Nadia curtsies back.

But Bodhi keeps coming until he reaches me. 'Want to come for a swim?' he asks me. 'Maybe at your private beach, over at Shearwater.'

Darith crosses his arms in that sports-team photo way that pushes out his biceps, making him look like an impostor. 'Thought you were hungry?'

But Bodhi already has my hand and a quiver of electricity burbles through me. 'Come on, let's go,' he says.

Ash pulls up next to Darith, hands on hips in a fair impersonation of our father. 'Don't be too long!' he yells. 'If you're not back by dark, I'll come looking.'

We almost skip along the path that winds through the scrub to Shearwater's beach and jog down the stairs, which are not as steep as at Oceanview, dropping our towels and thongs and racing across the empty sand to the water. No tentative wading for Bodhi: he leaps in, bounding over the breakers, dragging me with him, and when we emerge he pulls me close and kisses me.

On the lips.

'You're beautiful,' he says. The ocean's roaring and the swell lifts me off my feet but he holds on. 'I've got you.' My stomach, pressed up against his stomach, chooses this moment to let out an unholy growl that trails off to a strangled gurgle. Bodhi whoops with delight. 'You really are hungry! Come on, a few more waves and we'll go get something to eat.' He kisses me again and his tongue darts past my teeth and does weird things to my middle school science award. 'Watch out!' he says, letting me go to dive under the breaking wave while gobsmacked-me gets dumped a beauty.

I come up spluttering a few metres away. When I find my feet, sand has filled my bather-bottoms.

Bodhi waves. 'Hang on. I'm coming!'

I bob down to shake the sand out but it's jammed into the panty-liner part, a turdish sausage roll. I fumble around down there like a creepoid, dipping under twice to avoid being dumped again, and when I finally sort my bottoms out and stand, breathless, holding onto Bodhi for balance, the water sucking out and dropping below my thighs, my bikini top has come undone at the back and swings loose around my neck and my boobs are hanging out.

I push them back into their halter and Bodhi ties the bow. I'm pretty sure that's his erection against my hip. My face must be the colour of a tomato. I don't ever want to turn around. Bodhi presses even harder, puts his lips to my ear, says, 'Here we go,' and pulls me down with him, under the wave.

It takes quite an effort to escape the sucking tide without a further drubbing and by the time we make it to the wet sand and sit, his hard-on has gone away. Maybe I imagined it.

Salt water stings my skin, drying in the wind. The sky is a broadsheet of hazy blue: cloudless above the sharp line of the horizon and the deep rumble of the waves. A gull wings low, right over us, and even as I wonder at it, I'm also ninety-eight per cent sure it's going to poop on my face.

It doesn't.

'The shearwaters are out there somewhere,' I muse. 'Diving, fishing, fattening up. How do they know to do what they do?'

'Magic.' Bodhi falls back to his elbows on the sand.

I rebuff his assertion. 'Science.'

He runs his hand from my hair down my spine, coaxing me into reclining. 'Same thing,' he says. 'In the end.'

A big swash laps us with its fizzling chaos. Currents shift and move but it's only where the water breaks that the wave becomes visible. A pandemonium occurs, where substances collide, and then something new comes into being. Maybe it is a kind of magic.

I jerk, slapping at the sharp sting of a march fly and – horrors! – it falls, twitching belly-up on the wet sand, legs gesticulating violently. Bodhi doesn't seem to have noticed my un-Buddhist-like lashing out against God's innocent creatures; he's talking about the surf. It's a pity Ash has gone off him – they have a lot in common. With herculean effort the march fly flips right-way-up and, staggering, bunny hops into take off. I give an inward cheer.

Bodhi smiles. 'So it'll probably be ripper on Thursday.'

I nod, approvingly. Recovered, the march fly resumes the attack and on reflex, I whack it again.

The assault is witnessed and this time, it's fatal.

'Oh dear,' says Bodhi.

'Well,' I say philosophically, 'the little vampires only live three or four weeks, so let's hope this one was coming up to its month anniversary.'

That's not what I say. I gulp down tears and blurt, 'I didn't mean to kill it – they're just so slow.'

Bodhi nods. 'It takes a lot of practice to become mindful.'

Just as I'm plummeting to the depths of embarrassment he kisses my shoulder and takes my hand. 'Your skin's so soft.'

Like one wave chasing another, the thrill of his approval washes over me. Hyper aware of my shoulder all of a sudden, I also realise this wind is deceptive: I think I'm burning.

Bodhi stands and offers me his hand. 'Tide's going out. Let's go for a walk on the rocks.'

He crosses lightly like the Pan that he is, his toes gripping the black rock, but my feet are still citified and I'm grateful for the invention of rubber. 'I love igneous rocks,' I say when we get out to a favourite patch of mine, taking off a thong to rub the sole of my foot against a polished nub. 'How good is this lumpy black stuff when it's all smooth – the victory of watery Neptune over fiery Pluto.'

Or … considering that the volcanic strata remains despite all the swashes of the sea, is it the other way around? I must remember to jot that down in my *Book of Observations*.

'Most of this stretch is still rough with the sedimentary veneer, not to mention the limpets. Ash got dragged out by a rip once and had to walk back over it carrying his surfboard. His feet were shredded.' Wind whips my hair and I turn to the shoreline. 'These cliffs are like the big, noble faces out of the movie *Labyrinth*, don't you think? But more serious. And a bit genuinely scary because of the depth of some of those notches at the base—' When I turn back, Bodhi is fossicking in a rock pool. 'Watch out for blue-ringed octopuses.'

He jerks his hand out of the water and wipes it on his shorts. 'It's all volcanic around here,' he informs me, regrouping, and nods to the cliffs. 'That's part of what we're trying to save by revegetation, to stop the basalt from eroding.'

'They're pink granite along here. I learned a bit about the lithosphere when—'

'Correct: granite. It's the strata rocks that are being washed away.'

Strata rocks? It's a weird sensation to have pretty much what you've just said repeated back to you as if you know nothing about it. I consider mentioning that wave-cut notches can't really be combated by revegetation on the clifftop but I don't want to be mean.

We amble back to the stairs holding hands. When I do find my voice, all I can think to say is, 'I'm starving.'

Bodhi puts his arm around me when we've climbed to the top. Why is he so comfortable being this close? I try not to breathe in his face. What if my breath's bad? What if I smell of BO because my deodorant washed off in the sea? Mind you, even with the game of cricket my odour would be small change compared to Marlene's. But what if I've got visible snot in my nose? What if—?

'Come back to camp,' he says. 'I could make you something to eat.'

I must look as panic-stricken as I feel because he stops and turns me to face him. 'I'm not going to hurt you, Van.' He smiles and cocks his head to the side. 'It's only a bowl of curry.'

A lizard scurries from the scrub, sees us and skitters off. It's as small as I feel, though probably not as stupid. I skitter off too.

'Hey, where are you going?'

I have, as Alice did, shut up like a telescope. 'It's getting late,' I call back. 'I've got to go.'

'I'll walk you.'

'I've got cello practice.'

'Are you upset?'

'No.' I stop, run back and kiss him. 'Not upset.'

Well, I say I stop, run back, kiss him and say, 'Not upset,' but what I mean is, I wheel around like a seven-year-old pretending to be some minor kind of super jet, mash my face against his chest and make a gurgling noise, then run home as fast as I can.

And not only that: as I run off, I wave, super enthusiastically.

I actually wave.

∞

I burst into the foyer and throw my back against the wall for reassurance that I'm actually on the earth, in my body. I'm panting like a lunatic and Dad, poking around at the

modem wearing tennis shorts, slippers and an old David
Bowie T-shirt, straightens and looks me up and down. It's
sobering. In an instant, the word *Bodhi* is stamped in neon
on my forehead. Or maybe it says *Promiscuous*.

'What the hell are you wearing?'

I could ask Dad the same question. 'My new bathers.'

'Run out of material, did they? Where have you been?'

'The beach.'

'Who with? Your brother came home hours ago.'

'A friend.'

'What friend?'

'Bodhi.'

'Where's she from?'

I accept that gift. 'Melbourne, I think.'

'You've copped a lot of sun.'

'And salt. I need a shower.'

'You've missed dinner.'

'I'm starving. I honestly didn't realise it had gotten so
late.'

Dad leads me to the foyer couch and sits me down.
'Vanessa, I ...' He glances at my still-heaving cleavage
with dismay and peters out, as if he's forgotten what he
was saying. I take hold of my necklace, placing a casual-
cleavage-covering fist on my chest. Unless we're talking
about a piece of music I'm learning, or a test I'm about
to take, or a maths problem I'm contemplating, intimate
one-on-one chats have never been Dad's forte. Apart from
anything else, I'm the one who generally does all the talking.
But I don't feel like talking. My mouth is full of Bodhi's

kiss, my soul still burning with what a goof I turned into at the end, and in the face of my father everything about today seems like an act of betrayal.

When I say intimate one-on-one chats are not his forte, I mean he has visibly paled and seems to be sweating. 'You're not—' He practically flits to the modem, the lights flickering red, and stands, staring down at it before coming slowly back to rejoin me on the couch. 'You're not going off the rails, are you?'

The rails were Mum and Dad and everything the Way It Used To Be. The knot of guilt lodged in my sternum bursts into flame, a small comet of outrage. Show me the stupid rails and I'll get back on them. I open my mouth but nothing comes out.

'It still concerns me that you should be so spoilt as to think we should drop everything and buy you a new wardrobe but ... did you get everything you needed when you went shopping?' His eyes flicker to my bathers and back to my face. 'Rochelle said you had a good day together, that you were really bonding. Did you have a good day?'

'I—'

'She said you've been quite rude to her since then and it's hurt her feelings. That's not like you. Aren't you glad she took you shopping?'

'Yes, sorry. I didn't mean to be rude.'

'You don't know how much it means to me that you two get along.'

He's right, I have no idea how much it means to him. My estimate is that up to this point it has meant Zero. The lights on the modem blink green. 'Ah,' he says, 'Louise has sorted it out. Well . . .' He pats me on the knee. 'So you're all right, then?'

'Yes.'

'I'm glad we've had this talk.' He kisses the top of my head. 'I'd get some aloe on that face of yours – you look very red to me. Did you forget your hat?'

'Yes.'

'Well, remember it next time. Are you keeping up with your practice?'

'Yes.'

'It's a big night for us, this year. Important connections flying in, very important. Have you heard of Richard Marks, Vanessa?'

'Sure. Everyone loves the Marksman. Well, not Suyin; she reckons he's just an old tennis hack who's more famous for being famous than anything he actually ever did.'

Dad snorts. 'He won Wimbledon – and he's younger than me.'

'To be honest, I think Suyin only thinks that because zillions of people follow him and he reposted that "sounds of silence" clip and started the hashtag poorben. She loves Ben Affleck – and don't ask me why because I really don't know.'

Dad rallies. 'The point is, Marks didn't fritter away his prize money – not to mention the endorsements and then the clothing line and his TV career. He's an entrepreneur and now he's making a lot more money in property development – Marksman resorts are popping up all over the world. If your old man can broker this deal for his suite of companies, that will be three years' hard work come to fruition and then, poof—' he makes a 'poof' gesture with his hands, 'the sky's the limit. So you make sure you're a good girl.'

'What sort of deal?'

'It would just be terrific if you could make a good impression. You know how proud I am of you.' He kisses my head again and stands, businesslike. 'The chamber group will be here early in the evening of the party if you want to rehearse.' He and David Bowie pause with one foot on the bottom step. Dad smiles. 'The pianist is good, so you should be all right there.' He nods, as if everything is sorted, and jogs up the staircase.

I call after him, 'Lend me your thumb, Dad. I want to find out whether you're a criminal.'

Of course that's not what I say.

Ash leans over the balustrade, his dangling hands obscuring the panel where Orpheus bewitches all nature with the music of his golden lyre. 'So you're not dead, then?'

'Sorry to disappoint you.'

He graces me with a half-smile and disappears. I head straight for the kitchen to see what's been left for me in the fridge and then up to my room to write poetry about my love.

I'm a whale, bloated with longing, beached on the sands of desire but as much as I try to keep Bodhi in the picture, Darith keeps interrupting us and taking over until I give up and read Plato's *Republic*.

By morning, I'm less whale, more lobster, too burnt even to practise. Guilhermina lays in her coffin, admonishing me with her silence. Her potential for great beauty probably won't be fulfilled while she's in my hands. Still, as the Big O says, I've got to be grateful even if I never find success as a professional musician. In the olden days, nobody wanted women to play orchestral instruments, especially the cello. Pushbike, horse or the violincello – the space between a woman's legs has long been a touchy subject.

I laugh at my own lascivious pun.

Kelsey opens my door. 'Wow, your face is burnt. What are you laughing at?'

'Do you know that as late as the 1930s, women weren't allowed to play the cello for the BBC Symphony Orchestra?'

'I did not know that.' She tilts her head. 'And it does not seem funny. Why weren't they?'

'Because you have to spread your legs to play.'

Kelsey bounces onto her back on the bed and throws her legs wide. 'Ooooh!' she shouts. 'Run everyone!'

I throw my legs wide too and shout, 'Be afraid! Be very afraid!' The sheet slides off and Kelsey scrambles to her knees. 'Oh. My. God. Van! I thought your face was bad!'

'I know. And I'm really sore.' I groan because the stinging is intense. 'I shouldn't have done that.'

'It's because you went off to the surf beach after the cricket. You should have stayed in the shade.' She peels back the skin of one of the aloe vera spears piled on the bedside table and begins to wipe the sticky coolness on my sunburn.

It's heaven.

'Sooo,' she says, sliding a plump, fresh isosceles triangle of aloe along my radiant thigh. 'Spill.'

'He kissed me.'

'God. How old is he again?'

'Nineteen.'

'God. Did you kiss him back?'

'Yes.'

'Oh my God!' She runs her thumbnail along the green flesh to release fresh juice. 'So, what was it like?'

'Salty.'

'What, like anchovies?'

'Not that bad.' I roll over so she can do my back. It's impossible to explain how after the initial thrill, the *thought* of kissing Bodhi was somehow better than the actual kissing. 'I know this might sound weird but it sort of happened before I … it felt like I was *watching myself kiss him* rather than *actually* kissing him. Do you know what I mean?'

'Not really.'

'I dunno.'

She puts down the aloe vera and lies next to me, considerately not touching any part of my body. 'Are you all right, Van?'

I mustn't be, because I'm crying. I sniffle and compose myself. 'I've probably got sunstroke.'

'Didn't you want to kiss him?'

'Yeah, I did. I think so. No, yeah, I did.'

'But you'd rather kiss Darith.'

'That is true,' I concur. 'I would rather kiss Darith.' I point the remote at the sound system and 'Fall' floats on, cocooning us like bubble wrap.

'I'll never get to kiss the Biebs,' whispers Kelsey and she sighs as if her heart were truly broken.

I didn't think my skin could be pinker, tighter or more stingish but then I wake up. There's nothing I can do today but lie about like a roasted couch-potato, sipping water and smearing myself with green slime.

It's days before I feel fit to go outside again. I choose something nice to wear that doesn't press too hard on my shoulders, which are still sore, zinc up my ankle creases, which remain achingly crimson, and remember my hat – but Darith and Ash are nowhere to be found. I return to the couch hoping Kelsey will come and save me, but she doesn't. I ring her and she tells me she's at her aunty's. She must have a thousand cousins.

Louise calls me into her office and pulls out a plastic tub with the Christmas presents in it, the tags handwritten by Mum, and starts sorting through them. 'I know he's a bigwig these days but you'd think Richard Marks was the bloody President the way his team is carrying on – insisting on their own security, own caterers, own dancing girls leaping out of cakes,' she mutters.

'You're kidding about the last bit, aren't you?' I ask.

'Only about the cakes,' she says darkly. 'I know he's Mr Success and everybody loves him, but I don't like it. There's something fishy about the whole thing.'

'What kind of fishy?'

She looks at me sharply, as if suddenly remembering who she's talking to. 'Oh, don't listen to me. You know what I'm like when I've got too much time on my hands.'

This isn't the slightest bit true as I've never known Louise to have any time on her hands but it's no use asking questions. She's clammed up now and I *do* know what she's like when she's decided not to spill the beans.

She reads from the list of pre-wrapped gifts. 'So, which ones do you fancy?'

'Whichever ones you reckon. I'm going to walk in to town.'

'Cover up,' she says. 'You've still got a hint of lobster about you.'

I take one of Mum's sun umbrellas for extra protection. It's quite a walk but feels charmingly Anne Shirley to be out and about in the world under a gingham parasol. Gravitating to the cafe for a jar of juice, I wonder what it was like for Anne, that first time with Gilbert Blythe. Somehow I can't imagine her giving him a head job in the horse and buggy.

Mum first found out about Dad because Rochelle was doing just that under his desk in the home office. Apparently Mum had a whole conversation with Dad about their tickets for the Sailing Club Gala and Rochelle was hiding down there and Mum only busted them when she dashed back in to show him the dress she'd bought so he could think about which tie might match. Rochelle was halfway out and Dad had his pants around his ankles and they were laughing.

I wouldn't have known about that except Rochelle told one of the cleaners who was also her friend from uni and I overheard that cleaner telling the other cleaner on their way out to their car one afternoon. They were laughing about it too, until they saw me.

Pain irritates me back to reality when someone taps my shoulder. Bodhi, having tricked me, pops up on my other side. 'Hello there,' he says. 'I'm getting lunch. Do you want something?'

When we're settled and I've ordered the recommended turmeric smoothie, Bodhi says, 'Where have you been?'

I pull back the neck of my dress. 'Sunburn.'

He says, 'Ouch,' and gently strokes my skin. 'I was worried you were avoiding me.' He lifts my arm and kisses me, right on the inside crook of my elbow.

Marlene swings in next to us. 'Get a room,' she says, dumping her small leather backpack on the table. 'We've missed you at Foxhole – not so easy to commit to the hard stuff, hey?'

Before I can answer, Bodhi says, 'She had sunburn,' and Marlene rolls her eyes. 'You're a harsh woman,' he says.

'Women are always bagged for saying it like it is,' she tells me. 'Men get called "assertive" and told they have

"leadership qualities" but women are "bossy" and "harsh".'
I slurp on my smoothie and she pulls a Moleskine journal
from the backpack. 'I've been hoping to run into you
because there's something I'd like to show you.' A few
photographs spill out: men meeting with my father and it
looks like they're on the grounds around Shearwater.

'My dad wouldn't.'

Bodhi sips his chai. 'Wouldn't what?'

'Do anything illegal.'

'The trouble with men like your father,' Marlene slides
Bodhi's lunch towards herself and forages through the
salad, 'is that they change the laws to suit themselves.'
She sprinkles unrefined sea salt on her stolen stockpile of
lemon cucumber. 'And just because something becomes
legal doesn't make it moral.'

'My dad's not immoral.'

Bodhi turns a fork over and over.

'Anyway,' she says, crunching on cucumber and sweeping up all the photos but one, 'have you seen this guy
around?' She points to a fattish balding guy shading his
eyes and seemingly looking straight at the camera.

Who prints photos? And how dare they take them of
my father without permission? I should go to the police.
'Who is he?'

'Eddie Glasshouse.' Marlene picks at her teeth with
a toothpick she seems to have pulled from her hair. 'He's a
parliamentarian, a legislator: a lawmaker, that's who. And
one who shouldn't have anything to do with investing in
land development in protected areas.'

The name does sound vaguely familiar but I shake my head and hand her back the photograph.

'No, you keep it,' she says. 'If you do see him, could you let me know?'

Bodhi runs his finger along my forearm. 'We're going for a surf. Do you want to come?'

'It's tempting,' I say, blushing. 'But I don't think I'm ready to come out from under my parasol.'

'That's an omen, buddy,' Marlene says, pointing a pretend-gun at Bodhi. She shoots. 'An omen.'

'Ignore her,' he says and kisses my cheek.

And then they're gone. I put the photo in the pocket of my dress and walk down to the foreshore where a small flock of seagulls appear to be doing yoga on the sand. 'An omen of what?' I ask them. They continue their stretching and are not forthcoming.

It looks like the land ends where the water begins but the topographers know the continental crust I'm standing on goes deep under the water until it meets the oceanic crust. Is that what my parents are like? There's the bit of them I can see but vast tracts of them are hidden below. The waves are relatively calm today. Still, the drag leaves hollows under my feet.

'Where's my mother?' I shout and the seagulls flap up, disgruntled. Several of them wing out to sea and disappear.

Walking back through the tidy foreshore park I spy Darith and Nadia talking to two Aboriginal blokes sitting on one of the benches: one about the same age as Dad and an old fella with white hair. Darith has his head cocked, listening. He shakes the younger man's hand and the old man laughs and pokes Nadia in the ribs with his finger. She laughs too, more shy than ever. The men stand and the four of them walk off together in the other direction, away from me.

Tim scares the crappers out of me by leaping into my field of vision saying, 'Earth to Vanessa Partridge,' and waving both arms like he's an aircraft marshal. 'Where's Kelsey?'

'Gone to her aunty's,' I tell him when I've recovered. 'She has thousands of cousins.'

'Want to go back to yours and watch something?'

I can't believe Tim Bickford has just invited himself to my house. 'Sure,' I say.

'I was watching some hooded plovers,' he informs me as we stroll back.

'You like birds?'

'Oh, yeah!' And he tells me all about how he started a school project to help save the helmeted honeyeater, an endangered species in Yellingbo, his local area. '*Lichenostomus melanops cassidix*,' he says. 'It's Victoria's state bird. You can adopt one, if you like. In the wild, I mean.'

How did I not know that Tim Bickford is a budding ornithologist? 'I'm really sorry I threw my ice-cream at you that time.'

He bobs, a half-bow, and I think that's him accepting my apology. 'Better than a brick,' he says.

'No one threw a brick at you, did they?'

'Uh-huh.' He nods exaggeratedly. 'They most certainly did.'

'Did it hit you?'

'Uh-huh.' He parts his hair to show me the scar on the back of his head. 'It most certainly did.'

'Shit. What did they do that for?'

He sniffs evasively. 'Wearing glasses or something.'

'Jeez.'

'Yep. Some people are threatened by the most innocent things.'

'What do you want to watch?'

'Have you ever seen a show called *The Mighty Boosh*?'

'No.' I feel suspicious. 'Is it good?'

'Uh-huh.' He does the nod. 'It certainly is.'

We split off, him to Oceanview to pick up his DVDs and me home to organise snacks with Sharif, but first I ask Louise to sign our family up as a Friend of the Helmeted Honeyeater.

'It's our state bird!' I inform her.

The sound behind the pantry door makes my heart skip: a high-pitched lament, almost a whistle. For a second I think Roger Federer must be back and trapped in there. Then there's a small crash and a muffled voice says, 'Crap.'

I open the door. 'Are you all right?'

Rochelle startles, knocking a jar of pickled artichokes that joins the mess of broken glass and Nutella on the pantry floor, brine spreading over the globs of brown. 'What are you doing?' she demands, wiping tears and chocolate smears from her mouth with the back of a trembling hand, spoon still clutched in her fingers.

I've seen Rochelle cry three times. Once when a cricket ball rolled out of Ash's cupboard and cracked her on the elbow as it fell; once during her and Dad's wedding when her bridesmaid best friend, Shara-Jane, read out a poem about how great she was and how lucky we were to have her wrecking our family; and once when Marion-Mum – the day she left with Roger – grabbed her by the arm and said, 'Are you proud of yourself?' and wouldn't let her go, just stared into her eyes for ages until Rochelle cracked. But even then Rochelle didn't look as devastated as she does right now, sniffing and shaking and wiping the pooling black from under her eyes.

I step in and pull the door shut behind me. Artichoke urine and Nutella faeces gets on my toe.

Rochelle doesn't say anything.

I wipe my foot and cover the mess with several layers of paper towel.

'Watch out for glass,' she murmurs. 'In those thongs.'

There's a plastic rubbish bin for storing Arborio rice. I sit on it. Rochelle slumps back against the shelving, sucks the last of the Nutella off her spoon, sighs and looks across at me. 'Your mother was a saint.'

This is so *not* what I was expecting her to say that I can't really make sense of it and reply, 'What?' in a voice that suggests that if I acquired a brain cell, it would be lonely.

She waggles the spoon at me. 'Your mother,' she explains, dropping the spoon on the nastily stained paper towel, 'was a bloody saint.'

'What did Dad do?'

She starts crying again. I tear off more paper towel and Rochelle blows her nose like a trooper. The effort leaves her pale and blotchy.

'Did he yell at you?'

'Sure did.'

I pass the roll. 'He shouldn't do that. It's not fair.'

She grunts. I think it's in agreement. 'Aren't you organising the party right?' I venture. 'He sometimes yelled at Mum about that stuff too.'

She shakes her head but looks surprised. 'Did he? To hear him talk, you'd think everything she touched turned to gold.' She takes me in. 'Sorry.'

Rochelle has lived with us for years now. I find it hard to believe she never noticed Dad yelling at Mum. Or maybe she thought it would never happen to her. Even before I knew they were 'at it' (as Ash puts it), I thought he was always especially kind to Rochelle. When she stuffed up, he didn't yell (though he did get Louise to 'discuss the matter'). The paper towel underfoot is soaked through and I throw on a few more layers. 'What is it then?'

'I'm—' The leak springs up and she quells it, pressing her fists to both eyes. She lets out a breath, changing her mind about telling me. 'Never mind.'

Then it's over, whatever this was, and we're sitting in the pantry feeling uncomfortable. Well, I certainly do. I reach peak awkward when the chef opens the pantry door and peers down at us from his Sudanese heights.

We stare at him.

He blinks at us.

Rochelle steps over the wee-poo chocolate artichokes disaster as if emerging from a limousine and making her way up the red carpet. I try my best to imitate her but Sharif pulls me up. 'Oi,' he says. 'What's this?'

'They broke,' I say. 'On the tiles.'

'I can see that.' He puts his hands on his hips. 'But who do you think is going to clean that up?'

The glint in his eyes suggests that me proposing we wait for the cleaners is *not* a good idea.

When I gather it all up and stuff it into the plastic bag he pointedly hands me, I'm so deep into my excrement metaphor it even smells bad. When I've disposed of it in the rubbish bin, Sharif pats me. 'Thank you, Vanessa.'

I pat him back. 'You're welcome, Sharif. What can I take for snacks?'

Tim wanders up the drive with his mouth open. 'Kelsey said it was a mansion,' he says at the front door, running his fingertips over the bird in flight on the building's pewter nameplate. 'But I didn't really believe her.' He traces the lettering under the image. 'What does *yolla* mean?'

I point out the word *Shearwater* stamped above the bird. 'It means shearwater.'

'Huh,' he says. 'The seabird.' He touches the plaque again. 'What language is it?'

'Aboriginal language,' I say, absurdly pleased with myself to have looked it up. 'Boon Wurrung, to be precise.'

'Cool.'

It's strange to see the place through Tim's eyes (and fingers) as he wanders about saying, 'Wow.'

'It isn't a "mansion".'

'Oh, it is,' Tim says. 'It really is.'

'It's just a house,' I snap, but neither of us believe me. 'Come on, the TV's upstairs.'

'That's not a TV, it's a home cinema!' he insists, when we get up there.

I say, 'It is not,' and technically, it isn't, but taking in the stretch of sand-coloured carpet between the doorway and the back of the red-leather six-seater couch that faces the wall-to-ceiling window, its view partially obscured by the retractable screen, the ping-pong table to one side and a pile of red corduroy beanbags and shelves of books and games on the other, I guess it is pretty lush.

'Oh, it is,' Tim repeats. 'It really is.'

I begin to understand why someone hit him with a brick.

Darith and Ash turn up halfway through the second episode and apparently love *The Mighty Boosh*, too. 'Things were so much simpler at the turn of the century,' Tim says, shoving prawns into his face.

After morning practice, I call the Oceanview office because Kelsey's not answering her phone and apparently that's because she's *gone to a movie with Tim Bickford*. I retreat to the kitchen. Sharif pauses his chopping. 'Louise has ten minutes ago informed me that we're to cater for six extra security staff this year. Richard Marks's people. Six!' He slides the vegetables into a stainless steel tub for the fridge. 'And we're not allowed to take photographs – apparently there's an official photographer this year. And a yacht-load of VIPs.' He taps a list on the side of the fridge. 'Wilbur Wilde and the Troublemakers, you ever heard of them?'

'No, have you?'

'I have not.' He taps it again. 'But I do have a soft spot for Marcia Hines.' He puts the vegetables away and pulls a covered tray from the fridge. 'No offence to your father, but do you have any idea why the Marksman is coming here? The Shearwater New Year's Eve is very fine but hardly the usual haunt of the celebrity set . . . or the highrollers.'

'Not really. Some business thing.'

'All very mysterious.'

Every nerve ending wants to tell Sharif everything the Foxholers have told me but all I say is, 'Very.' Watching him pipe the finishing touches on tonight's incredible chocolate torte, I add, 'Hope no one tries to headhunt you for some fancy New York restaurant.'

He shakes his head. 'No thank you. I've done my time in a four-star and the stress nearly killed me – this quiet corner of the world suits me just fine.'

'Can I have some of that now?'

'No, you may not.'

'Do you know where the boys are?'

'No. But they told me at breakfast that they're taking the girls out to dinner tonight. Maybe they're with them?'

I take my sorrows to the pool, dragging out a lilo, my barge to Avalon. Since we've been on holidays together, I've got used to seeing Darith, even when he has his stupid arm around stupid Nadia's stupid shoulders. When he's away from me the hours seem to drag out for small eternities and the feeling of not being close to him is tears, rolling down my face.

Rochelle appears, tossing her book down and making herself comfortable on the deck-lounge. 'You're a dramatic little thing, aren't you,' she says, which seems a bit rich after the pantry affair. 'What are you, the Lady of Shallot?'

I slither off and dive under and when I come up, swim laps with the fervent hope that my exaggerated splashing will drive her away. As if in answer to my prayers, Kelsey and Tim turn up with the Lepski brothers. Coop runs and does a screaming bomb into the deep end and then all hell breaks loose.

I thought Rochelle would flounce off but she lies there reading her book as if we're all a mirage.

The boys adore Tim and if he was a show-off before, he's impossible now that Kelsey's encouraging him with her big laugh. Leading by example, he soon has them doing a strut like they're Hollywood toffs on their way down the red carpet but falling into the deep end as if they don't realise that the pool is there. Coop yells, 'Oh, no!' every time, as if genuinely surprised to find himself flailing about in water.

It's irresistible and of course I'm doing the stupidest swagger ever and pretending to wear a sneeze-inducing feather boa and win my tenth Academy Award when Ash, Dana, Darith and Nadia arrive, Ellen trailing them like the fifth wheel. I splash in, feet first, and wish there was a secret passage back to the house through the bottom of the pool.

I'm down there so long, I break the surface gasping.

Lachie spear tackles Harry and the small tsunami they cause splashes Nadia.

'Sorry,' says Ash. 'I was hoping we'd have the pool to ourselves.'

'Let's get away from the little kids,' Dana says and they file off after her to the house.

Darith looks back. 'Season's greetings, everyone.' He waves.

God, it's true, Christmas is only days away. I can't bring myself to join the chorus of replies but change my big sigh to a pretend jazz trumpet when I realise Rochelle is watching me watch them from behind her sunglasses and I shout, 'Stacks on Bickford!' to put her off the scent.

The boys settle into a game of swimming-pool soccer and Kel and I lie on our towels in the sun as far from Rochelle as we can get.

Well, I say *on* our towels but I'm under one, too, being already parbaked. 'Sooo,' I say. 'How was the movie?'

She rolls her eyes. 'Mum clearly neglected to add that she insisted we take my brothers.'

'Oh, God. No smooching then.'

'Not with Coop around – he's like his own personal news outlet.'

We're distracted by Tim shouting, 'Rogue shot!' and the ball smacking me in the side of the head. Kelsey grabs it and whacks it hard between the goalposts and they shout 'Score!' and everyone cheers, even Rochelle.

'He's actually a really nice kid,' Kelsey says when she's settled again.

'Is he?' I mutter, rubbing my still-burning ear. 'You guys should stay. There's a whole kids' channel going to waste up there.'

'All of us?'

'Why not.' I sit up. 'Mum . . .?' Rochelle takes off her sunglasses and we stare at each other, fast-tracked back to peak awkward. 'Rochelle,' I recover, 'can everyone stay for tea?'

'If it's all right with Chef, it's all right with me,' she says, slipping back behind her shades.

I leave Kelsey at the pool with her superhero to ask Sharif if it's too late to add five to the dinner table. 'They like plain food,' I say. 'Sausages and mashed potato, or something like that.'

'How about peas?'

'Yeah, and peas.'

He bows. 'Your wish is my command.'

'In that case, serve me Darith on a platter thanks and chuck Nadia in the compost,' I say.

That's not what I say.

We drag out the beanbags and occasional tables and eat

up in the lounge and I may be imagining it but I'm pretty sure when the others leave, Darith looks like he'd rather stay with us and watch the 1963 version of *Jason and the Argonauts* than be dressed up to go out to dinner like he's a grown-up, or at some school function.

Even if he does look so handsome I could cry.

When the movie's over, Harry offers to lead the way home and the boys head off before it gets too dark. That leaves me sitting between Kelsey and Tim, who both stare fixedly ahead at *Star Wars*, which was Tim's choice, not mine. 'Right,' I say. 'I'll go and ... yes, well ... snacks.'

When I get back with a camembert and a box of crackers the room seems empty, the backs of their heads having disappeared. I hear slurping and snuffling and stand in the doorway not knowing what to do. Kelsey's head pops up over the back of the couch, staring – she must have sensed me. 'Oh,' she says. 'Come in.'

'Are you decent?'

Tim jumps up, right to his feet, scandalised. 'Yes!'

'Settle your petals,' says Kelsey, pulling him back down.

They manage to refrain from grossing me out but I don't think either of them are aware of the actual film so we might have been watching something interesting and when *Star Wars* is done, Kelsey drags Tim off the couch, announces he's going to walk her home, and pulls him out of the room, chucking me an air kiss. Tim waves, grinning stupidly.

'See ya then,' I say to nobody. 'Season's greetings.'

∂◯

By the time I lurch out of bed in the morning, Ash and Darith have gone surfing with the girls in Dana's combi; Dad and Rochelle have set out for brunch before some fancy party at the marina; and when I wander down to the caravan park, Kelsey and her brothers are heading out with their dad to visit another set of cousins. 'It's Uncle Peter's family's Christmas Day,' she tells me when I get there, disappointed, 'and therefore compulsory.'

Tim appears around the back of their Tarago, gives me a wave and climbs in, high-fiving Coop on the way. Kelsey has bloomed a deep red. 'Um,' she says. 'Did you—? It's just that we're picking up my Grandma Laurel so there was only one spare seat—'

And they gave it to Tim Bloody Bickford. I jump in the Tarago, grab him by the shirt and push him out shouting, 'Yes, I want to come! Of course I do. How can you want to take Tim and not me?'

That's not what I do.

There's only so much dramatic-lonely-walking-on-the-windy-beach a person can do before they die of boredom. I set myself up on my bedroom balcony to practise in the shade of the magnolia, an evergreen variety planted and nurtured into a giant: the backdrop for a zillion wedding photos. I force myself to begin working through my practice schedule but can't resist skipping half the tech work to have a crack at the Mendelssohn even if the middle section lurches like a discordant fingernail down the blackboard of art, to coin the Big O's encouraging phrase.

I regroup and play the beginning and the end again – I do love them so – and feel revitalised. I've spent most of the year on *The Swan* and with the approaching sunset chorus as my accompanist it doesn't take long for the music to colonise me. Sometimes embracing Guilhermina pushes out all thought, leaving me a trembling carapace for the swell, sustain and plunge and then I think maybe I can play. I mean, really play.

Louise comes out in her blue pinstripe pyjamas. 'You okay?' she asks. 'I'm going to bed.'

'Yes – but it's not even nine.'

'I know, but I'm done in. Goodnight. Don't stay up too late and make sure the lights are turned off. And eat that dinner.' She shuffles off, yawning.

I play a dreamy largo and am contemplating stopping to eat the dinner that sits cold as stone on the balcony table when a voice floats up so spooky and sweet I wonder if I've fallen asleep. 'But, soft! What light through yonder window breaks?' it says. 'It is the east, and Vanessa Partridge is the sun. She plays the cello, yet says nothing: what of that?'

I rock my chair to the side on two legs to peer over and Bodhi is standing at the edge of the clearing where the gravel drive meets a stand of old gums. I'd *like* to put out my hand and say, 'What man art thou that, thus bescreen'd in night, so stumblest on my counsel?' but what I *do* is squawk, 'Cripes!' as the chair slides out from under me and I land heavily in a clump of terracotta pots full of geraniums, cracking a few and only narrowly avoiding smacking my beautiful cello into the pavers. Trembling with the near tragedy, I slide in the end pin and lie her in her case, panting, then peep over the balustrade.

Bodhi is still there. His perplexity shifts to a smile and he beckons. 'Come down.'

'I can't,' I whisper-call back.

'You can!'

'I can't!'

'You can! Hurry – before someone sees me.'

'Hang on!'

I clip Guil into her case, dump her inside and run down to the front door, passing Dana, Ash and Darith on the stairs. Ash follows me down asking, 'Where are you off to?'

'Nowhere.'

'Nowhere, where?' He watches from the doorway like some kind of Capulet as my Romeo steps out to meet me.

'Don't worry,' Bodhi calls to Ash, taking my hand and leading me into the woods. 'I'll look after her.'

Ash shouts, 'Van, come back!' but I'm already running and it's like being lifted onto a carnival ride – everything is different and there's music playing and the wind is in my hair.

Bursting onto the beach is exhilarating and lush Venus shines fat and glimmering through rents in the veil of thinly spread cloud. He leads me along the soft sand and turns up a track I don't recognise. The thump of drums gets loud and we step into a camp site like I've never seen before.

Fairy lanterns that appear to have been made by actual fairies hang in the trees and the tents are a mishmash of tarps and cloths and carpets and couches. Bodhi's still holding my hand and I follow him to a deep fire-pit with an impressive hearth of huge flat stones. This . . . village . . . seems like it's been here forever, as if it grew out of the forest, but at the same time there's an almost Hollywood feel about it, like everyone here has landed from outer space. The drumming peaks and comes to an end with a crash, then there's laughter and people break away from the circle around the fire. I recognise some of them from the cafe but there look to be about thirty people camping here.

Bodhi invites me to the fire and reaches into a nearby esky, pulling out two beers. 'Want one?' he offers and makes a winning face. 'It's organic.'

I take it. I've drunk beer heaps of times.

Well, I say I've drunk beer heaps of times but I mean I did have a glass once at one of Ash's parties but he caught me and tipped most of it down the sink. I'm rather keen to try it again without having to look over my shoulder for my brother. I wrestle with the lid.

Bodhi laughs. 'It's not a screw-top.' And pings off the lid with a bottle opener. He escorts me to a banana lounge that's seen better days, lays back and pulls me beside him, half on top of him. I'm relieved not to have spilled anything. He drinks. 'You haven't tasted your beer.'

It's malty and almost sweet with a horrible aftertaste – no wonder people keep drinking, to get rid of that flavour. 'The scientific name for hops is *humulus lupulus*,' I observe, hoping there's no foam on my lip like there is on Bodhi's. 'Apparently it's related to the cannabis plant.'

'Is it now?' Bodhi asks, lighting up with interest. 'Well, fancy – I happen to have a little of humpus lumpus's richer cousin right here.'

'*Humulus lupulus*,' I correct him as the drumming starts up again, in time with my racing heart.

The sun has gone and lights spring from the dark. Bodies everywhere, dancing, dancing. Everything about it is so right, so right, so right. So wrong. Wrong. I am out of my place, out of my depth. The music, the lights, all swimming close and now far and laughter coming from somewhere but it's my mouth open, my laugh loud even against the noise of the drums, and more drums inside my head. I fall against something. 'Whoa,' Bodhi says. I straighten up, fall into him and he lowers me to a seat. 'You're a little bit drunk.'

The world is soup, debris in the ocean floating, thick soup and the ocean, tides, surging and the music and drums. 'Which metaphor is this?' I ask, my voice a quiet rumble, a mumble, a quumble.

'Here,' he says. Something under my nose and a thrill, wide open awake, shooting stars and all the love in the world.

'That's more like it.'

'That's more like it,' I echo and the laughter again, from my other body-self.

I wake dry-mouthed, my cheek flat against Bodhi's chest, a dark patch of drool on his shirt, a darker shadow of nausea deep inside me. We're on a mattress covered in sarongs, his face is turned away from me, one dreadlock awry and sticking up to the sky. The camp looks dirty in the morning sun but in a warm and friendly way, as if no one here could mind you being a bit filthy and hungover. Marlene enters my line of sight and squats by the fire swizzling bacon and eggs in a frying pan. 'Want some?' she says.

The nausea-shadow hovers on the horizon and the promise of food makes it shimmer. I don't know if that's good or bad.

'It's organic fakin' bacon,' she warns.

'Okay,' I say. 'Is it good?'

She nods knowingly and smiles. 'Oooh yeah.'

I disentangle myself from Bodhi and come closer. 'What's it made of?'

'Tempeh.'

Marlene looks at me from time to time as we're eating. Finally, she puts down her plate and wipes her mouth with the back of her hand. 'So,' she says.

'My head's full of cotton wool,' I reply, my face full of fakin' bacon.

She smiles but doesn't seem happy. 'Won't your dad be wondering where you are?'

This sparks a little unease but I don't seem to be able to care. Perhaps I am still drunk. I certainly feel strange.

Marlene takes my empty plate and I crawl back to Bodhi. Cuddling up in bed is surely the best feeling in the world.

∽◯

When I open my eyes again, Bodhi stirs, stretches and pulls me close. 'Good morning,' he says and as snoogly as it is, his breath stinks. He kisses me.

I peer over his shoulder. Children sit on upturned logs around a table made of milk-crates and a red-speckled Formica tabletop. One of them is eating a sandwich. Another bites into a peeled boiled egg, leaving smeary fingerprints on the white flesh.

Lunch.

'Oh my effing gosh it's halfway through tomorrow!' I say and wriggle out of his arms.

He sits up and looks blearily around.

'Where are my sandals?' I'm scrabbling around in the dust like I've lost an earring, not a pair of size 8 shoes, stopping in surprise to see that my arms and legs are striped and flourished with fluorescent paint – yellow, orange and lime green. The children are looking over at me now. My bra and underpants are dotted fluorescent orange and I'm not wearing any other clothes. It's hard not to scream. 'Where's my dress?'

Bodhi fishes around under the sarongs and pulls it out. 'Your dress, madam.'

I find my sandals on the other side of the mattress. Was I dancing around in my underwear?

Yes. The image comes to me. Yes, I was dancing around

in my underwear. I ate breakfast with Marlene in my underwear. I turn my back on Bodhi and fumble myself into my clothes. I'm feeling sweary and teary but even though the children have turned their attention back to their food and each other, I somehow feel obliged to set a good example. All I manage is to whisper, 'We didn't—?'

Bodhi reaches out and pulls me to him and looks earnestly into my eyes. 'I would never, ever, have sex with someone who was out of it and didn't know what they were doing, Van. Never.'

A feeling surges up in me that might be love.

He squeezes me and presses his hard-on against my thigh. 'As much as I would have liked to.' He kisses my shoulder. 'And man, I'd really like to. But I'd never pressure you – only when you're ready, Van.' The throb against my leg suggests he's hoping that time's right now.

'Do you want me to give you a medal for not having sex with me while I was unconscious?' I say, pushing him away.

That's not what I say.

I say, 'Thank you,' and kiss him, struggling to avoid the mingling of our bad breath and being pulled on top of his erection, and scurry off in the direction I'm hoping leads to home.

It's hopeless trying to find my way through the bush but once I get to the sand my compass kicks in and it's not long before I see Darith up the beach. He spots me and yells, 'Van!' like I'm a miracle, and turns and shouts, 'Ash! Ash, I found her,' into the wind.

We run towards each other like Heathcliff and Cathy and he wraps me up in the best hug in the world. So safe. 'We were about to tell your dad he'd better call the cops.' He sounds like he might cry, too. 'Where have you been?'

'Dad knows?' I sniffle.

'Sort of.' Darith pulls back to look at me and breaks into a smile. 'Have you been at a rave?' He laughs. 'You've been at a rave!'

Ash runs down the beach and Darith steps away, the spell broken. To my utter surprise, Ash hugs me too. 'Holy shit-knuckle, I thought you might be dead.' He steps back. 'You'd better wash that off before we get you home. I told Dad you went for a swim with Kelsey and then two minutes later she bloody turned up looking for you. I'd better call them – everyone's worried sick. Even Mum.'

Hope surges up like a revisitation of fakin' bacon. 'Mum—?'

Ash shakes his head. 'I messaged her.' He shrugs. 'Last time I saw you, you were running off with some strange bloke twice your age and then you never came home. I kind of panicked.'

'He's not twice my age.'

He narrows his eyes. 'But he is strange.'

I skirt this trapdoor. 'Did she ring you back?'

'No, just texts.' He smiles. 'She even threw in a complete sentence.'

I feel a stab of jealousy. 'Where is she?'

'Didn't say.'

'Where's Dad?'

'He drove Kelsey to look for you. The mobile library is in town, so they thought you might have gone there.'

Dad and Kelsey driving around together.

Ash waves towards the stairs. 'I've got a towel up there. Go clean off in your bra and undies.'

My orange-dotted bra and undies.

'What?' Ash pauses, phone in hand. 'We won't look.'

'It's a bit cold,' I reason. 'I'll just wash off in the shallows.'

'Cold?' says Darith. 'It's thirty degrees.'

Funny how a barometer feels the pressure most when the weather is still and clear and mild. I'm finding it hard to breathe and the fakin' bacon is definitely threatening to make a reappearance.

Ash says, 'Yeah, it's fine, Dad,' into his phone. 'She got lost. They must have missed each other. I know, idiots.'

As if powered by a force beyond my control, I kick off my sandals and my legs start pumping towards the water, clothes and all. Scrubbing at myself with handfuls of sand feels exquisite, as if I'm sloughing off an unpleasant skin. The boys join me and we float for a bit, lifted by the genial waves, toes poking out of the water. When we head in, Ash stops me to scrub paint off the back of my legs and one of my elbows.

'Do you remember when we used to have baths together?' I say.

He shoves me off balance into a sandy swash. 'I'd rather not.'

I have to wade back out to rinse the sand off before I can come to shore for the towel.

We head home and Ash asks, 'So, what's going on with you and Bodhi?' without looking at me.

I swallow. A darkening cumulonimbus is hovering over me and the storm in it is called a lie. 'Nothing. I was mostly hanging out with Marlene.'

Ash still doesn't look at me.

Darith says, 'Not Bodhi, then?'

I swallow again. My throat makes a weird clicking noise. 'Of course he was there. He invited me.' We walk on in silence and a light rain falls from the cloud above my head like invisible tears. 'Thanks for looking for me.'

Ash skips ahead. 'Of course we looked for you. I'm just glad we didn't find you washed up on the beach, bloated, infested with crabs.'

Darith chants, 'Those are pearls that were her eyes . . .'

And they run, bouncing like goats, full of restless energy. 'Was it fun?' Ash yells back to me.

'Yeah.' I nod. 'It was fun. I danced.'

He runs backwards. 'Ha-ha! The Van dance. The mind freakin' boggles.' Then turns away shouting, 'Remember your phone next time.' And they're gone, leaving me to walk the rest of the track by myself.

My sense of elation fades with every step and I'm soon chewing over the five billion innocent things Kelsey could have said to my father that might ruin my life. He'll put two and two together and come up with Bodhi. He'll think I'm – what will he think? He won't know *what* to think. He'll take all my privileges and confiscate my clothes. He'll search my phone for debauched photos of me dancing around in my underwear or waking up in the dirty bed of his worst nightmare: the unwashed masses. I have to let that one go because as Ash rightly observed, I stupidly didn't take my phone when I ran off with Romeo. But he might slap me. Not even the thought of seeing Roger Federer can shield me from the horror of the possibility that he'll send me to live with Aunty Sue. I'll be forced to volunteer for the Lions Club every weekend: Schumann at the sausage sizzle. Or worse: boarding school! I've been afraid of this ever since Rochelle suggested it after Mum left and we realised she wasn't coming back anytime soon. And now it's going to come true.

Anger clubs down the relief on Dad's face when he first sees me slouching up the drive. I scrunch up, trying to steel myself for the yelling, but a strange uncertainty seems to wash over him. 'No need for hysterics,' he says, giving me an awkward, one-armed squeeze. 'Just a mix-up.' He steps back. 'Why is your dress wet? Come on, all's well that ends well.' Then gives me a shake. 'Vanessa, pull yourself together.'

Kelsey's eyes are saucers of wicked curiosity but I can't stop the sniffling and blubbering. I think I might puke and she starts to look worried, too.

'Thank God you're all right,' Dad says, handing me over to her. 'Now, I've got to go. I'm late. Louise is in the office if you need anything. For God's sake, both of you, be sensible and stick to the tracks.'

'We will,' says Kelsey, dragging me up to the bedroom.

Dad feigns surprise. 'She speaks!' he jokes.

Kel presses her back dramatically against the shut door. 'Tell me everything.'

She waits while I slip into the bathroom to dump my clothes, rinse off, throw on PJs and crawl into bed. 'I'm sorry you had to drive all over the place with my dad.'

'He's scary.'

'Is he?'

'Yep. Louise kept calling him about urgent thises and thats and it was as if someone had blocked up the toilets. But I didn't mind. I was worried. Where were you?'

'Blocked up the toilets?'

'My dad really only stamps about like a maniac when punters block up the toilets.'

It's hard to imagine Mr Lepski stamping about like a maniac. He's always so affable in his white terry-towelling hat, riding around on the caravan-park lawnmower or endlessly cleaning things with the high-pressure hose. I reach for my phone and find some comfort from the worried messages from Mum. The same one three times:

Drlng, let me know yr ok.

I show Kelsey the messages.

'Have you texted her back?'

Maybe it's malicious but I put the phone down. 'Later.'

Kel bounces with impatience. 'Well?'

'I slept in the same bed as Pan after running off and engaging in debauchery with him and his coterie of wild nymphs and dryads,' I whisper.

She looks disappointed. 'Come on,' she says. 'Where've you been?'

My qualms rise up like floodwaters. 'Well,' I say. 'I ran away with a boy nearly four years older than me and I'm ninety-eight per cent sure I drunkenly danced half-naked with him and his friends, sixty-seven per cent sure I broke my own rule of never, ever, smoking tobacco, seventy-nine per cent sure it was mixed with marijuana, and thirty-four per cent unsure if I took other drugs besides. I'm also point-zero-zero-one per cent unsure if I'm still a virgin and seventy-five per cent sure I'm going to throw up very soon.'

That's not what I say.

I say, 'I forgot my phone and got lost and now I feel really sick,' which, despite being one hundred per cent lies, is also one hundred per cent true. Tears well up from the bottomless lake. I blubber, 'I want my mum,' and Kelsey puts her arms around me.

'How the crikey heck did you get lost?' she wonders out loud.

'I went a different way.'

She laughs. 'Well, don't do that again.'

'I won't,' I say.

But then, I do.

In the early morning, Bodhi calls up to my balcony and interrupts my practice. 'I've borrowed a car. It's down on the road,' he says as if driving around in a car that isn't being driven by somebody's parents is an everyday thing. 'Come surfing.'

Maybe I'm suffering from depersonalisation disorder because what I think is, *Oh no, that's a terrible idea. Anything could happen to me! I should tell my dad about you,* but what I *do* is nod maniacally, dash inside to get my hat, look in the mirror to make sure there's no snot in my nose or food stuck between my teeth, and run downstairs and out the front door shouting, 'I'm going to the beach,' to anyone who might care.

We avoid the driveway and head to the road through the bush. Holding hands and running seems to be Bodhi's raison d'être and I have to say, I approve, but I pull up short when we get to the car, which is not like any car I've ever seen before: old and boxy, a surfboard sticking its nose out the back window.

'What is it?'

Bodhi says, 'A nineteen sixty-five Chrysler Valiant Regal,' as if announcing the arrival of royalty at a grand ball. I give the car a curtsy and he laughs, then swings me around to press me close. 'Aren't you going to kiss me?'

My voice has disappeared into the back of my throat like a penguin startled into its burrow. Mrs Bhatt would know what to do – she's a dab hand at coaching us for speaking under pressure.

Bodhi swims into focus, looking perplexed. 'Van?'

'Not here,' I squeak. 'Dad might see us.'

He says, 'True,' and lets me go to open the passenger door. He skips around and jumps behind the wheel.

The interior of the car is not like any other car I've ever been in before, either. The steering wheel is huge and the gearstick juts out of it, and instead of two front seats, there's a long bench, and the safety belts are similar to the ones in a plane. There's a look of quality about the whole shebang, though. I doubt there's a thing made of plastic in here.

∞

It's nice to be at a different beach. The water seems to have grown wilder since the surfers paddled out. The rush of the foam and the drag of it receding is destabilising; the sand sucked out from under my feet. I wade back to shore to find a hollow out of the wind. It doesn't feel safe to go in alone, not without a wetsuit and board.

From the shore, the water is opaque green, shot through with foam. The further out Bodhi goes, the more I appreciate the ocean's power – the swell and fall of it, the thunder. The risk. He gets up for a wild ride and dives into the thrashing. Despite my panic and heartache until I see him resurface and paddle back out to the other bobble heads, frankly, when Bodhi said, 'Come surfing,' if I'd realised he meant, *Come and watch me surfing*, I would have brought a book to read.

Or stayed home.

Or killed myself.

Boredom drives me into the scrub sans gloves, sans boots, in search of kikuyu, careful only to weed when I'm one hundred per cent sure there are enough natives to mitigate the risk of erosion. Renate would be proud of me – I remember to keep an eye out for snakes and get so lost in the task of filling the empty David Jones bag I found in the Valiant with weeds and rubbish, it's a few minutes of hearing it before I register that the plaintive cry on the wind is Bodhi calling my name.

He's shivering. 'Oh, thank God,' he says. 'I thought you'd been kidnapped.' He gestures to the carpark with the surfboard tucked under his arm. 'Come on. As soon as I get dry I'm going to give you the biggest hug in the world.'

It's strange how a few words can transport me from the furthest galactic periphery to the centre of the universe.

I slide into the passenger seat and next to me, Bodhi shields himself from the wind behind the passenger door as he peels off his wetsuit to the waist and scrubs his torso and hair with the towel. Unsuccessfully keeping his back to me, he shoves the wetsuit down to his ankles and hops around, holding onto the car for balance while he yanks it off each foot.

Then he's standing there.

Naked.

There it is, the alien force I've felt pressed against me like a rock-hard cabana, all tiny and shrivelled and benign, the sac hanging below like a conjoined pair of Emperor Moth cocoons; the whole thing like some deceptive monstrosity in a science fiction film.

'It's the cold,' he says.

I blame science in general for the curiosity that overtakes me. I reach out and cup the lot in my hand. 'Yes,' I say. 'It is cold.' It twitches and moves against my palm.

'Shove along.' He scoots me across the bench seat. Then

we're sitting there, close, me in my orange top and shorts, him sitting on his towel wearing nothing at all. It's mysterious that a body can become so calm while the heart starts racing at a thousand beats per second.

His penis twitches again. I bend to examine it. I touch it, avoiding the moth balls, lifting the soft flesh. It's warming now – and swelling. I slide the gnomish hat back to reveal a pinky-reddish fat-stalked mushroomy thing, the head brain-shaped but smooth. Everything I do makes it respond as if it were alive, as if it were a pet, as if it were in love with me. As I examine it, the stalk keeps growing until it's quite hard and slightly bent like a peeled banana, the brainy knob glossy and fit to burst.

It's quite easy to move the foreskin up and down.

Bodhi makes a sighing sound, almost as if he were in pain, but which elicits in me a glowing sticky flush of pleasure. I look up. I had almost forgotten he was here. He's flushed too, looking down at me with astonishment.

I'm quite astonished myself.

'Put your mouth on it,' he whispers.

No, I think, the warmth gone as if it had never been.

'Go on.' His voice is quiet, strained. 'Please.'

I was sailing in a pea-green boat on a quiet sea and now I'm thrown into the breakers, the water moving fast and deep and I can't see a shore to swim to. What I want is to remove my hand and slide away from Bodhi to behind the wheel but what I do is put my mouth on it.

❧

I'm cold.

Bodhi wants to drop me home but I'm keen to walk back. He seems worried. 'Are you all right, Van?'

'Yeah, I just feel like walking.'

'You're not upset, are you?'

'No.'

'But it's miles.'

'Is it?'

He nods. 'Miles.'

So we drive and on the way he reaches out and holds my hand. 'You're amazing,' he says. 'Are you sure you're okay?'

ME: No. My throat is burning. My jaw hurts. I want to cry. I didn't like the way you put your hands on my head and pushed me because it felt like I was going to choke and die. I was a ghost looking down on myself but I couldn't stop it.

BODHI: What are you even talking about?

ME: And that spurt of stuff was hideous.

'Please don't tell anyone,' I say.

Bodhi pulls over and turns off the engine. 'Hey,' he says, unclicking his seatbelt. 'Hey, come over here.' He unclicks my seatbelt and pulls me towards him for a cuddle. 'Of course I won't "tell anyone". It was beautiful, Vanessa. I respect you so much and I am so glad I met you.' He lifts my chin and gives me a kiss. 'Feel better?'

I do feel a bit better, it's true.

'When we first met,' he says, almost shy, 'your brother said he might be able to get some information on the casino stuff – but he won't answer Marlene and by the look on his face the other night, I'm guessing he's not too keen on, you know: us. I was wondering if he'd got anywhere with that?'

'I don't know,' I say. *Us!* 'I could ask.'

'That'd be great. I'd really appreciate it. Marlene's pretty annoyed that we scared him off.'

'Scared him off?'

'Well, you know what I mean.'

I don't know what he means.

'Are you sure you're okay?' he says. Words seem beyond me but I nod. 'Great.' He smiles. 'You're such a little sweetheart.'

He seems quite relieved when I say I'd rather he dropped me at the gate than accept his brave offer to take me the extra few kilometres up the drive to Shearwater. It's not until I'm almost out of the Valiant that I realise I'm meant to give him a kiss. I lurch back in as he leans towards me and it's less a kiss and more a clashing of teeth. 'Oops,' he says and laughs, turning back to the wheel. 'Maybe you could bring Ash out to see us,' he says. 'He might come if *you* ask him to.'

I doubt that.

It's good to be on my own. It's like I'm outside my body and need the walk and the quiet and the bush to reattach myself.

After dinner Suyin Skypes me on the iPad and I'm so happy to see her, I could cry. 'Look,' she says, thrusting her pelvis towards the camera.

A tattoo!

The camera weaves in and out of focus but it looks

like Chinese characters under cling wrap. She pulls up her waistband, sits back and smooths her skirt. 'It means integrity,' she says, this New Suyin Without Braces but With a Tattoo, and then she makes an excessively worried face. 'At least, I hope it does.'

I laugh, but I'm also floored. 'How did you get permission?'

She leans forwards and whispers, 'They don't know about it. Only Chao.'

Suyin's oldest brother has left school already and works for her father's firm. She's always been his favourite sibling. 'What, you just snuck off and got a tattoo by yourself?'

'Sort of. I went with Chao and his took about nine hours – it's amazing. I got talking to them about what I'd get and somehow we managed to talk Chao into it, so . . . it didn't even hurt that much.' She peers into the camera. 'Anything exciting happening your end?'

My throat closes over. There's a stupidly long silence but Suyin doesn't break it; she sits there, waiting.

'I sucked a cock,' I blurt at last. I don't know why I tell her or why I use those crass words or why I practically shouted them and now wish to die, but Suyin seems a whole lot less appalled than when I told her Ashton had smashed his violin on purpose.

I say she looks less appalled but what I mean is, she registers the information with a composed lengthening of the spine, alert, as if suddenly competing in a maths competition. She looks around furtively to make sure her door's still shut. 'Whose?'

'Bodhi's.'

She tilts her head and leans in, curious. 'What was it like?'

I spend a moment considering this. 'Salty.'

She sits back. 'Huh.' She seems bemused by this information, as if it's the unexpected answer to an equation she's been pondering.

'Sort of cheesy-salty,' I clarify.

'That sounds disgusting.'

'It didn't taste bad, if you know what I mean.'

'I don't. On what planet is cheesy not disgusting when associated with human flesh?'

'It was a bit like going to another planet, actually,' I admit. 'Somehow, the same rules didn't apply – and time was different too. It sort of stopped. As if we were outside ordinary time. Does that make sense?'

'No.'

'I don't know how else to explain it.'

'So ... how? I mean, how did you end up sucking his cock?'

There's something so funny about her saying those words that we lurch breathlessly over into hysterics. 'Well ...' I say at last, sighing, getting up to double-check no one's out in the hall, 'we went surfing – well, he did, but that's beside the point.'

'What *is* the point?'

'When he took off his wetsuit it was just ... there.'

Her eyebrows lift, ever so slightly. 'It?'

I nod. 'It.'

'Okay, spare no details.' She sits back with her exam-study face on. I half expect her to take notes. When I'm done, she says, 'Did it make you feel bad about yourself?'

Classic Suyin: straight to the heart of the matter.

'A bit.' I feel the tears well up. 'Yes.'

Now she looks appalled. 'Oh no, why?'

'I kind of gagged, to be honest. And you know, it's not very ... moral. I kept wondering what Mrs Bhatt would think of me.'

'Huh.' She seems somehow displeased by this answer. Her gaze sharpens. 'Would you do it again?'

I shake my head. 'Not in a hurry. Probably not, no.' There's a part of me that would love to get hold of another penis, preferably Darith's, and see what I could do to him – but I never want to feel invisible ever, ever again. 'I mean, I'd have to trust the person,' I say. 'Like, really, really trust them.'

'So you didn't trust Bodhi?'

'I don't know if I trust him or not.'

She taps a pen against her forearm. 'So, why did you do it?'

In a flash I'm back in those breakers wondering how I got from there to here. I don't know what crosses my face but Suyin puts up a hand to stop me speaking. 'Okay,' she says and pins the table down with her pen like she always does when an idea excites her. 'The important thing is: did it give you *grist for the mill*?'

I waggle the *Book of Observations* at the camera. 'It did.'

'Well,' Suyin rolls her hair into a bun and clips it tight,

'that's probably about as much as anyone could ask for after— Oh my God, Mum.'

Her mother barges on screen, waving at me. 'Hello, Vanessa! Are you having a wonderful time?'

I wave back. 'Yes, Lin.'

She leans in close but I can tell she's looking at the little version of herself in the corner of Suyin's screen. 'Wish your mother a Merry Christmas for me.'

Suyin says, 'Oh my *God*, Mum.'

'Oh no,' says Mrs Wang. 'I forgot. You poor children – such a terrible thing. They always seemed such a happy couple.'

'Oh my God, *Mum*, will you stop?' Suyin shoves her face into the camera and gives me a look of classic horror. 'I have to go.'

I laugh. 'Probably for the best.'

I shut the laptop, flip my book open and turn it to the right page.

Truth is not appearance.

Underneath I scribble: *Does visibility depend on being observed?*

CHAPTER 4

We don't even have a Christmas tree because that was Mum's thing and now Dad's announced we're booked to have Christmas dinner with Rochelle's parents at a restaurant in town. 'Do we have to go?' I ask Ash as we slouch downstairs for coffee.

'I think we do,' he says. 'But Dar's going home to spend Christmas with his folks and I'll be catching up with Dana afterwards. Do you . . .' he swallows with the effort, 'Do you want to hang with us?'

'Thanks.' I pat his hand to acknowledge the sacrifice. 'But I'll be all right. I'll go over to see the shearwaters come home from hunting – I haven't been once this year.'

He nods, relieved. 'How did you go with Mum? Did you get to speak to her?'

'Nup.' The truth is, I didn't even answer her messages. 'You?'

'Nup.' He stops and I stop with him. 'She can't have just *left*. Can she?' The thought settles on us bleakly, like a layer of dust. Ash shakes it off. 'I'm going surfing.'

'Will you come with me and meet with Bodhi and Marlene? Later today maybe, when you get back?'

'I don't trust those guys.'

'But—'

'I'm going. I've already missed the sunrise. See you later.'

∞

Kelsey bounces out to my balcony. 'I heard you squawking away up here.' She laughs. 'No, seriously, it's sounding amazing.' She touches Guil, tentative. 'I'd love to be able to play a musical instrument.' Her eyes gleam. 'So, tell me about Fairy-man and the Great Surfing Expedition.'

'It was . . .' Maybe it's because she's almost a year younger than me that it feels like to tell her the truth would be to slap her right in her open, gleeful, mischievous face.

'What?' she says.

'Boring.' I put Guil away. 'Like, sooo boring. All he did was leave me on the pretty-much empty beach and go surfing with some randoms who were already there.'

'Ugh.'

'Triple ugh,' I agree. 'How's Tim going?'

'Tim Bickford,' she says, pulling a dead leaf off the geranium, 'is a very good kisser.'

I find this simply impossible to believe. 'So is that all you've done?' I ask. 'Kiss.'

She looks perplexed. 'What else?'

I shrug, prickling with shame. 'I dunno – maybe you got married?'

She laughs. 'Noooo, I'm marrying Justin Bieber. Anyway,' she sings with fake-opera glee, 'it's nearly Christmas! You coming to the Christmas Eve shindig?'

'Will it be the same as always?'

'Pretty much. Non-alcoholic eggnog, Old Jack's gumleaf rendition of "Silent Night", the annual Christmas hamper darts competition and Mick as Santa giving out crappy Kris Kringles to all the kiddies – why would we mess with perfection?'

'Why indeed,' I say.

Ash is back after lunch but there's no Darith and when I ask Ash to walk over to the Foxhole with me, he doesn't even want *me* to go.

'You're the one who introduced them to me,' I reason.

'Yeah, and look how that turned out.'

'What do you mean?'

'I mean that guy's been sleazing on to you ever since he laid eyes on you.'

'So what if Bodhi likes me? That doesn't change what's going on with Champion.'

Ash shakes his head. 'I hate to say it, Van, but I don't think Bodhi really likes you – they just want the dirt on Dad.'

I slam his bedroom door and storm off, swing around and jerk it open again. 'You just can't believe someone likes *me* and not *you*,' I yell. 'You're a stuck-up, selfish *idiot*.'

He offers me his dactylion. 'Well, that makes two of us.'

I slam the door again and stalk off, stumbling down the staircase in a wash of tears. Ash hangs over the balustrade, this time where the lovers marry, the fatal snake curling out of the undergrowth. 'Seriously, I think they're full of bullshit.' As I reach the front door he yells, 'They're gonna ask you for money – you wait. It's a scam, Vanessa.'

Shearwater's front door is a thick polished slab of local messmate culled when the first trees were logged on the property with a slow return arm to prevent it from flying closed and crushing someone; when I try to slam it in righteous anger, it barely budges and I propel myself to the ground instead.

⌑

When I arrive at Gomorrah alone, Bodhi's disappointment is written all over his face. Marlene waves some kind of burger at me and demands to know why Ashton isn't coming.

'He doesn't trust you,' I stammer.

She swears under her breath and throws the food on the ground.

'I'll go home,' I say.

'No, no, it's not your fault,' Bodhi assures me, kicking the burger-debris off into the scrub. 'Don't worry about her. Stay. I've organised something.'

His face seems so earnest, my heart skips a beat. 'What?'

'A cello.'

My heart trips over its skipping-rope. 'What?'

'Well, I knew you'd never bring Guillerwhatsername down to camp, so I've borrowed one. It's a bit beat-up, but I think it's okay.'

'What for?'

'So we can hear you play!' He laughs. 'Don't look so surprised.'

I unstick my tongue from the roof of my mouth and struggle to swallow. 'But I didn't bring any music.'

'Yes, you did.' He puts his hand on my sternum. 'In here.'

'You don't understand—'

'Shh,' he says. 'Come on.'

There is, indeed, a cello. It belongs to some kind of psychedelic Gandalf with rainbow-tie-dyed trousers, no shirt and a flute, who Bodhi introduces as Hawk. And there are drummers. And several guitarists. I vaguely remember them, and Gandalf, from my rave adventure. But I'm not that girl who dances around in her underwear and improvises on the spot. I back away, sweating. 'I can't play for you without rehearsing.'

'Yes, you can,' says Hawk, smoothing his white beard. 'Come on.' He nods at a hard chair, lifts the cello, fixes the end pin, and swings her towards me. 'She won't bite. Tell me a few things you know by heart.'

Everything is in slow motion.

Tuning from Hawk's 'A', I'm encouraged by his nod of recognition. It really is a beat-up old beast. The scroll is quite lovely but there are various dings: one of the pegs has been glued back together and there's a fair crack in the body that's been glued, too. I fine-tune at the pegbox but can't see how it will possibly stay stable long enough to play anything. Negotiating the bow, I'm struck by how completely for granted I've taken my Henry Jay's smooth response to the touch.

Hawk takes no notice of the hints I'm trying to drop with my dubious face and strikes up Dvořák's *Humoresque*, a well-trodden student piece. I play along, but he stops. 'Quiet is fine,' he says, not unkindly, 'but tentative is torture. Come on, you know this instrument – let her sing to you, and speak for you.' He taps out the time signature with his foot and we begin again. From there he trips into Largo from Dvořák's *New World Symphony* and my heart lurches into it. There's such a freedom to Hawk's playing; his carnival showmanship and irreverent bare feet on the earth, his long white hair lifting in the wind. Drawn in to the pure joy of him, something unclenches inside me.

'Told you,' I overhear Bodhi say behind me when we're done and I rest my burning bow-arm and flex my fingers.

'Let's play it again,' Hawk instructs but this time the others join in, accents and accompaniments at first, then shifting the music to suit their own desires. I stumble into silence; it's impossible to hear over the 'ensemble' if I'm flat or sharp or completely off-key. I'm happy to rest my chin on the cello and listen to Hawk and his flute ride the wind-rafts of melody above the rhythm.

I thank Bodhi and ask him to put the beast away. 'I told them you were fantastic,' he says, kissing me on the lips.

Accepting the djembe passed to me and buoyed by Hawk's exhortation to 'fake it till I make it', I dive into drumming as best I can, laughing at my ineptitude, chuffed when I catch on; connected to strangers by the 'rhythm and joy' the Big O is always waxing lyrical about in orchestra until the afternoon waxes and begins to slide into evening.

Marlene bangs a lump of wood against a forty-four gallon drum, belligerent and tuneless, and the mood sours. The jam falters and peters out. People smile and nod at me but drift away, Hawk among them, and that's when I notice that Bodhi is gone.

Marlene is obviously drunk but she lays wood on the fire confidently, expertly, as if she's creating a piece of art. 'You're really scared of getting things wrong, aren't you?' she says to me, slinging herself into a camp chair. It's hard to tell if she's being mean or if it's the most insightful thing anyone has ever said to me. 'You think too much about shit that doesn't matter,' she concludes and the statement is like a gauntlet she's throwing down.

I pick it up. 'What should I be thinking about?'

It's as if this is the question she's been waiting for. 'Your privilege.' She jerks forwards to poke at the fire with a long stick, the orange flames leaping upwards. 'And what you might do with it.' She slouches in her chair and rubs her chin with the back of her hand, leaving a smudge of ash. 'It's all because of pretty, spoilt boys and girls like you ...'

I'm reminded of her spitting over the idea of working for Monsanto and sit there like one of the injured shear-waters Mum and I occasionally take to the ranger; its eyes covered, passive, too terrified to flap a wing. They get hit by cars all the time during breeding season.

'... all the money-hoarding, the selfishness, the disaster capitalism.' Marlene stares into the fire as if it's all unfold-ing there. 'All so ego-trippers like your dad can amass wealth to pass on to brats like you.'

Bodhi returns to dump a load of wood and tosses in a couple of logs. The sparks fly up. 'Leave her alone.'

'It's not even your privilege that shits me the most,' she says. 'It's your *ignorance*.'

Bodhi pushes a log further in with his foot. 'Knock it off.'

'I'm going home,' I manage, as assertive as a skink.

Marlene pushes herself to her feet. 'That's right, run home to daddy.' She rounds on Bodhi. 'You just couldn't help yourself, could you?'

He says, 'It would be good if you could handle your gin,' and doesn't look at her.

'And you—' She spears me with her pointing finger. 'Your father is *scum*.' She staggers with the effort of her vehemence. 'This whole place would be better off if you and your poxy family just went ahead and bloody killed yourselves.'

Bodhi stands, bristling, as if he can protect me from words with his body. 'You should go.'

Renate emerges from a tent and swings in next to Marlene, hugging her. 'Come on,' she says. 'These two haven't got a clue.'

They walk into the twilight and I think Marlene is crying. I know I am. Bodhi drags his camp chair close to mine and sits down. 'Sorry. She didn't mean that.'

'What does she expect me to do?'

'Van, we know your dad has been bribing government ministers to change the laws and now he's doing it again to lift restrictions on the siting and design guidelines. He's—'

'He's not.'

'He's making it worth their while by greasing the right palms so they can secretly invest in the casino development—'

'They can't do that.'

'Yes, they can.'

I feel like I'm struggling through cotton wool. 'Dad would never do that. The birds—'

'We've seen the development plans and Shearwater is the key – it's smack in the middle. They've been saying they can make a profit *and* preserve the local environment and now with Champion's money to really oil the wheels, it looks like it's all going ahead.' He takes my hand. 'But you know what they're like – how can this place survive a casino? Residential sprawl alone has brought it to the brink of disaster – habitats shrinking and introduced species—'

'But Dad loves this place.'

'He loves money more, Van.'

Bodhi's words are flames, burning me. I pull my hand away.

'If he brokers these contracts for Champion and reaps the benefits of the investments, not to mention the profits from securing the gaming tech for his own company, Simon Partridge will be stepping into a whole new level of wealth.' He says 'Simon Partridge' as if Dad's an institution, not a person – and as if it's not my name, too. 'The Americans have set precedents that are deadset gonna kill this planet.'

The urge to flee pulls me to my feet. 'My dad wouldn't have anything to do with gambling.'

'Yes, he would, Van.' Bodhi gently pulls me down again. 'He's bankrolled a whole new push in gaming development *and* there's a heap of new hotelier technology built in to the designs – I'll say one thing for him: he's leading edge.' His hands curl into fists. 'Simon Partridge and Champion want to turn this coastline into a sort of temperate Gold Coast.'

'Why do you care?'

'I grew up here. My parents still live in one of those shitty old fibro houses in the estate behind the shops.' He shakes his dreads. 'I don't suppose you've ever been down there – our whole house is probably the size of your shoe cupboard.' He seems to shake off the image. 'But, just look around, Van—'

The bush, expectant, quiet but for the crackling flames, seems to be looking back at me.

'You've got to agree: they have to be stopped.'

'That's why you've paid all this attention to me,' I say, the truth Ash tried to tell me finally dawning.

Bodhi fidgets at his rainbow scarf as if it's a school tie. 'Yes . . . and no.' He brushes the back of my hand with his fingertips. 'The minute I saw you, I fell in love.'

Fell in love . . . with *me*?

He pushes back his dreads. 'We *were* hoping you'd help us. Well, that Ashton would, initially. I met him at a few rallies and he seemed like a decent guy. We thought he might be angry enough to do the right thing but he's just another rich little show pony, demonstrating to get some attention from daddy.' He touches my hand again. 'I promise we didn't even factor you in.'

'But why does Marlene hate me?'

Bodhi's arm around my shoulder is as comforting as a boa constrictor. He has a new tattoo, a little one, the plastic still covering it. 'Marlene doesn't hate you. Van, she started volunteering for the rangers seven years ago – she could be earning real money, you know – she's smart; but she fell in love with this magic stretch of coast.' He sighs heavily and sits back, his arm sliding off me. 'She found out about the Shearwater stuff a few years back from a law-school friend who works for Eddie Glasshouse now—'

'Why don't you get them to help you, then?'

'He did, as much as he could, but then he dried up, pretty much: he got promoted and isn't prepared to lose his job over it. That's why Marlene got the Foxholers properly organised – we're going to protest the hell out of this casino thing if it gets going. But in the meantime, we got the grant, which keeps us close.' He reaches up to massage his own neck. 'But now the money's nearly run out and we haven't achieved anything, not really. We're trying to crowdfund but unless someone—' His hands fall into his lap. 'I don't know how we're going to finance an effective protest campaign.'

I feel cold, despite the campfire. 'Is that what you wanted Ash for? To get you money?'

'Sure, why not?'

'He's at school. He doesn't *have* any money.'

'But he could *get* money if he wanted it – right? And anyway, what we really need is *evidence*. The plans, the bribes, the corrupt vested interests – anything.'

'I thought you had the plans. Those photos?'

'Knowing about them and having them are two different things. Anyone can make a brochure. If we had something stronger than conjecture then even threatening to expose their correspondence might be enough to scare them off – the dodgy politicians, at least, especially Glasshouse – and they're the ones lobbying the new legislation in the parliament.'

'But Ash told you to piss off and you realised I was an easier target – more stupid and vulnerable than my brother.'

He slumps. 'No.'

'But I am, aren't I?' Bitterness pricks me all over like the sting of sunburn. 'A bit more stupid and vulnerable?'

He jerks forwards in his seat, startling me. 'You're *smart*, Van – you *know* something is going on. It's all over the news that Richard Marks is arriving soon. His yacht is heading for the marina as we speak and he'll be spruiking this casino thing as a done deal just as soon as he can, and once they've started building, even if some of them *are* exposed as corrupt, it'll be too late. It's got to be busted open before the investments are finalised and the bulldozers move in.' He leans into me. 'Marlene's guy did let her know Eddie's been invited to your father's New Year's Eve party; and so has Marks. They reckon Marks always has over-the-top security: there's no chance we can get close but *you* could. Maybe take some photos? Record conversations—?'

I'm on my feet again. 'Leave me alone.'

He shows me the new tattoo on his wrist. 'It's a mutton-bird.' My heart turns over but twists and wrenches me away from him. 'Van—' He offers up the tattooed shear-water. 'Van – it's too dark for you to walk back now.'

But I have to try.

Bodhi walks with me, just behind, and the darker it gets the more grateful I am that he's there, especially when he uses his phone as a torch. 'Good luck at the party,' he says when the circular driveway comes into sight. 'Your performance, I mean. Wish I could see it – or maybe hear it.'

'I couldn't get you into Dad's party even if I wanted to, so there's no point in—' He tries to grab my arm, saying, 'That's not what I was trying to do,' but I brush him off. 'And you're right, there'll be security – lots.'

Shearwater's gravel underfoot feels like safety. 'Thanks for walking me home,' I mutter.

Bodhi's voice follows me out of the shadow. 'I didn't mean to hurt your feelings.'

Ash hangs over his balcony. 'You all right?'

I look up and say, 'Yes,' and when I turn back, Bodhi's gone.

'Are you sure?' Ash calls, then disappears to meet me on the staircase. 'I'm sorry about before. Of course Bodhi likes you. I'll—'

'No,' I say, stopping him. 'You were probably right. Anyway, doesn't matter.'

He puts a hand on my arm. 'Are you sure you're okay?'

'Yep. What's Dad doing tonight?'

'The Marksman has docked his yacht at the marina and they're going out there, lucky bastards.'

'But what if he's a crook?'

'I read on Facebook today that he's just donated a heap of money to the World Wildlife Fund – I think the Foxholers are full of shit.'

'Isn't it a bit late for them to be going out?'

'It's a "late-night soiree".' Ash seems impressed. 'You'd better get inside before Lady Macbeth gets out of the bathroom and they realise you were still out.'

But it's not Rochelle that's Lady Macbeth in this scenario. It's me. This opportunity is like Duncan trotting under the battlements, and a vague plan that struck me when Marlene first mentioned hacking Dad's computer clicks into place. 'Look like th' innocent flower, but be the serpent under't,' I hiss theatrically. I'm always being roped into playing cello for the annual school Shakespeare play. This year Ash was Malcolm in *Macbeth* but he was terrible, so it's no surprise he doesn't even recognise the words. 'Come, you spirits that tend on mortal thoughts . . .' I chant, 'fill me from the crown to the toe, top-full of direst cruelty! Make thick my blood; stop up th' access and passage to remorse—'

Ash puts up his hands in surrender, says, 'Yup,' and peels away.

I double-check the night's plans in Louise's diary, swing by Dad's office to grab his laptop and head over to the bridal suite. I know it's a public space for most of the year but walking through the Turquoise wing, I feel Mum's presence more than I do at home now that her stuff's in storage and Rochelle's redecorated everything.

I stop to touch Mum's silver and crystal toiletries set, still proud on the mahogany dressing table she imported from Austria. Her trinket tray. The hand mirror and brush with the fuchsia repoussé. Pa-Albert's Russian portmanteau with its carved coat hangers and hidden drawers that I loved so much when I was little, the fine flower-spray carving on its curved outer panel inlaid with mother-of-pearl. Of all the things I don't understand about my parents' divorce, Mum giving up this place is the most baffling. When I pressed her, she said she 'just couldn't bear the nastiness'.

There's none of Mum's hair in the brush – it's just for show. I suppose it's weird to wish there was. I take the brush with me.

I find my father lying down in their bedroom with a damp face washer covering his eyes.

'Are you sick, Dad?'

He pats the bed for me to climb on. 'Just a headache. There's a lot happening.'

'Is Louise on strike?'

Dad rubs his chin. 'No.'

'Then isn't she doing most of it?'

The face washer slides off when he sits up and he catches it. 'Not this year.' He rubs the back of his neck, and throws it on the bedside table. Rochelle's bedside table has a pile of ratty looking Ian Fleming paperbacks and a photo of her and Dad on their wedding day. It's only been six months and he already looks about ten years older. 'So,' he says. 'You off to bed?'

'Not yet.' I show him the brush. 'The Statue of Liberty is made using the repoussé technique.'

'Is it now,' says Dad. 'And what's that when it's at home?'

'Like this – metalwork in relief. It looks like it's sculpted from solid silver.'

Dad touches the brush.

'But it's hollow. They beat it out from the inside.'

'So . . . is that what you came in to tell me?'

'Well, no.' I settle myself beside him to make my serpent-sneaky treacherous play. 'The Lepskis open their presents on Christmas Eve – it's a German thing, I think.' I don't seem to be able to stop turning the brush over and over in my hands. 'Anyway, they go shopping for presents themselves, even Coop, and they buy things that they think the person would really like, not just— Anyway, I know it might not get here by Christmas but I want to buy Rochelle a present. Something special. Just from me, I mean.' I'm hoping he'll mistake the sweat dripping off me for sincerity.

He seems absurdly pleased. 'So you want my credit card?'

'Yes.' I drop the brush on the bed and screw my courage to the sticking place. 'And to use your computer.' I draw it out of the bag.

He sits up to take it and frowns. 'Why mine?'

All my panic wells up. 'Don't be mad,' I say.

He darkens. 'What have you done?'

'I left mine down at Kelsey's and she took it to her cousin's and forgot it. I can get it back – but she's not going to see her cousin until next year, ha-ha and—' I recover from the near hysteria of attempting a cajoling laugh. 'I just have to do this now.'

'Vanessa! I've never known you to be so reckless: let Kelsey use her own laptop. And why now?'

'She doesn't have one.'

'Good lord.' Dad shakes his head. 'Some people live like barbarians.'

My brain is whirring like a storybook clockwork. 'If it doesn't come for Christmas I could give it to Rochelle at the New Year's Eve party – because she took me shopping and everything.' Dad looks positively *moved* and I press my advantage. 'If I don't order it now,' I say, 'it'll be too late even for that.'

He pats my hand. 'She'll love that.' He reaches over to his wallet and tosses me his credit card. 'Use an iPad.'

My palms are sweating. 'Louise says *never* to use a credit card on an iPad because she doesn't run the same security.' This, at least, is true. 'I'd be too scared.'

'Use your brother's laptop.'

'Don't make me tell him what I'm doing,' I complain. 'He'll say I'm sucking up.'

Dad narrows his eyes and I put on my most pleading, winsome face. I don't know how it looks but he laughs and I feel him relent. 'Suppose if we're quick,' he says, opening the lid.

'But—'

'But what?'

The clockwork clicks and whirs. 'I want to do it by myself – and get something for you, too. A surprise. Please?'

He mock-bows his head. 'Okay – but just shopping, no downloading anything.'

I cross my thundering heart. 'Promise, no downloading.'

He yawns and stretches, pointing his toes and flexing his ankles. 'Go on, then.' He knocks gently on my head. 'I wish some of your smarts would rub off on your brother.'

ME: Make up your mind, Dad – is he the boy genius or dull as dishwater? And has it ever occurred to you that I might exist independently of an assessment of him?

DAD: Jealousy is not attractive in a young lady, Vanessa.

I don't say anything, just watch him put in his thumbprint. He hesitates, then hands over the laptop and kisses me on the forehead. 'Promise you'll shut it down properly when you're done.'

'I promise. Have a great night.'

'It's nice – what you're doing for Rochelle.' He gives me another forehead-kiss. 'Oops, now I'm late for the shower.' He swings his legs over the edge of the bed and pads away.

I want to rest here, in the comfort of this lovely, well-ordered room, but time is running out and I, like Lady Macbeth, have stopped up the access and passage to remorse.

Any hope I was hanging onto that Bodhi was wrong dissolves like a solute of doubt in the solvent of a whole folder of correspondence with Eddie Glasshouse with maps and Department of Environment and Primary Industries documents marked *confidential*, as well as several brochures for an imagined monstrosity built of glass and stainless steel called Shearwater Towers that sits exactly where I'm sitting now. *Offshore transfers are a doddle*, one of the emails says. *ICAC don't have a clue.*

There's a file called *Atlantabank-Swiss* but I can't open it without a password. Ash reckons that because of Dad's encryption no one could copy anything without 'beaming the hack out to NASA' so I photograph as many of the emails as I can with my phone.

The door opens and I jump, clicking out of everything at speed. Rochelle says, 'What are doing with your father's computer?'

'Shopping.'

'Does he know?'

'Of course he knows.'

'Where is he?'

I shut the laptop. 'In the shower.'

She follows me out like fricken Macduff and if I resented her any more I think my head would explode.

I should have remembered the dark spirits are only on your side until the deed is done and not a minute after. The photos in my phone are like a stone in my shoe. A stomach-ache. A bomb. Back in my room, I ring Mum. She doesn't answer. I text.

Please come home.

Nothing.

Even Rochelle misses you.

Nothing.

She said you're a saint.

Nothing.

Are you missing us or having a really good time?

Something!

Yes.

That's what she writes. Yes, she's missing us, or yes, she's having a really good time? I ring again. She must be there – she's texting. But she doesn't answer.

Please call me. I need your help.

Nothing.

Mum!

Nothing.

I hurl my phone. It leaves a heart-shaped hole in the rattan-weave bedhead and a dint in the plaster of the wall behind.

∞

My howl of despair is loud enough to draw Ash to my room.

'I've killed my phone,' I sob, pressing uselessly at its carcass. 'It's dead.'

He turns away. '*You'll* be dead if you do that to me again.'

My father appears, and he is also unamused. He's in his suit now and shakes me by the arm. 'Is this because of something you saw when you were shopping? Did you do this on purpose?'

'Do what on purpose?'

'Smash your phone so I'd buy you a new one.'

I say, 'Wow.'

All my life I've been a goody-two-shoes, trying my hardest, doing my best – and for what? One sneaky empty suitcase and now I'm an arch-criminal-mastermind, lying at the drop of a hat.

'Well, too bad,' he says. 'You only get to play that trick once. You'll have to do without a phone until we get back to Melbourne and you can see if it's fixable.'

'Get lost!' I scream, climb into bed and hide under the covers. I *am* an arch-criminal-mastermind-*spy*, lying at the drop of a hat. I wish I was back with Bodhi, dancing in the jig of bodies, in love with everyone and everything. I always feel like I might love him when we're not together.

Darith's voice floats to me from the doorway. 'What's going on?'

I sniffle, wipe my face and emerge from the doona. 'Has Dad gone?'

'Yeah,' he says. 'Do you know Bodhi's outside?'

I sit up.

'Do you want me to tell him to go home?'

I climb out of bed. 'No, I will.'

I shepherd Bodhi into the shadows because I'm ninety-seven per cent sure Darith and Ash are spying on us. 'I had to come back,' Bodhi says, pulling me into his body. 'I really do like you.'

Part of me wants to slap him for being so casual about manhandling me but the other half wants to melt into the feeling of being held and have a good cry.

Ash shouts, 'Tell him to piss off or I will.'

'Look,' I say, dragging him further into the bush, towards

the cubby. I pull back the branches. 'We sometimes camped in here. As long as you get into the grounds before New Year's Eve, you might be able to hide long enough to sneak out and get pictures of the guests or something at the party – enough to at least bring attention to the corruption claims.' I hear Ash calling my name. 'I gotta go.'

'Thank you,' Bodhi says. 'I mean it.'

I pull away. 'I'm not doing it for you.'

♠○

It's half-past three on Christmas Eve and Louise is fresh home from delivering Darith to his parents. 'Ash and Dana have gone camping for the night,' she says stiffly. 'And your father and Rochelle still haven't come home from yesterday's party. I presume they'll all turn up for tomorrow.'

'Are you coming to the caravan park shindig?'

'Spare me.' She stomps off to the kitchen, calling, 'But you have fun.'

♠○

We might not have a Christmas tree but Oceanview does and the rec hall is hung with a mishmash of decorations collected over the years. I'm pretty sure the Lepskis haven't thrown anything out since 1919 and this year someone has contributed paper chains made from recycled wrapping paper. Mick the Maintenance Guy's old Santa suit that Harry tells me got partially melted in last year's near-tragic campfire incident has been stuffed as an effigy and jammed into an impressive cardboard chimney.

To seal the perfection, Kelsey and Tim are wearing matching reindeer headbands *and* red noses. 'I kissed Kelsey,' he tells me when she's called off to draw the raffle.

'I know.'

He blanches. 'I didn't do it wrong, did I?'

I put my hand on my heart and say, 'I swear on my grandmother's grave that she told me you were a very good kisser,' and the delight on his face feels like redemption for the snow-cone affair.

'What's that blob hanging from the ceiling?' he says.

'A bell?' I hazard.

∽

'So isn't it funny?' I say as Kelsey and I watch Tim lose the semifinals of the darts competition. 'All these years and no one hooked up with anyone and this year there are girl-friends and boyfriends all over the place.' I sip my terrible eggnog. 'Do you think it's because we're older or are they putting aphrodisiacs in the water supply?'

'Tim and I aren't girlfriend and boyfriend.'

'Yeah, but you're kissing.'

'We just tried it out,' she says. 'Like an experiment.' She gives me a sideways look. 'I'm going to try a girl next.'

I feel a jealous stab. 'Who?'

'Dunno, yet. Here we go. Old Jack's getting his gumleaf out.'

Lachie helps Old Jack up onto the stage and I don't think I'm the only one who holds my breath as he takes his seat – skinny as the old fella is, it doesn't look like Lachie's going to be strong enough to hold his weight; then he's settled, clutching Lach's hand in recognition and thanks. He looks out at us and rubs the stubble on his chin with yellowed fingers. 'You're all a pack of heathens these days,' he says. 'But whether you know it or not, it's a holy night, tonight, so here's to peace on earth for men of good will.' He lifts the leaf to his lips, thinks better of it and says, 'and ladies, too,' takes a deep breath, and closes his eyes.

The melody of 'Silent Night' peals out on the sweetest, strangest notes, melancholy and otherworldly; like a piccolo flute morphed with a theremin, as if Old Jack is beaming reverent love out to the farthest spheres of the cosmos; and when his carol is ended, we stay quiet, because it's as if the stars are streaming it back to us.

'Merry Christmas, everyone,' says Mr Lepski at last, giving the old man a squeeze around the shoulders as we begin our applause.

'Are you coming back to our place?' Kelsey asks.

I shake my head and retrieve her present from my pocket. 'No, Christmas is just too weird without Mum. But I've been waiting all holidays to give you this.'

She unwraps the bracelet that says *Kelsey* in silver script and throws her arms around me. 'I love it!' She steps back. 'You have to come: Mum's made you a very special gift from all of us.'

I groan. 'It's one of her painted wooden folk art things, isn't it?'

Kelsey's laugh is wicked and contagious. 'Going home and being miserable by yourself isn't going to help,' she says. 'Come on – your personalised shoe-rack awaits!'

∾

Louise picks me up at eleven and seems as quiet and lonely as I am as we walk home together through Old Jack's holy darkness.

∾

When we were little, we'd wake up so early on Christmas morning it'd still be dark and we'd run to Mum and Dad's room to climb into bed with them and open our first presents, which would always be picture books. Then Mum would read them to us – Ash's first, then mine – and if we fidgeted, Dad would say, 'Shh, your mother's reading,' as if she were the most important person in the world performing the most important task. It's been a long time since we did that, but I wonder if he misses her this morning, just by mistake.

Ash comes in and sits on my bed. 'Merry Christmas,' he says, and I think he's been crying too.

'Merry Christmas. Is Dana here?'

'Nah, at Ellen's.'

Dad texts and as requested, we troop down and outside to open our presents.

'Jet ski!' Dad announces to Ash, as if he might not recognise the gleaming beast on the trailer in the driveway.

'Dad,' Ash says, 'I hate to sound ungrateful but jet skis are like, poison. Didn't you read that stuff I sent you?'

Dad's face breaks my heart. 'I just glanced at it,' he says. 'I thought it meant you wanted one.'

'Thanks, Dad,' Ash says, giving him a hug. 'I love that you tried.'

'I'll have a go on it,' says Rochelle, climbing into the trailer.

'Be careful!' Dad cautions, rushing to help her up. She takes his hands and laughs. 'I'm not made of glass,' she says. When she's safe in the saddle, Dad gives his attention to me. 'Now, Vanessa,' he says. 'Here.' It's a new phone and a beautiful case. 'Real garnets,' Rochelle adds, pretend revving the jet ski.

We exchange our presents from the plastic box. Louise has replaced some of my mother's neat tags with her own semi-legible scrawl. The presents themselves are lovely, and I do like the fine gold ring with its delicate black opal – Mum's favourite. Maybe it's because they're as close to her as we're going to get that the whole thing feels hopelessly depressing, and a far cry from the spirit of Old Jack's gumleaf. 'Are you going to tear down Shearwater and build a casino?' I ask.

Dad just about chokes. 'Where the hell did that come from?'

'Are you?'

'Shearwater will be fine.' He turns away from me, reaching up to lift Rochelle off the trailer. 'Now get ready for lunch. Come on, let's not have any fuss. It's Christmas.'

∽

Rochelle's brother looks pretty much the same age as Ash and I can't tell if that's a problem for her family but it's certainly as awkward as heck for Ash and me. Rochelle's dad made a very nice speech at the wedding, so perhaps he's fine with his daughter marrying someone twenty-three years older than she is? I don't know. Maybe the older you get, the less it matters. I mean, who'd care if a sixty-year-old married an eighty-year-old? But then I look at Rochelle's cousin, Rob, who's thirty and what would people think if Mum ran off with him? They'd probably say he was after her money, or had mother issues, or was blind. Marlene is right: people are much meaner to women than men, overall. Rob gives me an uncomfortable smile and I realise I'm staring at him like a loon. I drop my eyes, and my fork lands on my plate with an unfortunate clatter. Ash's little groan and the normalness of his exasperation is strangely cheering.

'Do you want to try calling Mum soon?' I ask him quietly while the seafood is being served. 'What time is it in France?'

'I think it's about six-thirty.'

'Today or yesterday? Or tomorrow?'

'I'm not sure. But let's try it anyway.'

But we don't get to try it anyway because just as we're dropping the last prawn-heads on the crustacean's Mount Doom piled between us, she sends Ash a message.

Mry Mry Xmas my drlings Ash pls show this to yr sister I will call u soon I prmse luv Mumx

Ash shakes his head. 'Why does she leave out most of the vowels?'

I shake my head too. 'Why does she leave out most of the information?'

The turkey arrives. Rochelle's dad raises his glass. 'Merry Christmas everyone!'

Ash and I raise our virgin banana daiquiris to mutter, 'Merry Christmas,' and offer our father-pleasing smiles.

When the turkey has been reduced to bones, Dad stands and there's something about the nervous way his hand is twitching in his pocket that makes me uneasy. He clears his throat. 'We've been waiting until we were all together,' he looks down at Rochelle as if to remind us who the 'we' refers to, 'because we've got an announcement.' He looks over at us and clears his throat again.

Ash says, 'What now?' under his breath.

Dad addresses himself to Rochelle's parents. 'We're having a baby!'

A brief vortex opens up, pinning us all to its periphery, until Rochelle's mother claps her hands and says, 'Oh, wonderful,' and the hugs and congratulations begin.

Ash and I look to each other like a couple of cartoon-characters frozen into shock. 'Crikey Moses,' I say and the pair of us burst into hysterics.

Rochelle and Dad look our way, tentative, seeming to take the laughter as approval.

'Come on,' Ash says, getting up.

I throw my napkin onto the table more than ready to skedaddle, scrambling for my shawl.

'Where are you two going?' Dad calls.

Ash waves. 'Congratulations, Dad, Rochelle, everyone. Thanks for everything. It was really great, delicious. Merry Christmas.'

'Well, hang on,' Dad says. 'We haven't even had pudding.'

'We're going to see if we can get to the rookery in time

to see the shearwaters come home,' Ash says. 'We'll see you back at the ranch.'

I wave, too.

'Really?' I say, following him out of the restaurant.

'Sure – don't you want to?'

'What about Dana?'

'She'll be fine.' He pulls out his phone. 'I'll call her now and ask her to meet us there.'

'Do you think this means Mum will never come home?' I ask, puffing as we walk, glad to be in the fresh air.

Ash keeps his eyes on the path. 'I don't know what to think.'

'Maybe you'll get that little brother you've always wanted.'

'Maybe,' he says. 'But I'd prefer a puppy.'

∽◯

The three of us walk along the beach in the other direction from Oceanview, the cloudless sunset a gradient of light from pale, pinky almost-white through yellow into orange and red, deepening to match the indigo sea at the horizon, a rainbow band. It's windy and I'm glad I accepted Dana's offer of a jacket. The shearwaters are already gathering above the waves but still out at sea.

'There's one,' Dana says.

I shake my head. 'Nah, it's only a seagull.'

'Is that one?' says Ash.

'Nope, that's a seagull, too. They won't come in until it's dark enough.'

Ash sniffs against the wind. 'I can smell the nests.'

The sandy cliffs dotted with burrows, three or four to a square metre, do let off a pong – warm, sweaty and rich. 'I like the smell,' I say. The chicks sit safe in there until they're ready to migrate, unless someone drags them out to squeeze for mutton-bird oil.

By the time we climb the stairs and reach the rookery proper, the sunset has faded to grey and the Milky Way has begun to push through. There's a kind of agony in the waiting, scanning the twilight sky, because it seems impossible that the shearwaters exist. That they'll come home. The chicks begin their chirruping, just here and there at first.

'Looks like we're not going to get any clouds tonight,' Dana says.

Ash snorts. 'Looks like we're not going to get any birds.'

But, as if called by my prayer, the first of the shearwaters fly over our heads and back out to sea again, and before long the flock return in their mysterious, silent circling patterns of gradually falling altitude, and the perfect starlit dome of the sky becomes Hamlet's *most excellent canopy, the air—*

Look you! This brave o'erhanging firmament.

This majestical roof, fretted with golden fire!

But the fire is silver and white-light and the birds are glorious shadows, silent, no sounds but the wind and waves and the burble of chicks calling for their suppers.

'Oh my God,' Dana murmurs. 'The stars! It's so clear you can even see the Pleiades.'

Ash follows her line of sight. 'Which one is that?'

'Like a renaissance queen's hairnet studded with tiny diamonds – see it?'

'I think so.'

'Oh my God!' she says again. 'One's landed right near me.'

'They're not afraid,' I say.

Like a duck, the bird's short legs and webbed feet are positioned far back on its body. After a brief rest, it waddles to a cheeping hole and hops inside.

'That's the most gorgeous thing I've ever seen,' Dana breathes.

Soon the birds are thick and low, partners sitting outside the burrows taking turns to feed the chick before settling in for the night. It's a busy metropolis now, complete with greetings, arguments and property disputes.

'Mry Christmas, Van,' Ash says, giving me a one-armed hug. 'I'm glad we did this.'

I hug him back. 'Mry Christmas to you, too.'

Boxing Day dawns with my determination to tell Ash about Dad's dodgy emails but he's already left with Louise to pick up Darith and when they get back, he's itching to get to the beach. 'Not now, Van,' he says. 'We're camping with Dana tonight. Find something else to do.'

'But, Dad—'

'I can't *do* anything about Dad.'

Darith bounds down the staircase and the two of them disappear outside. 'Hope you had a good Christmas,' Dar calls back to me but the door closes before I can answer.

CHAPTER 5

I'm in the foyer pressing modem buttons for Louise when the police pull up in the driveway. I stare in horror through the long window. This is it. They've come to tell us they've dragged my father away and put him in prison for corruption. A cop steps out and opens the back of the divvy van and Darith climbs out wearing nothing but board shorts and a face of thunder.

Louise beats me to the door.

'Sorry to bother you,' says the cop. 'But this young fella's been insisting he lives here.'

'Of course he lives here,' says Louise, pulling Darith into the house. 'What's going on? Are you all right?'

The officer plants his legs apart, as if now it's Louise who's in trouble. 'We found him sleeping in the park with ...' He gestures to the paddy wagon. 'Some other fellas.'

'And that's a crime?'

'It is an offence to be drunk in a public place and we don't like anyone to sleep in the park. I'm sure you'll agree it's in the public interest to deter vagrants.'

'I'm not sure I do agree, thank you very much.' She gives Darith a quick once over. 'He doesn't look drunk.'

Darith says, 'I'm not.'

'Anyway, I'm happy to let it go here.' The cop nods at Louise and turns his beady eye on Darith. 'But you want to keep out of trouble.'

Darith heads upstairs. He looks bowed down, like he's been punched in the chest.

Outrage boils out of me. 'You can't be a vagrant on your own land!' I shout after the cops and there's a muffled cheer and laughter from the back of the van.

I run upstairs but Darith doesn't want to talk. 'Just shut up about it,' he says.

He still doesn't want to talk about it later when Dad insists on calling his parents, and then on making a formal complaint.

'Mum and Dad are on their way to Hawaii now, remember?' Darith says.

'Well, they'll still have a phone,' says Dad. 'And at the very least you deserve an official apology.'

Darith puts his hands in his pockets and stares at the floor. 'Not much help to those other fellas though, is it?'

When Darith comes back upstairs after speaking to his folks, Ash says, 'I hope you're not leaving.'

'Nah, they asked if I wanted to go but I'd just be in the way.' He flops on the couch. 'They're having a "second honeymoon" – even more sickening than you and Dana.'

'Good. Yeah, fair enough. She's hanging out with Ellen tonight – there have been *words* about how she came down to spend time with her but has been hanging out with me instead.'

Dar puts his feet on the coffee table and a few board games slide to the floor. 'Yeah, that'd be a fricken rude thing to do – invite your friend on holiday and then spend the whole time with somebody else.'

Ash snorts. 'Jealous, brother?'

'Over a pasty like you? In your dreams.'

Ash launches over me and they wrestle to the carpet, laughing their heads off.

At breakfast the next day, Nadia and Ellen come to the kitchen door looking for Darith and the three of them wander off, heads together, Nadia reaching up to rub Darith's back between his shoulder blades.

I slather myself in zinc and take to the lilo.

Darith seems a bit cheerier when he gets back, in time to watch the cricket highlights with Ash, dubbed by me as the 'Boredom Olympics'. I, however, am gripped by growing panic. Why have I been practising such fiendishly hard pieces full of impossible sliding, and double stops, and crazy arpeggios? What makes me think I'm not going to make a complete fool of myself, squawking away? My *Swan* is more like a headless chook.

Ash throws a cushion at me. 'What's wrong with you this time?'

'I have to practise.'

'Now? We're meant to be going out – I was just about to tell you to get changed. Don't you want to check out Richard's yacht?'

That idea strikes me with a shiver. 'No, I already told Dad I don't want to.'

'You're such a weirdo – it'll be amazing. Kate Ceberano is playing the ballroom.' He peers at us. 'The *ballroom*, on a boat.'

Darith yawns and stretches. 'Want an accompanist?' he says to me and then laughs. 'Don't get too excited. I'll have to play it by sight so I'll be pretty shit.'

'You're kidding,' says Ash. 'Do you really not want to come either? What about Nadia?'

'She can't. She and Ellen are saving all their brownie points for New Year's Eve – so if Van's not going tonight, I'll just be the third wheel. Again.'

Ash groans. 'You can't be the third wheel at a party.'

'I don't want *my* not going to stop *you* from going,' I say to Darith, even though I really want him to stay. Bodhi and Marlene will definitely be down there watching Richard Marks. What if they saw me swanning onto the Marksman's boat? I'd die of shame.

'Nah, it's not that,' Darith says. 'Sorry, I'm just not in the mood.'

'No need to be sorry. I don't care. But I'm going,' Ash says and there's a frosty space between them until Dana turns up looking like some kind of Aussie-Nordic princess and Ash taps Dar on the knee. 'I made the correct choice, friend,' he says.

∽◯

Dad isn't overly fussed about leaving us at home because Louise isn't going to the party, either. 'I wasn't invited, apparently,' she says, stiff with indignation.

'We've been over this—' Dad starts but Louise turns her back on him. 'I'll be in the kitchen if you guys need me,' she says and flounces off, as much as Louise can flounce, which is similar to the way a brick might.

An impetuous thought grips me as Darith and I head through to the baby grand. 'Can we try the Elgar? Just the first movement?' I scramble over his trepidation. 'I know it's a conversation between the cello and the violin—'

'No, between cello and orchestra.'

'—but you could do it with a piano arrangement. I know you could.'

'It's more than a conversation,' he says. 'And we've only got four days.'

'Five, if you include New Year's Eve day.'

'So I'm performing now?'

'Please?'

'How did I get here?' he says, opening the lid of the Steinway and setting up his iPad. We find the score and a selection of piano reductions but he looks stricken. 'I dunno, Van – I'll never be able to bring the lushness of an entire string section. It's gonna be like trying to play Motörhead on the kazoo.'

'If it doesn't work or it isn't fun, we won't do it.'

We listen to a few versions online and then beaver away but it takes him sitting at the keyboard with headphones until late into the night just to flesh out an interpretation for the opening recitative and Louise shoos me off to bed before he's done; but now it's got us, like a puzzle that demands to be solved.

⊸⊙

I'm all technique before sunrise but we're back at the piano as soon as breakfast is eaten, forced to build ourselves a bubble of concentration as the house erupts with a stream of preparations – the house-cleaners, window-cleaners and the pool guy, caterers, the florist, and security-Ron with his new offsider, Ariki. It's worse than trying to practise backstage at a school concert.

'Stop,' I say. 'I've gone out of tune.'

'*Moderato*, next time.' Darith jiggles his leg with impatience.

'I'm trying.'

'Well try harder – you keep going ponderous and squashing it.'

'Now I know how Tubby the Tuba felt,' I mutter.

We begin again but the pads of my fingers are sore and I'm struggling with feeling the harmonic. I keep hitting the same wrong notes. 'Flat,' he sings out. 'Sharp.' Then harsher, 'Sharp!'

'I know!' I yell, stopping to towel my sweaty face. 'I'm not missing them on purpose.' The injustice of all the lonely hours practising to get vibrato and pizzicato right furzle up in me and I accuse him with the bow. 'It's all right for you; your notes come in convenient individual packaging – the cello is fretless, remember? And how am I supposed to hear if I'm sharp or not if you keep shouting "sharp" all the time?'

Darith starts packing up the piano. 'We don't know what we're doing. There are too many modulations. It sounds like shit.'

'Fine.' I lay Guil on her side and flounce off, or I would if my legs weren't made of jelly. 'I'm going to the beach.'

'Good.'

Kelsey doesn't believe I hate Darith Laurie and after a swim, neither do I. 'Are you coming to the party after you've finished wowing the celebrities?' she says, pouring sand over her knees. 'On the back beach. Bring everyone, why not?'

'I'll be there. Not sure about the others but I'll definitely be able to disappear without even Louise noticing. It wouldn't be New Year's if they weren't still kicking on till the wee hours.'

When I get back, Shearwater looks stupendous and Darith's tinkling at the keys, trying stuff out.

I take my seat.

'What about this?' he says.

'Hold your horses.' I swing Guil up and tighten the bow, inspect its hairy untidiness and reach for the rosin; give it three strokes and draw the whole length of the bow, tip to base, across an open string. Guilhermina responds with a lovely, even tone. 'Right,' I say, drinking in the woody smell of her. 'Give me an A.'

Days spent practising music between swims and cricket scores and Skyping Suyin for technical advice are days spent in heaven.

Rehearsal time has run out but at last it's beginning to feel alchemical, this fusion of body and instrument, note, pitch, rhythm and tempo; the unstable combination of unquantifiable isotopes: connection, memory, confidence. The transfer by repetition from learning to knowing. Elgar demands control and abandon in equal measure – is that the 'sensitivity' the Big O is always pushing me to strive for, being 'present' for the shifts in time and beauty and 'meaning' of something so much larger than myself? But I'm not in it alone. Dar and I accompany each other and share the magic of the creation itself. Landing the timing or swerving to avoid disaster brings a mutual glance and smiles to our faces.

As the drama builds, it's as if something of the earth below and the ocean, always churning in the distance, pours itself into the music – and though it was written in another land, another time, it's *now* and energy bursts from the wound in Darith's chest and is ignited into the crescendo; and in the aftermath, to attempt truth in the cello's final notes demands all my soul's attention, and yet none because I'm carried on winds of love and grief that my bones somehow *know*; that Elgar has wrung from the human heart of me.

'That was almost it,' Darith says, looking a bit shocked.

'Thank *God*,' Ash chimes in, swinging open the connecting door to the kitchen. 'I am sick to fricken death of the first fricken movement from Elgar's fricken Cello Concerto in E fricken minor. Let's go – it's madness around here and they want you out of the reception area.'

Darith slides his marked-up sheaves of music into a tidy pile. 'Well, I guess that's as good as it's gonna get. See you in the music room about eight?' he says to me. 'The keyboard will have to do for a warm-up.'

'It's bloody fantastic.' Ash catches my eye. 'And I mean that.'

Darith almost touches my shoulder, and then they're gone.

The cocktails and canapés are a hit and Sharif is in his element, commanding the busy kitchen. He shoos me away. 'I'll come and hear you play,' he promises.

Shearwater is one hundred per cent elegance tonight and I'm eighty-eight per cent dowdy in my orchestra blacks, provided by Louise who 'knew they'd be wanted'. I wander up to snoop around Mum's stuff. It must be a bit strange for Rochelle because it's sort of 'fixed' in the Turquoise suite in the way Mum's family have kept to Pa-Albert's original art nouveau vision, updated in parts to art deco by Ma-Gladys in the thirties, after he died. I love the mix of organic and geometric, the impeccable style. Rochelle's preference for eco-friendly boutique reclaimed timber and vegan repro-duction leather can find no purchase here. Even if Dad does want to develop Shearwater, surely he doesn't want to destroy it? He *must* have plans to protect it. And the beach. And the mutton-birds.

Mum's collection of evening dresses that usually hangs in the wardrobe has been tumbled into a cheap-shop striped bag and shoved behind the bathroom door. I drag the bag out and take it to my room.

My mother is a bit shorter than me and somewhat thicker these days but there are a couple of dresses that fit. One is the softest-grey silk and the skirt has the most wonderful fall. There's a flexible corsetty thing sewn into the bodice and an inbuilt bra support because it's off the shoulder, the scalloped sleeves sitting on the forearm merely for show. Slipping it on, I feel like Jane Eyre on a bender, though I'm sure she would have worn a modesty kerchief to obscure the vulnerable flesh of her heaving bosom given her lascivious thoughts about Mr Rochester. It must be vintage. Maybe Mum bought it and never wore it – I can't remember seeing her in it. I lift my hair into her signature French twist and it's almost like she's wearing it now.

There's a knock and I let my hair fall.

'Wow,' Darith says when I let him in.

'It was my mum's. I think I'm going to wear it tonight.'

He nods. 'You should.'

'Those people downstairs—' I plump into the armchair, Mum's skirt puffing out like a parachute. 'They seem kind of awful.'

'Some American guy just asked me if I know Jessica Mauboy.'

'Do ya?'

'I wish.' He pulls me up to look at us together in the mirror and I twist up my hair again. 'I should find a suit,' he says.

Rochelle appears at the doorway, making us jump. 'This is becoming a habit,' she says.

'Just going,' says Darith and slips off.

She looks me up and down. 'Lovely.'

I can't help but wish she didn't sound so surprised.

'Do you want to wear this?' The box she hands me houses a pendant in the shape of a teardrop. 'Topaz and marcasite,' she says. 'It's your mother's. I think it was her grandmother's – same vintage as Shearwater.'

I love it.

She slides it around my neck and does up the clasp. 'Would you like me to help you put on a little make-up, maybe?'

'Thanks, Rochelle,' I say to her reflection. 'I would.'

When Richard Marks walks into the party, it's as if he has already claimed the kingdom as his own. He isn't as good looking in person as he is in photos but there *is* something magnetic about him. Or maybe it's that he brings his magnets with him; a dozen lovely-looking people trail him like a cape, and Shearwater has come alive: this is what she was built for – glamour.

He seems quite sociable for a sinister destroyer of lands and lives and seabirds.

Dad shows him around, proud as punch of the very thing he's apparently plotting to demolish. I can't figure out whether it's Richard's glow that makes people seem better looking, or Shearwater's, now that she's in all her glory – but Rochelle and Dad are practically gleaming. Darith always looks beautiful but seems shyer than usual, as if he feels as out of place as I do. Ashton, on the other hand, is radiant, keen to shake the Marksman's hand and show off his beautiful girlfriend. He puts his hand on the small of Dana's back exactly like Dad does to women but she pulls his arm round her waist, bringing Ash closer, and her other hand flutters to her cleavage. The sporty nerd can't help but ask about Wimbledon and the coterie gather round to hear the stories as if Richard were Socrates on the steps of the Agora but showing off his aces with a tennis racquet rather than scoring against Roman rhetoric. He's as bad as Ash nostalgically crapping on about Revisor.

By the time Dad introduces me, I'm so paralysed by the conflict between the adoration in the room, Lady Macbeth guilt, the truth of Bodhi's words clanging about in my head, and Richard 'the Marksman' Marks's eyes lingering on my immodest bosom, all I can think is to shout,

OUT, DAMNED SPOT! So I say nothing, nothing at all, and finally Dad says, 'Starstruck,' and the entourage rescues me by laughing kindly and sweeping Richard away.

There's such surety to these people, I feel like a visitor in my own home.

I guess it wouldn't be me if I didn't step on my skirt negotiating the six-inch portable stage and jerk forwards, clunking my accompanist in the back of the knees with the cello and eliciting a suppressed chortle from the audience. We recover, and preparing to introduce the piece, I call upon the spirit of Mrs Bhatt to sustain me and chuck in the powers of the Ladybird People because after that warm-up, I'm pretty sure we need all the help we can get.

'I'd like to begin by acknowledging that we meet tonight on the lands of the Kulin Nation,' I begin, longing to get the Acknowledgement right. 'We pay our respects to Elders past ...' I pause to let the room echo with the distant roar of the sea; 'Present ...' I look around at the people in the room who seem suitably solemn; 'And future ...' The words and the spaces around them have made my heart feel both full and broken and when Darith Laurie takes his place at the piano wearing jeans and his Aboriginal flag T-shirt under the jacket of Ash's tuxedo, I nearly burst with love.

I sit, open my legs for Guilhermina, and can't deny that the hum of adrenaline feels a lot like pleasure. Maybe that's why I launch into the dramatic opening chords with my hand in the wrong position, which makes me seem horribly out-of-tune, and fade off in mortified confusion. Darith and I make faces at each other that would be worthy of a Suyin Snapchat and the audience laugh, which helps, but I have to breathe the tears away and the urge to flee is strong; he raises his hand like Olga and with the other plays the tonic note three clear, confident times; E for Elgar, not lowering his hand until he's sure I've composed myself and my hand is in the right position. It's either run and abandon him, or put the false start behind me and trust myself to leap off the cliff again. We settle properly into the hush of preparation. I relax my shoulders, take a breath, and offer all of myself over to Darith and Elgar; to vibration and heartbeat, to playing in harmony.

Between us, we fudge a few moments and I'm aware that the musicians in the room would have heard them but if the souls of the listeners didn't thrum with the sensitive thunder of Darith's interpretation of Elgar's lament for a way of life destroyed by war, they are dead inside.

Dad steps onto the stage, clapping. My legs are trembling and I'm grateful when Louise takes Guil out of my sweaty arms so he can help me up and give me a hug. 'My daughter,' he says to the audience, beaming, and I am exhaustion and elation in equal measure. We applaud for Darith, who takes a quick bow before taking my hand and the two of us take one final bow together.

The chamber group take back their seats and say kind things to us about our eight minutes of fame. 'This would be a good time to give Rochelle her present,' Dad whispers.

'What present?' I whisper back, then, 'Oh, no, sorry, Dad. It hasn't come yet.'

Darith pecks me on the cheek and says, 'See you, Van, and thank you.' Dad shakes his hand and says, 'Well done,' and I take the opportunity to escape.

It's only when I wander around the party with my non-alcoholic sparkling grape juice being smiled on and nodded to, I discover Darith, Ash and Dana have escaped, too. Permanently. Off to meet Nadia and Ellen somewhere, I presume.

Louise clinks my glass. 'Fantastic.'

'Thanks. Wasn't Darith amazing?'

'He was.'

'Maybe I'm delusional,' I whisper, 'but I feel like every time I look, Richard Marks is watching me.'

'And why wouldn't he be? That was very well done.' She tears up. 'I wish your mother had been here to see you.'

'She's probably doin' the cancan and playing honky-tonk piano in some fabulous bar in Paris.'

'No.' Louise shakes her head and takes a swig of her beer. 'I don't think so.'

'Anyway,' I say. 'Love to chat but I've got to sneak out now to an underage drinking party on the beach.'

That's not what I say.

I figure the boldest thing is to wander nonchalantly out the front door. These sandals Rochelle lent me may only have a low heel but I ditch them and fossick for a pair of thongs or Crocs from the assorted lost-property store.

Richard Marks shadows the doorway and smiles. 'Cinderella, I presume.'

'Spill the beans,' I shout and whip out my Sherlock Holmes hat, pipe and magnifying glass.

That's not what I do.

I stand there as stiff and guilt-stricken as if I've been caught swearing by Skutenko ... or, as is actually the case, been caught by an adult nicking off to an unsuitable party.

He smells familiar. Ambre Topkapi, the same cologne Mum used to buy for Dad but that he doesn't wear anymore because Rochelle prefers Poivre – it's unisex and they can both wear it – but it's all a bit overpowering if you ask me. But that's not what he's asking me.

He's asking me if I want to sit with him in one of the eatery nooks that flank the entry and share one of the two frosty champagne flutes that wait on the table. He pushes the door, which swings slowly closed behind me, and gestures for me to sit. When the door clicks shut, the night becomes quiet. We settle into the nook, his thigh pressed alongside mine, and he serves the drinks, fizzling and bright. He clinks my glass and the crystal chime is pure. 'You played wonderfully,' he says.

His admiration feels both sweet and oppressive, like being smothered by marshmallow. I'm repulsed and yet fascinated by the patch of hairy leg between his sock and trouser, his lumpy swallow, one too many shirt buttons undone. What would happen if I tried to steal his mobile phone? Who knows what evidence might be on there?

He smiles, catching me looking, and I flush, stuttering, 'Thank you.'

'Very sexy.'

This seems a bit perverted coming from someone who must be forty at least but I say, 'Thank you,' again anyway, embarrassed by my own discomfort because maybe he means it in the same way Kelsey means Crocs are very sexy. I gulp the bubbles down.

He laughs. 'Easy. It's good champagne.' He takes the empty glass, putting it with his own on the table. 'But it's nice to see you're keen.'

I lurch up in horror thinking there's a snake or something sliding up my leg only to discover it's Richard's hand. He rises, quick and sure, steering me to the wall, his arm up, cutting off my exit, stepping in close to shove me against Shearwater with his body. The back of my head smacks against the render. He presses hard, one hand squeezing my breast and then sliding over my throat, the other pulling up my skirt, pushing my legs apart, wedging them open with his knee. His hand drops from my throat to fumble at his trousers. I don't speak or move or think I'm breathing but he says, 'Shh,' breathing hard. 'Shhh.' Under my skirt his scraping finger hooks the crutch of my underpants. The elastic of my undies saws into me and rips where he's pulling it to the side and he jostles me further up the wall. 'Oh,' he says with pleasure, 'that's gotta be so tight.'

Like a hallucination, Marlene strides up shouting, 'Get off her!'

Even now, Richard's eyes are fixed to my bosom. 'We were just talking,' he says and lifts his eyes to mine and winks. He seems smaller now with Marlene shoving his shoulder but he's not fazed. He zips up his fly and winks at me again.

'I saw your *talking*,' Marlene snarls. 'Now piss off.'

Richard straightens himself, doing up his belt and tugging on his cuffs. 'You're trespassing. I'm calling security.'

Marlene brandishes her phone. 'Go ahead. I'd be more than happy to show them and Simon Partridge the video of you sexually assaulting his fifteen-year-old daughter.'

With a sportsman's reflexes, he bats her phone to the ground, stamps on it with his heel and puts the remains in the inside pocket of his jacket, unmoved by her swearing and demands. He pulls his own phone out and all the panic in me froths to the surface. I crack open the front door and slip inside, then run, unsteady from the champagne, yelling, 'Dad!'

Richard follows me in, locking Marlene out. I'm nearly across the foyer when he grabs my arm. 'Stop it,' he says, then composes himself. 'Come on, shh. There's no need for all this. Nothing happened.'

Marlene bangs on the door a few times and then there's silence. I find enough voice to plead, 'Please let me go.'

He pulls me away from the entrance to reception and steps back, hands up in surrender. 'Of course,' he says, more kindly, lowering his arms, sliding one hand into his trouser pocket and leaning against the wall as if suddenly posing to have his photograph taken. 'I misunderstood. You were so ... anyone might have thought you wanted me.' He smiles. 'A lot of women do. I had no idea you were only fifteen.' He crosses his arms as if I've been disobedient. 'The fact is, if you're going to dress like that and flirt like you do, you're going to have to learn to accept the consequences. You're a pretty thing.'

He grabs my arm again to stop me pushing past him and his voice is hard now, like his grip. 'Your daddy and I are about to cement the most important deal of his career – a real game changer for him,' he says tightly. He pulls me around and sits me firmly on the lowest rungs of the staircase. 'He won't thank you for trying to make a fool out of me and trust me—' Marlene bangs on the door again and he nods towards her. 'No one is going to be interested in the ravings of the lunatic fringe and sweetheart . . .' He pulls out a pack of cigarettes. 'Simon is so proud of you. He said so himself, just a few hours ago. How do you think he'd react to the news that you're not quite the little lady he thinks you are: sneaking out of the house to meet up with drug addicts and God-knows-who? How do you think he'll feel finding out how you led me on – quite the tease – at your age?' He taps a cigarette on the packet. 'Now, the last thing I want is to get you into trouble so I'm going to call security and make sure they do a clean sweep of the grounds and then rejoin the party and you're going to get yourself straight to bed, like a good girl, and I promise I won't say a word or tell your father what you've been up to.' He wanders casually back to the noise of celebration, pulling out his phone and releasing a plume of smoke that trails behind him.

All I seem to be able to think is that my mother would never let guests smoke in the house even if they were famous and American. Richard's certainty has carved out a hollowness in me; sucked out the oxygen and left a paralysis. I'm Christopher Robin on the stair neither here nor there but not happy about either. No, not Christopher Robin; he's pure and I'm sullied now.

More door-banging shakes me into action and when I open it, Marlene appears to be almost wrestling with Bodhi. She grabs me into a hug. I collapse against her for a moment, the sharp smell of her, the soft fabric of her shirt. My body shakes so much my teeth are chattering. 'God, Van – are you all right?' she says into the top of my head.

Bodhi's dancing with agitation. 'Let's go before they get here.'

'Let them,' she growls.

'They'll get you arrested for trespassing,' I say dully. 'It's happened to people before.'

Bodhi tugs my hand saying, 'Come on,' and I let myself be pulled along and Marlene lets herself be pulled along with me. 'What a complete prick,' she says. 'You have to report him to the police.'

I shake my head and she jerks me to a standstill and my hand slips from Bodhi's. He keeps running but Marlene takes my shoulders in her bony fingers. 'That guy assaulted you. I think he was going to rape you.'

'Nothing happened.'

She drops her arms as if she's disgusted with me. 'It makes me so angry that girls won't recognise the patriarchal bullshit they're mired in even when it jumps up and bites them.'

Bodhi calls, 'Come on,' cutting through the rush of shame and I turn away from Marlene, down the track after him.

The kick takes me by surprise. I scramble forwards, off balance, begging Ron and the other guy to see it's me, Vanessa, just Vanessa.

'Shit,' Ron says. The two of them help me up. 'Sorry, Ms Partridge.'

Marlene and Bodhi are gone, just sounds crashing through the bush. Ron moves off after them. 'Don't,' I say. 'Let them go and I won't tell Dad you kicked me.'

More security arrives and they square up as if they're rival teams. Richard's Americans are slicker somehow but Ron and Ariki still look like they could crush them; I almost expect the pair of them to break into a haka.

'What's going on here?' the slickest one says with his cop-show accent. 'Those trespassers won't be back, damn fools. Who's this?'

'Simon's daughter,' Ron says. 'She's okay, nothing to worry about.'

When we get back to the house the floodlights are on and Dad and a half-a-dozen guests have spilled out the front door. One of them is Eddie Glasshouse. My father draws me inside and looks me up and down. I am a bit bedraggled. 'What happened?' he asks Ron.

'Trespassers, sir. I think it's the same mob from the marina. All clear now.'

Dad turns to me. 'But what happened to you?'

Richard wanders into the circle and Rochelle touches his hand. 'I'm so sorry about all this,' she says.

'No, no, not at all.' He smiles like the wolf in one of the old picture books Mum used to read me. 'What's all the excitement about?'

Rochelle says, 'Oh, your dress!' and takes my hand whispering, 'What's going on?' as we make our way up the staircase.

'Nothing,' I whisper back.

'False alarm,' Dad calls, jovially raising his glass to the group. 'More champagne and someone tell Wilbur it's time to bring on the jazz.' He takes the stairs two at a time and puts his arm around Rochelle. 'Time for a little dancing.' He pecks me on the cheek and as they sashay down, calls back, 'Well done tonight, Vanessa. Never mind about the dress, you clumsy clot. Now off to your room and not a peep. I'll be sending Louise up in an hour to make sure you're all right.'

Richard and the sound of laughter follow them through to the dancefloor. The band strikes up and Rochelle whoops, 'Simon!' in an utterly delighted way.

I pull off Mum's dress and my torn undies under the running shower and kick them wet to the bathroom floor but a shower's no good.

Bed feels safest but I can't read or bear to watch anything or go on Facebook or answer Suyin's messages about how the performance went or Kelsey's texts about where I am and whether I'm coming to the beach party. I don't really sleep, just lay there in an adrenaline-fuelled coma of horrible nothingness. When my door creaks open,

I stiffen and my throat closes over but if it's Richard I'm going to find a way to scream and scream.

Louise flicks on the light. 'What's wrong?'

'Nothing. I was asleep.'

'Sorry.' She flicks the light off. 'You were making a funny noise.'

Later when I get up to see if Ash has come home, there's an American security guard outside my door. 'No moving about the house, ma'am,' he says.

'What?'

Over the music, I hear a scream and splashing in the pool.

'The privacy of the partygoers,' he explains. 'Adult only,' he adds and winks, as if associating Dad's party with porn is supposed to make me feel better about being kept like a prisoner in my own house. A wash of tears swooshes up, surprising me, and instead of arguing, I grab his arm. 'Don't let anyone into my room,' I insist. 'No one.'

He pats my hand. 'Yes, ma'am.'

Dad wakes me to say, 'Happy new year!' He doesn't even look hungover, his eyes are sparkling. 'Not getting up?'

'I have dysania.'

He pulls out his phone, asks for the spelling, and taps away. 'Ah, the chronic condition of not being able to get out of bed in the morning,' he reads aloud. 'Well, guess what? It's the afternoon.'

'You seem happy.'

'I am! Richard is extremely pleased with our progress. It looks like there are only a few hoops to jump through and then it's full steam ahead. We're off to Richard's yacht. The *Iphigenia* has been causing quite a stir down at the marina, I believe. And not just with those ridiculous trespassers. Louise will be here to keep an eye on you. Do you know anything about those greenies here last night? Some people have nothing better to do with their lives.'

'What hoops?'

'Nothing you need to worry about. Just a few small hoops.' He practically rubs his hands in glee. 'Next year we might be taking our summer holidays on our very own *island*!'

'I don't want an island.'

'Vanessa, everybody wants an island.'

'So you *are* selling Shearwater?'

'Not selling it, no. Opening up its potential. Unemployment down here is at a record high – a bit of industry will put the place on the map.'

'What industry?'

'Let's just wait until the ink's dried on the contracts.' He pats me as if I were seven. 'Then there'll be a big announcement.'

Words and images tumble around in me. I feel more lost than when I got separated from everyone at Disneyland. 'Richard—' cranks its way past my closed-over throat.

'A fantastic guy. I know I'm always saying it's dangerous to put all your eggs in one basket but I think we're pretty safe with Richard Marks. He's not just a star athlete – well, *was* – he's a business genius.' Dad pats me again. 'He was quite taken with you, too. Told me you're the kind of talented young woman he admires.' He jiggles his eyebrows at me. 'Compliments from the Marksman: that'll impress your school friends.'

He clearly does not know Suyin.

A thought seems to jolt him. 'Rochelle thinks you might have struck up a bit of a romance with that boy, Tim. Is that right?'

'No.'

'Ah, well – stick to the school books if you ask me. Trouble with boys is that they're only after one thing.'

'Not like you men,' I croak, but Dad's not listening.

'But invite him over for another swim in the pool, if you like,' he says. 'Yes, invite him over for a swim in the pool. Later in the week when things settle down.' He jumps up. 'I'd better go.'

My father kisses me on the head and rushes towards the bathroom, realises he's gone in the wrong direction and laughs. 'Out the door, Simon,' he says. 'Out the door.'

He's replaced by Ashton, who sits on my bed. 'Bloody hell, is Dad buzzed off his head or what? Must have been some party last night. Did you have fun?'

'No.'

'Did you go to the back beach with Tim?'

'Why does everyone think I'm going out with Tim?' I feel a sudden hatred for everyone and everything. 'Thanks for sneaking off like a—' Words fail me. 'Like a *sneak*.'

'Aw, Van – don't cry. Jesus, the girls thought you'd be— Bloody hell, when you carry on like this it makes me glad we left you behind.' He storms off but I storm faster, pushing past him to rush to the cubby and cry.

But I don't cry. I lay there on the Foxholers' abandoned sleeping bags and shake.

There is a silence in me; a hush that's fallen. I guess even to myself, my blithe chattering was like the drum of rain, like dog-panting, like the orchestra warming up; sound that lives in a world of its own, that completes itself, paying perfect non-attention to the intentions of others; but my childhood has clattered to stillness.

About time, I suppose.

Funny that it should be Ash who notices, even if he's wrong about why. He thinks I'm annoyed with him for not taking me to their New Year's party. We're down in the kitchen and he's been busy telling Darith about how cold it is all of a sudden, as if Dar might have some other reason to put on a jumper and jeans. 'The sky's full of cloud,' Ash tells him. 'Like it's still blue, but covered in a thin layer of cloud – sort of stamps of cloud. Bizarre. It was thirty-five yesterday.'

'Very bizarre,' says Darith. 'Probs global warming.'

Ash turns on me. 'So what's with you? You still sulking?'

I twitch a shoulder, stirring my hot chocolate.

He hoicks himself with an effortless twist to sit on the kitchen bench, which he'd never do if Sharif were here, and crowds me with a knee. 'Aren't you going to illuminate us with some rare and pointless fact about clouds?'

'Just because *you* don't know something doesn't make the knowledge *rare*,' I say and slump to the table to half-heartedly shift around what's left of the puzzle, all blue.

Darith snorts. 'You've been owned.'

But it's as if my brother somehow sees the new shadowy hollow that's sprung up where my enthusiasm used to be. Not even approval from Darith shines a light in there. Ash slides off the bench and drags a chair to sit too close next to me, causing a hot chocolate tidal wave. 'Are you sick?' he says.

I twitch both shoulders. Darith chucks me a tea towel saying, 'You didn't miss much, to be honest,' and I toss it over the spill.

'Yeah,' Ash pipes in. 'Funbags here chose New Year's Eve to break up with Nadia, which meant we all had a wonderful time.'

A day ago this news would have had me dancing around the room but all that swells up in me is a dampening hush, like mould spores I don't want to breathe in. I can't even *look* at Darith.

'What's wrong, Van?' Ash is still serious. 'What's happened?'

'Richard Marks tried to rape me,' I say.

No, I don't.

I dump my cup in the sink and stomp out yelling, 'Cirrocumulus, all right? Happy? Mackerel sky, colloquially, if you really want to know, which I know you *don't* and you mean climate change, Darith – global warming isn't a description of the freaking *weather*.'

∾

I'm watching *Spartacus* when the boys leap over the couch, one on either side. 'Sorry, we should have at least told you we were pissing off,' Ash says. 'I'm putting the cricket on. You can watch this any time.'

I shrug. 'It's so unfair that no one cares if *you* sneak off to a party but *I'm* put into lock down with hourly cell inspections.'

Ash yawns. 'It's because you're a girl.'

They both seem entirely comfortable with and certain about this fact.

'So what?'

'You could get pregnant.'

'Oooh,' they shout at the TV. 'Not out!'

'Well, that's a disaster for both parties, surely?' I say. 'I mean – wouldn't you feel half responsible if Dana was pregnant?'

Ash looks horrified.

'So why aren't there a million rules to make sure boys don't get girls pregnant then?'

'Or worse stuff can happen,' says Darith.

'So why aren't the rapists the ones who have to stay home and not wear miniskirts or whatever?' I snap. 'It's not fair.'

'What are you rabbiting on about?' Ash points to the screen. 'That was a beautiful shot.'

'I'm *talking* about people saying, "Sorry, but you're not permitted go around socialising with girls unsupervised because we can't trust you not to be a total creep."'

'It's not like they *let* me – I just went.' Ash leans forwards to watch the replay. He sits back. 'Not that I'm a creep, by the way.'

Darith settles his feet on the coffee table. 'No one's gonna think their own son is a rapey creep.'

'Then why are they so quick to believe their daughters are "asking for it"?'

Ash tries to dismiss me with his eyebrows. 'Aren't you the little feminist? Is Marlene rubbing off on you?'

'Don't be a tool.'

He brushes me off with a shoulder-raise. 'It's obvious why it's easier to believe your daughter wants sex than that your son is a rapey creep. Oh, oh, yes! And it's another six.' They high-five over my head.

'But wanting to look nice or to have sex or to sneak out to get drunk at a party isn't the same as wanting to be *raped*.' I feel the pressure of Richard against my chest, his hand across my throat, his scraping fingers; and Bodhi's hands on the back of my head. 'Nobody *wants* to be *raped*!'

'Calm down, Van. You're freaking me out,' Ash says.

But I can't calm down. 'You can't ask for it,' I scream. 'The word *rape* means that *no one asked you*.' I run to my bedroom but Ash lurches off the couch and wrestles me down in the hall with an unyielding tenderness that makes me sob into his chest. Darith hangs back, watching.

'Van,' Ash says, so hushed it's like he's scared to hear what I might have to say. 'Did Bodhi do something to you?'

I shake my head and suck back the tears.

He holds me tight. 'You can tell me.'

But I can't tell. All the words in me are empty shells. 'I'm okay,' I sniffle. 'I just miss Mum.'

'Do you promise?'

'I promise.' I climb back into my blank place. 'You can let me go now.'

He lets go and we sit there. 'Maybe you shouldn't hang around with Marlene and Bodhi so much – you've been pretty emotional since you met them.' He wraps his arms around his shins. 'Are you doing ice, Van?'

'What?'

He shrugs. 'Are you doing shard, crystal meth?'

'Why would you say that?'

'I dunno. Erratic. Gone all night. No appetite. Angry. And you look, I don't know – thinner. Or like you've aged or something. It just makes sense.'

'No. At least – I don't *think* so.'

'You don't *think* so?'

'I did take something at the dance party but I don't think it was ice, it wasn't cold.'

'Oh, Van, you really worry me.'

'Ice pills aren't cold, are they?'

'No. And it's not even pills. Stay away from that shit. Will you promise me?'

'Promise me back?'

He smiles. 'Too easy.'

We shake on it.

'I think it's my hair.'

'Your hair?'

'That makes me seem older.'

He appraises me, like he's zooming out to a wider frame. 'You've had it cut.'

Darith says, 'Have you only just noticed?'

'I knew *something* was different. I thought it was just the no plaits. And your new clothes.'

Darith claps his hands, breaking the weird mood. 'Come on you two. *Guitar Hero* – I'll be Prince.'

Ash pushes to his feet, dragging me with him. 'Bullshit, I'll be Prince.'

'You're too white,' Darith scoffs. 'You can be Peter Frampton.'

'Who?'

They wrestle and Darith reaches out an arm to snag me and drag me along. 'You can be Nigel Tufnel,' he says to me and they laugh.

I pack up Richard Marks and put him in a small iron box with a big padlock and throw away the key. 'No way,' I say. 'I'm Annie Clark.'

Ash pulls free, breaking our scrum. 'Who's she?'

'St Vincent,' I say. 'You philistine.'

We google St Vincent and forget *Guitar Hero* for three-and-a-half hours of eating junk food and watching YouTubes of female lead guitarists, finishing up with a documentary on Patti Smith. I think it may well be the best three-and-a-half hours of my life.

But later, alone in my room, Richard comes burbling out of his iron box like theatre fog mixed with the stink of cigarette smoke, suffocating me.

CHAPTER 6

I wake to birdsong but it's still darkish outside. It's the second day of the new year already and before we know it, we'll have to go back to school. What will I tell Suyin?

Nothing.

I'll never tell anyone anything.

Darith half-blinds me by turning on the light, sits next to me on the bed, says, 'I don't know how else to do this,' and plays me a video clip called *Marksman Rapes Teenager*.

Everything I know scatters like a dropped box of Scrabble. You see me sitting with Richard and then banged up against the wall, the fabric of my skirt thrown up and some of my leg exposed; his trousers slide down and it looks like he's humping me before Marlene yells and starts running. The whole thing goes for less than two minutes. It's had hundreds of thousands of hits and more than five hundred comments.

'How—?' I ask Darith. 'When?'

'It was posted as clickbait to a website called *Eddie Glasshouse is Corrupt – Save the Coast*. And someone's turned it into a YouTube.' He flicks through his phone. 'People are already writing articles about it.'

Darith seems a long way off, like one of us has zoomed through a telescope to the far end. I can't feel my feet. And I'm cold. 'What people?' My voice is calm. Shouldn't I be screaming?

'Article-writing people.' He scrolls through his phone. 'Like, *The Huffington Post* and *Mother Jones* and *TMZ* and *The Sydney Morning Herald* and *The Age* and the feminists: that kind of thing. YouTube have taken it down twice, apparently, but it keeps popping up again.'

I take his phone and scramble out of bed mumbling, 'I have to show Dad—' suddenly convinced my father can save me but Dad's already marching along the landing with his iPad, shouting, 'What the hell is this?' He looks drunk. He brandishes the iPad at me.

Darith steps between us. 'Why are you yelling at Van?'

'What the bloody Christ would you know about it?' Dad points at me. 'Do you have any idea what you've done?'

'I didn't want to—'

'Well, what the hell were you doing alone with him, then?' Dad leans against the balustrade and drops the iPad on the carpet to put his head in his hands.

The comment showing on Darith's phone reads: *she looks like she's Enjoying it to me she isn't even struggling.* The next one says, *Go Marksman! Legend! LOL*, then, *She's gagging for it.*

Darith is shaking.

Ash swings out of his bedroom, pulling the door slammed shut and looking ready to punch someone. 'What if it was me?'

Dad looks up. 'What are you talking about?'

'What if it was me and I told you I didn't want to? Would you believe me?'

All the blood leaves my father's face. 'Are you telling me—?'

Ash shakes his head. 'God, Dad. No. But see—'

Dad's phone rings and he jabs at it, striding away from us down the staircase, talking rapidly. 'I know, I know,' he says. 'Yes, yes, she's fine. Is there any chance—' and he's gone, out the open front door to pace around the garden.

Ash kicks his bedroom door open and it bangs again, bouncing brokenly behind him.

Darith takes the phone from my hand. 'I'm so sorry.'

He follows me as I shuffle downstairs with feet of lead. 'He's going to tell everyone I led him on,' I say, my voice sounding like it's coming from far away, even to me.

Darith says, 'Your dad?'

'Richard.' I look out to my father gesticulating at the rosebushes. 'He told me Dad would be disappointed in me.' A big sigh whooshes out of me and I run past Darith, back upstairs. Ash is on his bed, hunched over his knees with his hands drawn into fists and I can tell he's crying. 'He didn't get in,' I say. It seems urgent that he should believe me. 'He didn't.'

Ash wipes his face on his sleeve but doesn't look up. We faintly hear our father laugh and say, 'Of course I believe you.'

Darith puts his arm around me but I slip out from under it. 'I'm okay,' I say. 'I need a drink of water.'

In the kitchen, my phone buzzes and I'm scared to look

but it's only Suyin sending me a series of Snapchats she calls *the seven stages of grief*, each one more bizarre than the last, which I presume are messages of solidarity. There's a wad of cash and a note sitting on the kitchen bench under an amber paperweight. I leave the phone, take the money with me out the back door, scrunch up and throw away the note and keep walking.

The Foxhole is quiet. A bunch of tents have gone, only the bare essentials still standing; Bodhi said a lot of people only came for the lead-up to New Year's Eve. Whoever's left seems to be elsewhere or still asleep. The fire-pit has been filled in and the ground around it swept bare. A helicopter flies overhead, getting louder then fading, and the returning silence makes Gomorrah seem emptier than before.

Cockies caw into the air in a brief cacophony that settles into the general jazz of birdsong. There's the unmistakeable whomping of a kangaroo bounding off. A highway of ants streams up and down the smooth dappled trunk of a gum. The bush doesn't care about the internet and my utter humiliation: it's just glad to be alive. The cumulus mediocris are fat and fluffy like something from an olden-days cartoon. It's getting hot again. I shuffle over to the shady spot where Bodhi's curled in his swag and sit on a rock and tears roll out of me almost as if I had nothing to do with them.

Bodhi seems small. Maybe he couldn't stop them. Maybe

he posted it himself. Maybe Marlene did. Maybe I'll go bush. Into the wild, as it were. The idea of accidentally eating wild potato seeds and poisoning myself sounds pretty good right now even though I cried my head off when I saw that film at school. Maybe I should just walk into the sea.

Bodhi opens his eyes. He wipes spittle from the side of his mouth. 'It wasn't me,' he says and lifts the doona to invite me into his swag. 'Please?'

I don't move.

He closes the swag and his eyes. 'It wasn't me,' he repeats.

Marlene strides into camp trailed by Renate and a bunch of Foxholers carrying bags of weeds, fresh from early morning gardening. Her face crumples when she sees me and she drops her gloves and tools and runs to scoop me into a hug.

Needless to say, I'm confused.

Well, I say I'm confused but what I mean is that I dissolve into an incoherent blathering that sometimes turns into shouting but is mostly silenced by big snot-dripping tears.

'Oh,' Marlene says. 'Oh.'

'How could you?' I manage.

'I didn't.' She holds on tighter. 'Bodhi didn't.'

I push away. 'I don't believe you.'

Renate sniffs and takes off her bonnet. 'I did it,' she says. 'It had automatically uploaded to the cloud and I couldn't let the opportunity pass by.' She straightens her back. 'And it got the attention we wanted, so no regrets.' She offers me a shallow bow. 'It wasn't personal, if that's any consolation.

I didn't mean for those sexist bastards to turn you into some kind of Lady Godiva. You're a nice kid.'

It isn't any consolation.

Bodhi is out of bed. He puts his hand on my arm.

'Don't touch me,' I snap.

'Van, I—'

'Why are you acting like you're the one who's wounded?' I smack him ineffectively in the face. 'Don't shove your cock down girls' throats.'

Yes, that's what I say.

Then, I run.

෨○

Dana's combi pulls almost off the road to drive slowly alongside me. Ash leans out of the passenger window. 'Whatcha doing?' he asks. Dana lifts a hand off the steering wheel to wave hello.

'Walking.'

'Where you going?'

'To get Roger Federer.'

'From Aunty Sue's?'

'Yep.' My ankle turns on a grassy tussock sticking out of the sandy grit of the roadside and I have to stop and waggle it to see if it's broken. The van stops with me.

Ash sniffs. 'In Sydney?'

My ankle seems okay and we all set off again. 'Yep.'

'You're going to walk to Sydney?'

'I'll get the train.'

'Where from?'

'Don't know yet.'

'Have you got any money?'

'I took the three hundred bucks Louise left for the shopping.'

'Technically, that's theft, Van.'

I stop to face him and the combi stops again too. 'I'm applying the categorical imperative to that normative theory of ethics.' I slap at a mosquito and add, *'Technically.'*

'What does that mean?'

'It means I need my dog more than Shearwater needs another wheel of cheese.'

Ash looks flustered. He fiddles about in the cab, muttering to Dana, then returns to the window. 'Phone reckons it will take you fifteen hours to walk to the nearest train station.'

That throws me, especially as my ankle is starting to pound like it's been whacked with a rubber mallet, but then Ash loses his temper and yells, 'Look! We've got a music festival thing to go to and you're driving me crazy!' which is so annoying, it steels my resolve. I trudge on. He masters himself. 'Look, sorry. Come on.'

Tears are threatening and I drop my head: best not to look at him.

'Please get in the van, Van.'

I keep trudging but my resolve lags behind.

I get in the van.

It smells like incense.

I'm grateful to Ash and Dana for shutting up on the way home as far as the Richard disaster and my failed mission to walk to Sydney is concerned. I sit quietly in the back while Ash tries to seduce her by speaking French.

'What did you just say?' she asks.

Ash is beside himself with glee. 'I said, Could you please direct me to the police station, my beautiful cheese.'

Dana squawks with delight. 'Say something else.'

As we rattle over the bumps, they go back and forth. I hadn't realised that Ashton could be charming. It's hard not to love him when he says, 'I said, You are a thrilling gherkin at the end of my street.'

'Does Dad know about the money?' I ask, interrupting before he starts again.

Ash shakes his head. '*Je garde ton secret.*'

'*Merci,*' I say.

'*Pas de quoi,* kiddo.'

When we get home, Dana leaves the motor running and Darith, who must have been waiting, yanks the door open, throws in a backpack and climbs in after it. 'Everything okay?' he says.

Ash nods. 'Everything's okay. Go on, Van. You'll be right. Ask Kelsey to come over – you need your friends around.'

I want to ask them to take me with them but the words cram in my throat. 'What music festival?'

'It's like a Beyond the Valley afterparty,' Ash says. 'With tickets.'

'Why do *you* have to go?'

'Because we got tickets!'

Darith touches my hand as I climb out. 'We'll be back tomorrow,' he says.

I plod upstairs and turn on the TV. Hours later, Dad calls me down for dinner but I'm not hungry. He appears and stands between me and the screen. 'You have to eat.'

'Do I?'

He hovers for a moment and then stomps off muttering, 'For God's sake.'

After a few more hours I do slouch down to the kitchen for food. It's getting late and I've never been good at sleeping on an empty stomach. At the loom of headlights through the foyer windows and the sound of wheels on gravel, I run outside but the combi hasn't come back to save me.

Mum has arrived at Shearwater with a box of chocolates from Aunty Sue, and the dog.

Like the cockies and the kangaroo, Roger cares nothing for the internet. He bounds in perfect bounds and seems as thrilled to see me as I am to see him. Mum says, 'I came as soon as I heard. It's been a long flight.' I don't reply. What am I meant to say? She has no make-up on except a bit of lip balm and there's a wide grey stripe down the middle of her head suggesting she hasn't cut or dyed her hair since she left us, and she's wearing Birkenstocks and fisherman's pants so I'm not sure I even know who she is. I don't want her to touch me when she tries to and she lets her hands fall, then one rises to her chest as if regulating her breathing. The dog, on the other hand, is soundly himself.

'Roger Federer,' I whisper into his neck. 'I've missed you, missed you.' He licks my tears and we lay down together under the table like we used to do when I was little.

'You've cut your hair,' Mum says.

Sharif calls out a greeting from the kitchen, he sounds delighted, and Mum disappears for a moment to talk to him. When she gets back, my father hugs himself, looking puffy-eyed and dishevelled. 'She's gone off the rails,' he says. 'Richard wants our assurance that we can put the whole thing behind us and move forward.'

'What does Vanessa want?' Mum's voice is strained, small. Has it always sounded so calm?

Dad's is irritated but strangely weak. 'She was perfectly fine until this ... this video.'

Mum rubs her collarbone. 'Sue rang me. I haven't seen it yet.'

'Richard says—'

I hiss, '*So in very truth, whatever anyone may think, the real tyrant is a real slave to all coaxings and slaveries of the basest*—' The dog raises his ears as my voice blows up like a bubble of hate. '—*he must flatter the most worthless of mankind.* Plato's *Republic*!' I yell. 'Book Nine!'

Roger accepts my apology by letting me snuggle into him. We roll further under the table.

'See what I mean? Come on,' Dad urges Mum, then adds, stiffly, 'I'll show you to your room.'

I see his legs and her bag heading away but she says, 'I'll be there in a minute.' A chair moves and Mum sits on the floor, almost but not quite under the table. The legs and bags disappear – he must be putting her in the Yellow wing.

She pats Roger's head. 'I'm sorry I missed Christmas,' she tells me, as though continuing a conversation. 'I was hoping I'd be well enough to come home, but I wasn't quite ready.'

It seems a furphy, this 'being ready'. I cup Roger's paw in my palm and weigh it. 'What was wrong with you?'

'I was in retreat.' Mum's eyes and voice are full of tears and I wonder which one of us they're for. 'A sort of hospital, really.' She brightens. 'Then a ten-day silent Vipassana, then an ashram, and then Plum Village.'

This news floats above me, not quite landing. I kiss the paw and let it drop. 'What's that?'

She mists over. 'A mindfulness centre – remember that book I gave you by Thich Nhat Hanh called *Being Peace*?'

It's at home on the floordrobe but I say, 'No.'

'Well, it's a Buddhist meditation retreat that's grown from his teachings.'

So Mum's a Buddhist now. Somehow I can't see her and Bodhi bonding over their meditations on the dharma. 'Do you still hate Dad?' I ask and the little inner voice adds, *And me?*

Mum smiles. 'Hate's a strong word, darling.'

'You should have told us where you were.'

She gently pulls on Roger's ears in the way he likes best. 'Yes,' she agrees. 'I probably should have.'

I roll over and look directly at her. 'It's not true – what Richard says.'

Mum attends me closely, steadily. It's unnerving. 'What does he say?'

But I can't speak his words out loud. My throat closes up and burns. I don't seem to be able to cry, either. 'I'm tired,' puffs out of me like a child's complaint.

'Come on. Roger can sleep with you tonight,' she says. 'He'd like that.'

She follows me and the dog upstairs and as I crawl into bed, pokes around at my floordrobe. 'Are these your clothes?' she asks, opening drawers.

'Don't go through my stuff,' I say. 'Don't come back from nowhere and think you can just pick up where we left off.'

That's not what I say. I don't say anything, just hug Teddy when she rescues him from obscurity and tucks him in with me, and stroke Roger's ears, his chin resting right on the ache in my chest.

'You've changed your style.'

I find enough voice to reply, 'So have you.'

She peeps into the bag of evening dresses just as Dad comes to the door. 'I'll leave you two alone,' she says and kisses my hair.

There's a clumsy shuffle between them at the door and when she's gone, Dad sits on my bed. 'I didn't know you still slept with Ted,' he says. 'Look, I'm sorry about before. I've been under a lot of pressure but – look, I shouldn't have reacted like that.' He smiles but I can't smile back. 'I honestly think Richard is just a little too used to having women throw themselves at him – I've seen it myself, and they really do – and too used to taking the things he wants.

He misread the signals and got the wrong end of the stick. It's horrible what's happened but he really is so sorry about the misunderstanding.'

Maybe Marlene's wrong. Maybe some women do want to be groped against the wall. Maybe it is my fault. I hug Ted a bit tighter.

'So – are we all right, kiddo?' I nod and my father kisses my forehead. 'Now, listen, I want you and your brother to leave it to Rochelle and me to tell your mother about the new baby when the time seems right. Do I have your word on that?'

'Okay,' I say. 'Unless she asks.'

He pats me. 'Good girl.' For a minute I think he's going to ask me how I feel about Rochelle being pregnant but he doesn't and I'm not sure if I'm disappointed or relieved. Probably both. When he's gone, I pull out the *Book of Observations*.

People are not Things.

The note in the gift bag with Aunty Sue's chocolates reads, *Hang in there: you're stronger than you know.*

From reception I can see through to where Mum, Dad and Rochelle are eating breakfast on the dining room balcony. They're discussing the latest news 'article'. I've seen it. Suyin sent it to me: the headline reads *Teen Sex Bombshell* but the grainy photo is of me and Suyin holding up our orchestra medals that she used to have as her profile picture. We're jumping up and down like twelve-year-old loons. The article is basically about nothing except that they have *exclusive evidence to reveal* with a link to the Eddie Glasshouse page. The inset photo is one the official photographer took of me playing Guilhermina at the New Year's Eve party; Richard in the background, watching me. It's strange to see yourself from the outside like that: if I didn't know who it was with her poise and gravitas, I'd assume she was a real musician.

Dad shoves an iPad across the table to Mum. 'Does this mean we'll be besieged?'

'I don't know, Simon,' she says brusquely, her face drawn. 'I hope not.' And it dawns on me that their 'nanny scandal' must have been her Lady Godiva moment.

But Mum seems different, now – pared back, as if she's been washed in bleach. There's something calm about her. She's still not wearing any make-up, and hanging around in her Shearwater bathrobe and terry-towelling slippers. The animosity of 'Marion' seems to have faded with her hair dye. Or perhaps it was merely the unfortunate by-product of the vodka. Rochelle, on the other hand, looks like she's about to go out for dinner. I glimpse high heels under the table and a pang of compassion jags through me. Rochelle is like Mum was: wanting Dad to make her feel good about herself, and he never will; he never can. I guess that goes for me, too.

I wonder what will happen when they tell her Rochelle's new secret?

Sharif nudges my shoulder. 'Breakfast?'

I shake my head.

'I have rhubarb to die for,' he coaxes. 'How about a bit of rhubarb and yoghurt with my famous granola, if you're not hungry enough for eggs Florentine?'

I shake my head again.

'Then join me for coffee. Come on.' He leads me away from spying on my parents and busies himself at the cappuccino machine. Roger turns in a circle three times before settling by the back door, lifting his ears when Sharif bangs the portafilter on the coffee-grounds shoot. Sharif glances at me while he's wiping out its little metal basket. 'You ever heard the saying: *to starve is the cruellest death a man can die*?'

'Yes.'

He smiles. 'I thought you might.'

'But Plato says it's not good advice.'

Sharif laughs.

'He says, better to demand your heart to endure than to think about food and drink all the time.'

'Does he? Well, perhaps he's never been hungry.'

There's a wave of melancholy that ripples over our chef that makes me wonder what his heart *and* stomach might have endured but he banishes it with another smile, handing me a latte. 'Tell me what you think – new beans, locally roasted.' He nods. 'Fairtrade, of course.'

'Of course.' I sip. 'It's delicious.'

He seems genuinely delighted. 'Tell Louise that – she thinks I'm messing with tradition.'

'She's just not a big fan of change.'

'True.' He pours himself a piccolo and joins me at the staff table. 'So, how is your heart enduring?'

'You've seen the video?'

'I have not.' He spreads his hands. 'But I have heard.'

'Dad thinks it was just a misunderstanding because celebrities have people throwing themselves at them all the time and we're lucky Richard is still willing to go on with their business arrangements.'

Sharif's face clouds. 'Then your father is wrong.'

Roger's ears lift and then he's up, tail wagging like a mad thing. Ash, Dana and Darith barrel through the back door. Darith ruffles my hair in the most annoying way anyone could ever ruffle a person's hair. I slap his hand away. 'Watch out,' he says. 'Feisty.'

Ash rolls about on the kitchen floor with the dog, and pulls Dana down with him.

'Do you know Mum's back?' I ask, swirling my latte.

Ash lies on his back and Dana untangles herself to leave Roger licking his face. 'About bloody time,' he says at last, lurching up to join us at the table, Roger panting at his feet. He rubs his face with a tea towel. 'That coffee looks good.'

Sharif nods towards the coffee machine. 'I knocked off twenty minutes ago but you're very welcome,' he says. 'You're in luck, it's still on.'

Ash heads over and makes vague gestures at it like a confused puppet. 'I don't know how it works,' he complains.

Dana bumps him to one side. 'Watch and learn. Some of us have actual ... you know: life skills.' She and Sharif share a laugh.

'Are you going to go and see her?' I ask.

'Yep.' He turns to Dana. 'But first, teach me to make coffee.'

Sharif, Darith and I crowd around the Christmas jigsaw at the end of the table. Roger sighs and I wish I could stay here like this forever especially when Kelsey appears at the back door and plonks herself next to me but she says, 'Get your bikini on. It's swimming weather and my mum wants to see you.'

'Good plan,' says Ash, 'cos we'll be off shortly.'

Kelsey takes me by the hand to drag me upstairs. I overhear Sharif say, 'She's a nice kid,' and the rest of them say, 'Yeah.'

Kelsey pokes through my stuff. 'I can't wear a bikini,' I say. 'I just can't. From now on I'm going to wear the baggiest clothes and have the hairiest legs and plaitiest plaits this side of the black stump.'

'It's got nothing to do with your clothes, Van.'

'How do you know?'

'Mum says it happens to all sorts of girls and women. Even children.'

'That's horrible.'

'I know.'

We sit with the horribleness of it until she bounces back and rummages through the floordrobe to pull out the over-the-top-of-your-bathers swishy thing. 'Wear this over them.'

'It's too see-through.'

She uncovers my original pyjamas. 'Perfect, wear Snoopy. Come on, before it gets too hot.'

I groan. 'Noooo.'

But Kelsey is in no mood to take 'noooo' for an answer. 'There's hardly ever anyone at Shearwater's beach,' she says. 'The *No Trespassing* signs put people off.'

I have no powers of resistance. I'm just grateful she doesn't think I'm a *stupid s— who should think herself lucky*, who *had it coming* and should be *raped properly next time*.

When we get there, she hugs me and jumps up and down yelling, 'I love you, Van. So goddamn the internet! Come on!' She drags me to the sea.

The Channel 7 helicopter flies over and a vague sense of galeophobia sneaks through me, though technically the helicopter generally means there's a *rational* reason to fear sharks but Kel spear tackles me and we hit the water screaming and squealing as if it were years ago and we hadn't even grown breasts yet. The helicopter turns, hanging in the air, high up but deafening, a huge zoom-lens camera poking out and flashing, and with a part-hysterical conjoined scream of horror we realise it's there for me. I grab Kel's hand and we duck, staying under the water as long as we can, only bobbing up for breath. Just when I think it might be better to drown (or that I may, indeed, be drowning), it swings away. Its roaring fades into the distance, a wave lifting me slightly so I have to stagger backwards to keep my footing.

'This must be how Justin Bieber feels,' Kelsey pants.

The helicopter comes back to deafen us as we push out of the water, scurry up the stairs with towels over our heads and scamper off the track and into the bush, stuffing ourselves under an acacia and using our towels to protect us from the worst of the stabbing and prickling. After about three years of unbearable noise, squashed sweating and warding off ants, the helicopter finally goes away. 'I doubt they're going to look for you at the funny little caravan park,' Kel says. 'So you'll have to come and see Mum after all.'

We flit through the scrub like fugitives; fugitives that keep getting stabbed by sticks, scared out of their wits by sticks that look like snakes, and whacked by sticks still growing from trees. 'Remember when we used to pretend we were bushrangers being chased by the troopers?' I say.

'Yeah.'

'Am I remembering wrong or were we a lot better at sneaking through the bush back then?'

'I'll call on the powers of the Ladybird People,' she says. 'Our loyal subjects.'

'They can't help.'

Kelsey says, 'Pfft!' and raises her arms to wiggle her fingers at the sky.

I may be imagining it, but our journey does seem smoother and less stick-y after that.

At the edge of the park, Kelsey has a brainwave and heads off on a mission. Ten minutes later, her brothers arrive like a posse. Lachie lends me his bike, a spare set of clothes and his precious St Kilda football cap and I ride off. 'Don't show off,' Kelsey yells after us as she and Lachie follow on foot. 'Or she'll stick out like dogs' balls.'

When we get to their house, the boys spill inside and deliver me to their mother, who's on the phone. 'Thank you,' I say, grabbing them for hugs. 'Can you – sorry, but can you please not tell anyone I'm here?'

Kelsey's mum says, 'Hang on,' and puts her hand over the receiver. 'Coop? What will you do if someone asks you if Vanessa's here?'

Cooper's face is pure determination. 'Say nothing and find a trusted adult,' he says.

'Good boy. Now here's your brother, so go on, shoo.'

'You can keep the clothes for as long as you like,' says Lachie magnanimously as Kelsey pushes past him and plonks herself on the couch. 'Just take care of me hat.'

'I promise I will. Thanks, Lach.'

The boys leave and the house seems to take a minute or two to settle, like a whirlwind's passed through. The settling is safety, stealing around me like a blanket until shame sneaks in like a cold draft, making me shiver. 'Have they watched the video?' I ask.

Kelsey shakes her head. 'They know something's happened to you, though,' she says. 'If Harry or Lachie have googled it on the sly, I don't think they'd tell me anyway, in case I told Mum and Dad.'

'But definitely not Coop?'

'Definitely not Coop.'

I put my head on her lap and she strokes my hair until I'm done crying. 'Want to play Scrabble?' she says.

෨◯

'It didn't occur to me at the time,' I mutter as we pack up the board games and head in to watch TV, 'but since I've watched it again, I can't believe Marlene let that creepoid get so far before she did anything.'

'I can't believe they put it on Facebook too.'

'I can't believe people are being so horrible to me.'

'I can't believe you doubted the powers of the Ladybird People.'

That gets a laugh out of me. 'And I can't believe my mum has become the serene queen of fisherman's pants but is still agreeing with everything my dad says.'

'No offense, but your parents are idiots.'

'None taken.'

She rearranges the couch cushions, pulls out a bike pump and a crossword book and throws them on the floor. Something digs into my back – what the hell else is down the back of this couch? I pull it out, peer, and show her the plastic man. 'Who's this?'

After a quick inspection she says, 'Flash,' and kicks him under the TV cabinet.

Mrs Lepski comes in to sit in the armchair opposite, still on the phone. 'I'll put her on,' she says and holds the handset out to me. 'It's your mother.'

Kelsey reaches for the remote. 'Speak of the devil.'

She and my father and *Rochelle*, Mum's kind enough to add, have decided the best thing for me to do is to stay at the Lepskis' until the 'worst is over'. Mrs Lepski agrees. Apparently the media storm that follows the Marksman wherever he goes has picked up on the story, especially since sexual harassment has become 'news', and now at least three other women have come forward with new 'allegations' and Shearwater is 'surrounded'.

'You were smart to cover up today,' Mum says.

'Today?'

'You and Kelsey at the beach – it was all over everything almost straight away. Thank God for Peanuts and board shorts is all I can say. You both looked like tomboys. Happy, carefree tomboys.'

'What are they saying?'

Mum hesitates. 'I've learned not to read the comments.'

I know she's lying.

'Sue thinks Richard's probably paying trolls to bad-mouth you.'

'So Aunty Sue's read the comments?'

'Look, they don't seem to know who Kelsey is, so you should be safe there. Try to ignore it. All of it. We've sent clothes and your books – and Roger. Anything else?'

Kel dumps a glass of orange juice with ice cubes and a straw on the coffee table for me and toasts me with her own.

'The lawyer's advice ...' Mum says and I hear the conflict in her voice. There's a muffled sound as if she's put her hand over the phone. She comes back, clear again. 'Marks is an American citizen and it's unlikely he would be extradited on—' she pauses. 'On such a minor charge.'

'So they're going to charge him?'

Kelsey stops slurping to listen.

Mum coughs.

'So they're *not* going to charge him?'

'Richard has more lawyers than you've had hot dinners,' she says. 'I know it's awful but it seems better just to carry on.'

'But what about the video? What about the other allegations?'

Kelsey says, 'What about Harvey Weinstein?' and returns to her slurping.

'The claims of one of the women have already been debunked as a money scam of some sort, which makes the whole thing more difficult, to be honest. And the video . . . it's just not . . . conclusive, but I believe you, darling. You know that, don't you?' Her voice wavers. 'You haven't done anything wrong.'

'Hey!' says Kelsey. 'I just realised rapey guy's name is Dick Marks.' She laughs then kicks back and turns up the TV. Only free-to-air: the selection is terrible.

'. . . Vanessa, are you listening to me?'

I pass the phone to Mrs Lepski who puts it to her ear and says, 'Sorry, Fi, it's me,' and heads off to the kitchen. Roger sneaks onto the couch and even though we're all boiling despite the air conditioner noisily blasting away, we slouch there for hours watching re-runs of *Bewitched* on catch-up and wondering what Samantha sees in her stupid husband.

Well, I say we wonder what Samantha sees in him but we know exactly what it is: her mother doesn't like him.

My heart has retreated into a bunker and quietly, like a child might, is singing the same lyric over and over to itself in a corner. *What the hell is this? What the hell is this? What the hell is this?*

⁹○

Later, when everyone's gone to bed and I'm lying awake on the fold-out couch in the lounge room, Mrs Lepski comes to the door. 'Will you come for a walk with me?' she says. 'Let's go and have a look at the moon.'

'Do I have to?' I say. 'Because I'd rather not.'

That's not what I say.

The balminess of the night is offset by the relentless wind blowing out to sea and I'm glad I put on my dressing-gown. The moon *is* beautiful, hanging over the ocean like a silver plate. Mrs Lepski stops at the lookout and leans on the rail, her hair parting at the back of her head. She waits until I lean, too, and I can tell she's working up to something. 'I'm not going to embarrass you with the detail,' she says at last, her voice low but strong, even under the wind. 'But I know what it's like to be hurt that way and then blamed and disbelieved— Oh, this wind is ridiculous.' She hurries me back and down the few steps to the sheltered wooden bench tucked against the cliff and out of the wind that everyone calls the love seat.

Mrs Lepski smiles and sighs at the same time, both hands on the railing as if she's holding on for dear life. 'I was a little bit older – seventeen, and it wasn't quite on your epically public scale, of course.' A bird glides over our heads. 'Owl,' she says.

Dark cloud streaks right down to the horizon and in

the relative quiet out of the wind, I tune in the roar of the surf below.

'The thing is,' she says, 'that back then, no one told me that rape – or any kind of sexual abuse – is about power and control and about violence – not sexiness, or passion, or drinking champagne with your father's friend at a party.' She lets go of the rail to put her arm around me and squeezes tight. 'So *I'm* telling *you*, Van, because I really wish someone had told me.' She sniffs. 'It can never be undone, but if you're lucky, it will become something you forget most of the time. But when the anger comes – and it will, from time to time, and sometimes when you'll least expect it – promise me you'll find somewhere creative to put it and not turn it on yourself.' She relaxes her grip on me. 'Otherwise he'll always have power over you and we don't want that, do we?'

'No,' I manage.

'No,' she echoes.

The sky has cleared, the stars muted by moonlight.

'Do you think I'm a bad and immoral person?' she asks. 'Do you think it's my fault that boy did that to me?' She looks me square in the face and maybe it's the moonlight but it seems like her teenage face is peeping out at me from behind her round, familiar, middle-aged one. 'I went out on a date with him. I *liked* him.'

I say, 'No,' but the word gets tangled by the tears in my throat. How could anyone think Mrs Lepski was any of the things the comments say about me?

'Well,' she gives me another squeeze, 'please believe that

I know that *you* are not a bad or immoral person either and it's *not your fault* that man did that to you.'

'Thanks, Mrs Lepski.' I put my head on her shoulder and we sit like that, quietly, until the moon has nearly disappeared and the stars burn bright.

'Come on,' she says at last, her normal self again, clicking on an old-school torch that she pulls from her pocket. 'You'd better get some sleep if you're going to be match fit for the Oceanview totem-tennis championship tomorrow.'

∽◯

As it turns out, I'm knocked out by Cooper in the first round.

∽◯

Living with the Lepskis is like living with a family in a novel set during another time. We play a lot of Pictionary. The family only has *one* computer and it's not even a laptop and Mr Lepski is in charge of it because Mrs Lepski rules the one in the office that *no one* is allowed to use except her. And if you don't do your chores you can forget about your hour.

One hour!

And the boys don't even complain that much when their time's up, either. And twice I've seen Cooper give his hour to Lachlan because Lachie is obsessed with some Japanese game show and Coops would 'rather be outside anyhoo'.

It drives Kelsey crazy how much I love her brothers.

I say I love living with the Lepskis but the truth is: I have to get out of here. There's no space and they listen to commercial radio, which makes me want to tear off my ears. We tried listening to Classic FM but it was a terrible failure. I miss my cello. I miss my laptop. Mrs Lepski makes me leave my phone in a basket on top of the fridge. There aren't even any iPads. I'm so sick of hanging around the caravan park. The only movies we can watch are the ones available in the Oceanview DVD library in the kiosk and they're all blockbusters or films from the '80s, which seems to have been a truly terrible time for filmmaking. There are people everywhere all the time and the house is so small and everyone takes up so much room – and it's been raining and when the boys are all inside, it's bedlam. And Mr and Mrs Lepski have dropped strong hints that they think I should take a turn at doing the dishes, which seems utterly, utterly unfair on top of all the other unfair things. I burst into tears and Kelsey says, 'What's wrong now, you missing your servants?'

No wonder she's sick of me: I'm sick of myself.

But when Mum calls to say it's all clear for me to go back to Shearwater, I don't want to leave. 'Maybe tomorrow,' I tell her.

I hand the phone to Mrs Lepski, who looks conflicted.

'I'll take my turn at doing the dishes,' I plead. 'And I'll deliver Old Jack his supper: every night.'

They're always squabbling over who has to take Old Jack his supper in case the 'old bastard is dead'.

'Please, Mum?' Kelsey begs which makes me love her forever because I know she's had me up to her eyeballs.

'And his breakfast!' I add, desperate.

Old Jack is still grossly clicking in his false teeth when he opens his caravan door for his porridge the next morning. 'The sixth of January. Epiphany, for those who care,' he says and accepts the tray. 'Thank you kindly.'

'I don't think he even knew it wasn't one of you,' I tell Kel when I get back.

'Nah, he's getting pretty blind,' she agrees.

Her parents sit opposite me as if I'm an interview subject. 'Oh-oh,' says Kelsey. 'This looks serious.'

Mr Lepski has printed out the information from the *Eddie Glasshouse is Corrupt* website and Mrs Lepski has highlighted sections in yellow. Mr Lepski looks at the pages and then over his glasses at me. 'Do you know if any of this is true, Van?' he asks.

Mrs Lepski reaches out to take my hand and sixty-seven per cent of the story comes tumbling out of me along with the tears.

Ash texts and I head into town on the best of the Ocean-view bikes to meet him. I wear Lachie's clothes, despite the all clear, setting off early and arriving in plenty of time to wander down to the foreshore and back up to the mobile library. It's a relief to be on my own.

My brother sits on the metal step of the library truck and looks squarely at me. 'Nice hat,' he says. He looks tired. 'Mum sent me to ask you to please come home, so here I am. Rochelle's gone to her parents' so it's intensely weird, but Dad's heading up there tomorrow, apparently. The paparazzi have definitely moved on – they're following the blood trail to some other ocean because the *Iphegenia* has left the marina.'

'Is Dad—?'

'Dad's lost his mind, but this isn't about him. We need you home.'

We.

'Come on, Van. The Lepskis can't adopt you. You'll have to come back sooner or later.'

'Maybe tomorrow.'

'That's what you said three days ago,' he says. 'Come back with me now.'

'I can't just go home without saying thank you – and I promised I'd give Lachie his hat back. And besides, it's my turn to do the dishes.'

Ash snorts. 'You? Doing the dishes?'

I nod. 'By hand.'

'That's positively medieval.'

How can I explain that the most peaceful, purposeful thing I've done since everything went horrible is to wash the Lepski family dishes?

A lady and her adorable kid who says, 'Scuze me, scuze me,' want to get down the library steps at the same moment Dana arrives. Ash stands, both to move out of the way and to kiss Dana and the lady says, 'Naw,' out loud. With the 'n' sound.

'Mum's pretty shattered,' Ash tells me.

'I'm glad we had Nanny but I'm not going to have one for my kids,' I say, to chase away my thoughts. 'I want to be hands-on, like Mrs Lepski.'

'I never had a nanny,' says Dana, 'and I survived. Hey—' She nudges me with her shoulder. 'You have a fan page.'

Ash picks his nose and flicks it into the scrub. 'And a hate page. So what are you going to do about ... you know? Are you going to press charges?'

I half-collapse to sit in the sandy dirt because the thought of a fan page and a hate page and the recurring nightmare of everyone at school having seen the comments sucks all the strength from my legs. Dana sits with me and her arm around me feels like the only thing keeping me on the earth. I gather myself and try to shake away the awfulness. 'The cops have basically told Mum that nothing is going to happen to him so I don't feel like there's any big decision for me to make about trying to— I mean, it's not like doing something will stop it from happening to other girls. If I thought that, I would.'

Dana gives me a squeeze and says, 'Fair enough.'

'Apparently the video's not ... "conclusive",' I add.

Ash breaks the stick he's been fiddling with. 'I told you those Foxholers were bad news.'

'They posted it because they want to save the coast. Renate thought the video would embarrass them: Dad, all the politicians at the party. Generally put a bad smell around any deals they might be making, draw attention to the Foxholers' allegations and maybe, somehow, the corruption would come out. She wanted to capitalise on Dick Marks being – you know, famous.'

Ash looks down at me with his 'you talk too much' face but I persevere.

'I was thinking maybe we *could* whistleblow the information they want – about Champion and the bribes they've been paying to the government ministers, the shonky conflicts of interest and all that—' I feel the hated blubbering approach. 'I don't want them to turn Shearwater into a casino any more than Renate does and the Lepskis—' The thought of them is the end of me.

Ash rolls his shoulders. 'What are you talking about?'

'It would close the park.' I pull the tears back. 'Kelsey's family just lease the place – a gentleman's agreement from the old days. No compensation for them. They'd lose everything.' I swallow hard. 'Old Jack would have to go into a home.'

Ash unfolds his arms to push back his hair in exactly the way Dad does when he's stressed. 'Of course Dad will compensate them, he's not that much of a prick – and Oceanview's not a retirement village. They're not responsible for those old drunks—'

'Ash—' Dana sounds disappointed in him.

'You didn't see them at Christmas,' I argue. 'They're a *family*.'

He shakes his head. 'No wonder they never make any money.'

I feel heat bloom in my cheeks. 'And anyway, don't you think I should make it *mean* something – all this public humiliation? And if Dad—'

'I don't give two shits about Dad,' Ash spits, and it hurts and satisfies in equal measure to see his fury. 'Don't you get it? Freakoids on the net are already threatening to do – to do just the shittest things to you.' He dissolves into tears and it's a melancholy wonder to wrap your puny arms around your athletic big brother and feel that somewhere, deep down, you might be the stronger one.

'*Please* don't make yourself more of a target,' he says, pulling himself together, Dana comforting him now. 'What if something even worse happens to you? I couldn't stand it—'

The librarian steps out and stops halfway down the steps. 'Do you need help?' he asks, a bit suspiciously.

Ash pulls away, rubbing his face, and stands, taking Dana with him. 'Sorry, we've gotta go. I'll tell Mum you'll be home tomorrow.'

On the way back to the Lepskis, I stop at the lookout to google *Stories of girls who betray their fathers* on my new phone and it comes up with nothing. I dig around and find *King Lear* – trust Shakespeare to cover all the bases.

CHAPTER 7

Despite the offers of company, Roger and I walk back to Shearwater alone in the morning. I'm not sure what I was expecting but the utter domesticity of the place seems anticlimactic. All that fuss and then foomph, the story is only alive in the internet. I feel sad about shutting down all my accounts and guilty that Ash has had to as well. How is he going to cope in general when Dana heads back to Northern New South Wales?

I'm glad Roger's on the lead so I can stop him galumphing straight in, because Dad is arguing with Sharif in the foyer.

'This is none of your business.'

Sharif's voice is quiet but purposeful. 'With all due respect, Simon,' he says, 'it is my business. If men won't stand up to other men, what hope do women have?'

'Well, thank you for your input,' Dad says. 'Now please make sure Mrs— Fiona has a gluten-free menu.'

'Of course.'

'Someone will be in touch about the February bookings. For now, best to assume it will be business as usual. We'll be at the Marina hotel if you need to contact me.'

I peep through the window to see them shake hands. Dad looks haggard, and small, next to the chef.

I scoot Roger around the back to the kitchen door and run in to give Sharif the biggest hug in the world. 'Is there anything I can help you with?' I ask. 'Load the dishwasher. Peel a potato?'

'Okay,' he says. 'Wash your hands.' He hands me a mallet. 'I think you're going to enjoy this job.'

I'm pressing crushed biscuits into a flan base when Mum comes in with a rolled yoga mat under her arm. 'Well, hello,' she says.

'I'm making a lemon tart.'

'So I see.'

'You know the spare guitar in the music room?' I say, offering up my efforts to Sharif so he can tell me if it's even enough.

'Yes.'

'I'm going to give it to Kelsey.'

'Are you?'

'Yep. And I'm going to give the old student Yamaha to Lachlan.'

'I see.'

Sharif wipes his hands and tests my flan base with his palm. 'Better. Now, into the fridge.'

'Right,' Mum says. 'Well, it's good to have you home, Ness.'

When the kitchen's 'closed' I test out my hypothesis that there's only so much lonely-walking-along-the-windy-beach a person can do and live but spend a lot more time out there than I thought I would. It is undoubtedly calming and a balm for the soul. In the long run, however, my hypothesis stacks up: I am bored to death.

When I get back, the boys drag me upstairs to watch the first day of the Australian Open. 'It's tradition,' Ash says in response to my protest. 'And F him. So what if he won Wimbledon.'

But we're not that long into the broadcast before one of the commentators mentions that it's 'about time we got tennis back into the news for the right reasons'. They seem quite pleased that Marks never got past the semi-finals in the Open. 'It's certainly taken the shine off his reputation in the sport, there's no doubt about that,' he adds and when the other guy retorts, 'He's a bloody disgrace,' I feel like applauding; and minutes later when Roger Federer comes on screen, Ash puppeteers the dog's front paws and we all have a cheer.

Back in my own bed, I finally make good on my promises to answer Suyin's Skype call. All the Wangs crowd around her laptop. 'We hate that guy!' says Mrs Wang and they nod and wave and say various things over the top of one another like 'are you okay?' and 'someone should break his legs'. The last person to speak is Suyin's little brother, who complains that no one will let him watch the video.

'Good,' I say. 'I hope you never watch it.'

'You take care, Vanessa,' says Mrs Wang and they disperse off screen.

Suyin says, 'Oh my God, I'm so sorry.'

I laugh. 'It actually made me feel a bit better.'

'Are they going to put him in jail?'

'Nope.'

'What happens if you're pregnant?'

'I'm still a virgin, Suyin. It was only attempted.'

'Thank God. But just for the record, I, for one,' she leans away to check the door and swings back, 'would vote for abortion.'

'But I don't *feel* like a virgin,' I say.

'I do,' she says. 'I'm a *super-virgin.*'

I wake with a crick in my neck and the iPad still on my lap. Someone is moving about in my bathroom and panic rises up to gag me, but it's Mum, the ruined dress draped over her arm. She slumps to the tiles like she's been shot and I scramble out of the doona.

But she hasn't had a stroke, or a heart attack, or a brain aneurysm. She's found my torn underpants and is huddled over them sobbing. She reaches out, snatches me down, crushes me into her arms and holds me there.

When she sits back, it's as if she's staring at a ghost just beyond my field of vision. 'Your dad was so wild and handsome when I met him; he swept me off my feet,' she says softly. 'He was beautiful, clever, an IT "up-and-comer" – but he had no real money behind him and when it came to it, my father didn't want me to marry him.' She glances at me. 'Told your father to his face that he wasn't good enough.'

She looks at her hands, as if they hold secrets. 'He lost the money Dad lent him to invest in his first business – too big, too fast – and after that, everything I did and said upset him: as if I was doing or saying it to make him seem inadequate, or to prove my dad right.' Mum rubs the finger where her wedding ring used to be. 'He made the money back, and paid it back with interest, but I realise now he's been trying to prove himself, all this time.' She smiles at me. 'When you children came, it got better, and I told myself we were finally happy. I loved being your mum, Simon's wife, but I'm only beginning to understand now how I made myself smaller, made his dreams, my dreams, his way, my way, because it all seemed to matter more to him.' She tucks my hair behind my ear. 'Then you guys grew up. The less you needed me, the emptier I felt. I'm not surprised he started looking around for someone with a bit of life to them.'

'Mum—'

'I'm not trying to excuse his behaviour. Or mine. I'm just saying – don't give yourself away.' She kisses my forehead. 'Not to your dad, not to that horrible Richard Marks, not to anyone. You're full of life and dreams, Vanessa Partridge.' She kisses me again. 'Hang on to them.'

'Do you think Dad will ever forgive me?' I whisper.

'Of course he will, and there's nothing to forgive.' She puts a hand to my forehead as if feeling my temperature. 'The bigger question is whether you'll ever forgive your father.'

The day dawns cool and cloudy and Mum asks if I want to drive into town for a cafe breakfast. It's twenty degrees and we're all rugged up as if winter has struck but it still feels strange to be out in public, even wearing jeans and long sleeves. It's as though my skin were transparent and everyone can see into the rotten gagging-for-it, Duncan-betraying heart of me, but the fact is, no one takes any notice.

'The Owl and the Pussycat's certainly had a makeover,' Mum says, peering up the footpath. 'Or should I say "makeunder". What it's called now?'

'It's called No Sign and it has no sign. The food's great but I'm not in the mood for kale.' I pull Mum into Beachside Hair and Beauty. 'Nora,' I say, '*this* is my mum.'

Nora shakes Mum's hand and eyes her massive regrowth stripe. 'I have a cancellation at eleven-thirty. Shall I book you in?'

When Mum marshals us to sit at the kitchen table, I can tell she's feeling good about her new mostly-grey pixie-cut, artfully tousled by Nora herself. 'Come on,' she says to Darith who's loitering near the back door. 'I've got some exciting news. But first it would be good if we had a bit of a family meeting about ... well, what's going on.' She clears her throat. 'Mrs Wang has kindly offered us their city place until we figure out exactly how we're going to negotiate,' she waves her hand around, 'this new family situation.'

Ash jiggles his leg under the table. 'So you're home then?'

Mum clears her throat. 'Yes, home for good.'

Ash stops jiggling but now his foot is tapping. 'Is Dad coming back?'

'They've gone home to keep some sort of medical appointment. He said they'll be back in a few days.' She sips from her cup. The teabag tag says *Inner Peace*. 'Is there something going on with Rochelle?'

Ash deflects her by cracking his knuckles, which she hates. 'Is he still in business with that rapist?' he asks when she's finished admonishing him about his potentially arthritic future. He glances at me. 'Sorry, Van.'

Mum rubs her neck. 'I'm afraid so. I don't know what more I can do about that.' She smiles at me. 'I saw photographs of the party in *The Weekend Australian*. You look wonderful in my dress.'

Ash jerks to his feet and his chair makes a horrible scraping noise. 'I'm going for a swim.' A thunder rumbles under his voice. 'No offence, Mum, but you—' He drags himself back from whatever mean thing he was going to say and turns to me. 'You coming?'

'Wait,' says Mum. 'You haven't heard the real news.' She settles, preparing for the announcement, waiting until Ash resumes his seat.

'Vanessa, Dr Skutenko called.'

She's probably seen the video; and Mrs Bhatt, too. I've hardly 'upheld the excellent reputation of our great school' this holiday. The thought leaves me clammy with shame.

'Back in September, she submitted your earth-spheres composition to the Victorian Youth Orchestra masterclass series and ... you've got an audition!' The news washes over me like cold water over wax, leaving no residue. Mum is clearly perturbed. 'You might be able to workshop your piece with the assistant principal cello of the MSO, and the VYO will play it!'

'That really is great news, Van,' Ash says. 'Well done.'

'There's still the audition process, of course.' Mum smiles up at me. 'You'll have to play a chamber piece or an excerpt, some studies and the first movement of a concerto.'

Ash says, 'When?'

Mum sits up a little straighter. 'The end of Feb.'

He whistles. 'That's not much time.'

She fusses about with the iPad. 'Look, to be honest, the confirmation email with Olga's practice schedule came well before Christmas and I've only just found it. Sorry. But you've been doing great work this holiday. I'm sure you'll be able to catch up.'

Darith clears his throat but his voice is still nervous. 'You've got the Elgar. Maybe you could play the Mendelssohn?'

'I don't want to play anymore,' I say, surprised by how flat my voice is, as if it's coming from underground. 'And I'm going to live down here and go to Kelsey's school.'

Mum's hand flutters to her chest. 'You can't give up music – your lovely school.'

'Everyone—'

'Look,' Mum holds my hands as if pinning me down,

'that horrible man has taken enough from you already. Don't let him take your friends and your teachers, too. Don't let him take Guilhermina and orchestra and science club and all the things you love.'

'But everyone knows—'

'Knows what? That you were the victim of a crime, that's all.' She shakes her head. 'I don't mean "that's all" but the point is, you're the victim. No one can blame you for what happened. There's nothing for anyone to judge, only his behaviour. And with this "me too" thing—'

I pull away from her. 'But that's not true, Mum. People do blame me, and anyway, I don't want people to look at me and think I'm a *victim*. Argh,' I scrub at my face, 'I'm so sick of crying!'

'Give your school community a bit more credit than that. Your friends and teachers aren't the trolls.' She pulls me to her for a hug as if that can absorb the pain of what we're saying. 'And I can't think of a school where they wouldn't know about what happened to you, and certainly not one down here.' She strokes my hair. 'And where would you live? It will fade, Nessie – tomorrow's news is already on the horizon. And this is a wonderful opportunity.'

'Let me go.' I wriggle free. 'And don't call me Nessie: I'm not the fricken Loch Ness monster.'

Mum bristles. 'Are you sure about that?'

'I'm going to bed.'

She squints at me. 'In the middle of the afternoon?'

My dysania is genuine and lasts all the next day and night, too, despite pep talks from my mother, updates on the tennis from the boys, and exhortations from Kelsey to come to the beach because Tim is going home tomorrow.

'Wish him bon voyage,' I say.

On the third morning, Darith sends me a text.

I've learned the Mendelssohn (sort of). Ready when you are.

I haven't picked up Guilhermina since the Elgar. All the music in me has dried up. I'm sure of it. Richard's scraping fingers have hollowed out my confidence and Hawk is right – tentative is terrible. It's better not to try.

I reply:

That's nice

Then:

But I'm not doing it.

An hour later, Kelsey bounces into my darkness and flicks on the light. 'Darith says you're not going to do the audition.'

'I've given up music and I'm going to go to your school. It'll be better. People won't know who I am.'

'What about Fanny?' she demands.

I sit up, wishing she'd turn off the light and go away. 'Fanny?'

'Fanny Whatserface. The musician.'

'Mendelssohn?'

'That's her.'

I mooch out of bed to the toilet. 'What are you talking about?'

'Didn't you tell me once that she'd kill to have the freedom you've got? That you don't have to pretend to be a boy to get the chance to be, I dunno . . . whatever you want.'

'Fanny Mendelssohn never pretended to be a boy.'

'You know what I mean. Didn't her brother have to pretend her music was his? Didn't her dad say she should stay at home and you know – be a proper woman?'

'I can't do it. I don't want to.' I yank the toilet paper so hard it spools on the tiles.

I hear Kelsey pull the curtains back, click off the light and say, 'Come out here and look me in the eye and say that.'

It's remarkable how much she sounds like her mother when I can't see her face.

'It's not like sexism is dead, Kelsey. Orchestras had to have blind auditions so women could get a decent go – that's how *gender-neutral* music is.'

'Well, what about Clara Schubaker?'

'Who?'

'The first woman to . . . do stuff with music who faced down armed soldiers to rescue her family from . . .' She fades off. 'Some war.'

I stick my head out of the bathroom. 'Do you mean Clara Schumann?'

'That's it,' Kelsey says. 'Be like her.'

'She had to cancel her concerts half the time because of her crazy husband.' I slouch back to bed and pull the covers up. 'Why did you let my mother tell you to say all this?'

She balls her fists and stamps them on her hips.

'Whatever. But we don't even have a proper music teacher, let alone an orchestra. The parents had to fight to get us a *library*.'

'Well I don't play cello anymore so it doesn't matter. And why do you care, anyway?' I slam back against the pillows. 'You just don't want me to go to your school.'

'No, I don't!' she yells. 'Because you're a spoilt *idiot*.'

The door bangs and I roll over. 'I am not,' I mutter but Ted's glassy eyes tell a different story. 'Leave me alone!' I scream and hurl him across the room.

I text Kelsey.

I'm so sorry. Thanks for coming to see me.

My heart leaps when she texts back.

Me too.

A few minutes later my phone buzzes again.

It's not that I don't want you to come to my school. I love my school. It's just sometimes I wish it had the stuff that yours does.

I get up.

Guilhermina is in the music room, safe in her coffin. I open the lid. I never understood how Ash could smash his violin but I think I do now. He was desperate for something to change.

I pluck a string. She's out of tune.

We both are.

Darith and Ash rumble past the doorway with boogie boards under their arms. A second later, Darith reappears. 'Want me to play you an A?'

'No. Thank you, though.' I rest my fingers on the curve of Guil's body. 'I think I need to do this on my own.'

'Right,' he says, then calls down the hall, 'hang on, I am coming.' I overhear Ash say, 'You know she's still just a kid, mate?' and Darith reply, 'How long are you going to do this for?'

I shut Guil's case and look up recordings of Fanny's compositions, and Clara's virtuoso piano, and videos of Jacqueline's brilliant violincello, and each one makes me burn inside, not just because of the wonder of the music and skill but because of the courage of the women themselves, carving out space in a hostile society and filling it with beauty.

'And they all began when they were just girls,' says Mum, startling me, particularly because she appears to have read my mind. Roger trots in and makes himself comfortable on one of the armchairs. 'Come on,' she says, locking the cello case and lifting it to roll Guilhermina towards the staircase. 'The music's already down there, waiting.'

Roger groans and slides off again to trot after her and I follow him in a trance.

There's something peaceful about seeing Mum sit at Pa-Albert's piano, her smile when the birds of paradise come into view. She runs her fingers lightly over the keys the same way Darith does, as if acknowledging their mysteries with her fingertips. 'Let's start with a few exercises,' she says. 'And see if we can't work up to Felix's *Song Without Words* from there.' She looks up. 'If that's what you're playing?'

I take my seat and swing the cello up but the thought of opening my legs for Guilhermina makes me clammy. I lean on the cello and look down at my chest, expecting to see the skin jumping with the pounding of my heart. My body looks the same as it always does but I know it's not the same. I'm a stranger here now.

'I can't,' I pant, the hated tears lapping at me. 'Why didn't I fight or scream or do . . . something?'

Mum drags a chair next to mine and puts her hand on my back. 'Breathe with me,' she says, taking the instrument and laying her carefully down.

'I didn't even struggle. I just did . . . nothing.'

'Follow my breath. In through the left nostril, out through the left nostril.'

I glance at her for confirmation. 'Left nostril?'

She nods. 'Left nostril.' And taking my right hand, she presses my thumb against my right nostril. 'In through the left.' She straightens my fingers. 'Fingers pointing to the heavens. Out through the left. That's right – in, out. Keep going.' She rubs my back. 'It was shock, darling girl. At the violation. And fear. Sometimes the adrenaline just makes you freeze. There's no "correct" way to be assaulted. Keep breathing: you'll feel better soon.' She straightens my wilting heaven-pointing fingers. 'I promise.'

'Mum?' I say, after a few breaths.

'Yes? Keep breathing.'

'Why did you say we should call you Marion?'

'I never said that.'

'Before you left.'

'Nice, easy breaths,' she says, and blocks off her own nostril to take a few herself. 'I really have no idea. Are you sure it wasn't Marilyn? I've always wished I had a bit of Marilyn Monroe about me. Just a few more breaths. Well done.'

We look up and the chef is standing by the swing doors with a clipboard, observing us breathe through our left nostrils and make our strange cosmic salutes with an expression of carefully assumed neutrality.

'Sharif!' says Mum. 'How would you like to hear Vanessa and I play *The Swan*?'

Before I can choke out my protest, he takes a seat. 'For me? I would really be honoured.'

'Come on,' Mum says. 'Your father tells me you were rehearsing it like mad before Christmas and it's one of my favourites.'

'Will you mind if I close my eyes?' Sharif asks.

'Of course not,' says Mum.

I reach for my instrument trying to breathe through my left nostril without my thumb blocking off the right and simultaneously calling on the spirit of Jacqueline, and Lisa Cristiani and, of course, the great Guilhermina Suggia herself. The cello settles between my thighs where she belongs.

When we're tuned, I procrastinate a little longer by applying rosin to my bow, the puff of dust warning that I've gone overboard, and warming up with the tech work

Mum promised me. When I sense our audience of one shifting in his seat, I stop to say, 'Ready,' and Sharif breaks into premature applause.

Mum stands and bows. I'd forgotten what a ham she is at the keyboard. 'Camille Saint-Saëns, *Le carnaval des animaux*,' she announces in her corniest French accent. '*The Swan*.' She flicks out her imaginary tuxedo tails, sits, and plays me the opening note.

Tears fall from my closed eyes almost as soon as the bow enchants the string and the swan leaps into life, gliding over the water, seemingly unaffected by the somewhat frantic, but poetic, paddling going on below. She may have been a bit grainy and nearly drowned a few times and been deafened by a hideous squeak but what I'm left with is the warmest pulsation of joy. And pain; Skutenko is right: it doesn't pay to stop practising.

Sharif gives us a standing ovation. 'Bravo,' he says.

I join Mum in her ridiculous bows.

When I wake in the night, Roger's gone. I'm afraid that I imagined him; that Mum's not back. 'Roger?' I call, but he doesn't come and I return to the dark, to the aftermath of dreaming I was kissing Darith but he turned into Richard and I said, *I love you, Richard*, and a helicopter flew over us with spotlights and Richard was on morning television saying, *She performed fellatio in a Valiant, what was I supposed to think?* and Stan Grant answered, *That's right, and on Aboriginal land.*

Darith is at my door. 'I heard you crying,' he whispers.

I cry harder; I can't help it.

He clicks on the bathroom light and leaves the door ajar, coming back to sit on my bed and hand me a roll of toilet paper. 'I don't know where the tissues are.'

'Thanks.' I blow my nose and wipe my face and blow my nose again. 'Am I respectable?' I ask. 'Snot-wise?'

He inspects, and nods. 'As far as I can tell.' He gets up to shut the bedroom door. 'Everyone will freak out if they find me in here.'

'Everyone is already freaking out.'

I plump the pillows and we sit up against the bedhead for a comforting cuddle, him on top of the bedcovers, my ear against his heartbeat. He kisses the top of my head and I push myself up to kiss his cheek.

I could lie like this forever but he whispers, 'I should let you get some sleep.'

'Why did you break up with Nadia?' I whisper back. 'Didn't you love her?'

I feel him tense. 'I don't know about *love* her. We're still friends – she's a pretty special person and we had a lot in common.'

I flip the bedclothes back and settle cross-legged, opposite, so I can see his face. 'Because she's Aboriginal?'

'Torres Strait,' he corrects quickly, like thunder rumbling.

'Okay, sorry.' I push on. 'Because she's Blak?'

The lightning strikes and his voice is like paint-stripper. 'I dunno, Van: did you "go out" with Bodhi because he's *white*?' He lurches from the bed but the sheet tangles around his leg and he has to wrestle with it before he can storm off.

'I didn't sleep with him.'

He yanks the door open but stops, his back to me.

'Not in the way you mean, anyway.'

He turns, like I hoped he would, but shame surges up and spills out as fury. 'But what if I did?' I hiss. 'What would that mean? That I'm all the things people say I am?'

'No.' He looks so stricken the burn of tears sears my throat. 'Of course not.' A kind of shudder ripples through him. 'I'm just so sick of whitefella bullshit.'

'Sorry. It was a stupid thing to say.' I push away the tears, and the shame. 'I'm just jealous,' I confess, half to myself.

The tinder-brittle air between us softens with his shoulders and he clicks the door shut. 'So am I.'

We take each other in across the half-darkened room and the pause is as tense and rich as Debussy's space between notes until a resigned tenderness crinkles him into a smile. Something settles inside me, like the feeling of coming home to a warm house when it's cold and raining outside.

'Don't say anything to Ash,' he says, suddenly anxious. 'Not yet.'

'Say anything about what?'

'About this.' He scoots across to hover by the bed. 'Can I?'

I nod and he climbs in. We lie down practically nose to nose.

I swallow. 'Can I kiss you?'

'Yes.'

I put my hands on each side of his face and kiss him and it's the most peaceful dizziness.

'Or about that,' he says.

I kiss him everywhere and he kisses me back and his fingers brush over my undies and linger, causing a thrill I've never felt on my own – but a wave of horribleness comes crashing after it and claustrophobia closes in on me but the walls are my own skin and the pressure feels like hatred and for a moment I think of bashing at him, as if that would somehow make it stop. 'No,' I say and curl up, a slime of self-loathing where the glitter had been. He lies still, holding me, until the worst is past, fading to a bewilderment that I could ever think to hurt someone so beautiful.

Darith kisses my hair. 'Come on, let's crash.' He presses buttons on his watch, rearranges the doona and we spoon.

Despite the comfort, I'm restless. 'Did you sleep with Nadia?' I ask.

He shakes his head a little. 'Nah.'

I hug him to me and we rest in the snuggle until I feel his chest quietly shaking at my back.

'Why are you laughing?'

'Because you sounded so white when you said "Blak".'

'You sound so Blak when you say it.'

'Funny about that.'

Laughter is a benediction and I draw his arms around me and tuck them under my chin. I feel him swell against me but he shifts a little to make sure I'm not bothered by it. When I roll to face him, he lies on his back with his eyes closed.

'Have you ever watched porn?' I ask.

'Yeah.'

I can't tell if his voice is flat with sleepiness or distaste. 'What's it like?'

He pulls me closer. 'Nothing like this.'

'Is that a good thing, or a bad thing?'

'Good.' He finds my lips for a single kiss. 'It's a good thing.'

We relax again but a thousand questions whirl through my heart, swirled through with embarrassment. 'I don't want to be part of the whitefella bullshit, Darith.'

He snorts. 'Must be tough. I feel real sorry for ya.'

'Marlene told me people like me are the "cornerstone of imperial neoliberalism".'

'Oh yeah.' He yawns. 'And what did you say?'

'I asked her if she meant the sacred kind of cornerstone or the ceremonial kind.'

He smiles. 'Of course you did. So, what's the difference?'

'The sacred is structural, permanent; the ceremonial is decoration. A plaque or a stamp – you know, with the architect's name, or even the builder's. It can be removed, or changed.'

'Which one did she reckon you are?'

'She didn't say. But ceremonial, I guess, because later she told me the best thing I could do for the planet would be to kill myself.'

'That's horrible.' He puts his fingers in my hair and strokes my head, like I'm a cat. 'She told *me* you were one of the sweetest kids she'd ever met.'

I slide my hand over his stomach feeling the miracle of his body shuddering under my fingertips, against my palm. 'Do *you* think I'm one of the sweetest kids she's ever met?'

He reaches down to put his hand over my hand. 'I think we should go to sleep.' He pats me and we settle again but like the upward sweep of the Elgar, the thrill is building. I'm Juliet and when dawn comes, I'll want to deny the chorus of birds and the rise of the sun. It's hard to keep my hands off him.

'I do want you to touch me,' I whisper.

'Are you sure?'

'Yes.'

'How?'

'Do what you did before.'

And when he does it's impossible to go invisible or forget he's there because he whispers, 'There?' and 'This?' and when there aren't any words, he speaks to me with his eyes and his breathing and I have to press my face into his neck to stop from making too much noise and then he kisses me and kisses me.

'Your turn,' I say when I can breathe normally again.

He laughs, sheepish, and lifts the doona to show me his stomach, all sticky. I reach over and hand him the toilet paper.

'Am I respectable?' he says when it's cleaned up. 'Sperm-wise?' And we dissolve into hysterics, shushing each other, which only makes it worse.

When we've recovered ourselves and become comfy he says, 'Now we really do have to go to sleep.' I hug him because I can't hug him enough and say, 'I'll never get to sleep,' but he rolls us over and lets out a little snore.

∞

I suppose Darith might get the wrong idea if I wake him up to share my revelation that despite everything that's happened this summer I still haven't, technically, had sex.

Or have I? I mean, none of it has really been about actually 'Doing It'. Or has it? This sex thing has turned out to be a lot more complicated than I imagined.

I wriggle carefully and reach for the *Book of Observations* and my pen to write, *Sex is a whole soul conversation.*

I snuggle back but my mind ticks over and I have to get the book out again.

It should be up to me how much I want to say.

CHAPTER 8

I say I'll never get to sleep but startle awake to a snort of my own snoring. Darith's gone. Roger raises his curious ears at me and I wonder if I made the whole thing up until I look in my *Book of Observations* and there it is. I add, *Theory: all penises do not look or feel the same and therefore must be considered as variables in any hypothesis*, as a purely scientific observation.

I'm disturbed a second time by Darith creeping back into my room. 'Ash sent me,' he whispers. 'He wants us to sneak out and meet them.'

'Crikey Moses,' I moan, blearily reaching for my dressing-gown. 'Why?'

'You probably don't need your hat.'

'I'm not getting sunburnt again. My feet are still peeling.'

'It's dark outside.'

I knew I hadn't been asleep nearly long enough. 'What time is it?'

'Nearly four.'

A different kind of knowing stops me in my fumbling tracks. 'He's leaving, isn't he?' I say.

The combi is waiting in the waning moonlight, out of sight of the house, around the first bend of the driveway with its doors open and I suddenly feel about ten years old. Ash hops out and sits in the sliding doorway, Dana strolling around to join him.

'Where are you going?' I ask.

'Byron first to meet Dana's parents, then—' They look at each other. 'Not sure.'

'Maybe a few music festivals,' Dana says.

I cross my arms at Ash. 'What are you going to do for money?'

'Sold that jet ski on eBay for seven grand.' He laughs. 'Then we'll see.'

'He can make a decent coffee now.' Dana slips her hand into his and their fingers intertwine. 'There's hope for him.'

'What about school?'

Ash's face hardens. 'If I'd wanted to have that conversation, Van, I would have told Mum what I'm doing.' I must look as scandalised as I feel because a jagged sigh heaves out of him. 'Look, I've done half of next year's subjects already and so have you. If we want to go back, we can. I just want to do this now, with Dana.' He kisses her hand before he lets it go. 'School isn't everything.'

'What about Dad?'

'What about him?'

'Have you seen him?'

'No, and I don't want to.'

'What about Mum?'

'Mum's on her own trip. She'll be all right – we've got to grow up sometime.'

My arms fall and tears burst out of me. 'Don't go.'

'Van, I have to. You don't know what it's like to be expected to be mini-Simon.' He pushes his hair back and reaches out to pull me to sit between them. 'I've got to get away. And so do you. Come with us – we'll look after you.'

'We've left room for your cello in the roof pod,' Dana adds, encouragingly. 'Text when you're packed and we'll drive up and get you.'

I blush with the overwhelming warmth of it all but shock has turned me into a playdough person. My mouth opens and the word 'okay' lumps out.

Ash leaves me sitting there to hug Darith. 'Thanks again for everything, Dar. Sorry to leave you with this ... awkwardness.'

'I can handle it.'

Dana gives him a quick hug too and jogs around to climb into the driver's seat.

'Go on,' Ash says to me. 'I really don't want to have to deal with the olds.'

Darith and I hurry back holding hands but not speaking. He stands lookout while I throw my stuff into my suitcase and when I zip up and shrug, he carries Guilhermina out to the rose garden where we wait. He holds me so tight, I can't tell which of our hearts is pounding. I don't want to leave him behind but a thrilling sense of release burbles up in me, a kind of terror of excitement, but how can I be afraid when my brother is going to look after me?

The combi rattles to a halt and Dana slides the back door open while Ash climbs up to put my cello in the pod. I don't know how I'm going to say goodbye to Darith without wailing but he says, 'I'll come as far as the road,' and climbs in the back with me.

I glimpse Shearwater's magnolia as we round a curve, a silhouette against the dark of the sky. It's probably crazy but it always seemed like that tree was reaching down to me when I practised – as if somehow, it loved the music, too – and a competing urge swells in my soul: ambition. It's not going to be fun going back to school after everything that's happened but I *want* to be Olga Skutenko's student and workshop my composition with a notable cellist and I can't do that unless I prepare for the audition and I can't practise four or more hours a day in the back of Dana's combi.

And when the August auditions come, I'm going to try my heart out to get into VCASS, whatever Mum and the Big O say.

And if I can't get in there to do music, I'm going to maybe pursue a career as an environmental scientist and just play Guilhermina for joy, like Hawk plays his flute.

'I can't go,' I blurt and Dana pulls up. 'It's no good, Ash,' I sob. 'I'm epistemophilic.'

His face gentles away from looking like he's going to cry and he laughs. 'Okay, you pissed off who now?'

Dana nudges him with her shoulder. 'What does that mean, Van?'

'It means I have to finish high school.' I scrub the tears

from my face with the bottom of my pyjama shirt. 'And do the VYO audition.'

My brother's eyes become serious and sad in the twilight. 'Well, Skutenko is right – you do have a beautiful tone.'

'Olga said that?'

He puts on her accent. 'If you could be bothered to put in the practice you'd have a beautiful tone like your sister.' I pull Darith's arms tighter around me and Ash takes us in. 'So I'm gathering you two won't mind looking after each other.'

I launch at Ash for a hug and clamber through the front seats to curl up on his knee. 'Don't forget me.'

'I'm just on the end of the phone – whenever, wherever: promise you'll call if you need me.'

I squeeze him. 'I promise.'

'One twelve-point turn coming up,' Dana half-jokes, laboriously turning the combi around to let us out again at the rose garden.

'Sorry about the rigmarole,' I say.

Darith climbs up to release Guilhermina. When he's done, we lean on the sill of the passenger door window. 'I guess I'll see you in the internets,' he says to Ash, his arm around my shoulder.

'Thanks for everything, man. Smash those cricket trials.'

Dar steps back and Ash leans out to pull my hat over my face. 'You're still weird,' he says. 'And Skutenko also said you had to work on your phrasing.'

They drive off, Dana waving and Ash lurching danger-ously far out the window with his violin to play 'La Cucaracha'.

'He's so rusty,' I sob.

Mum opens the door in her nightie. 'What on earth is going on?' she demands.

Darith drops his arm and I pray Mum doesn't notice the cello case and bags strewn among the roses. 'Ash's gone with Dana.'

'Surfing? They must be mad. And what are you two doing?'

'Heading up to the rookery to see the shearwaters taking off to go hunting.'

'You're all crazy. I'm going back to bed.'

We wait a few minutes and Darith helps me stow the baggage. 'It feels like we've been up for days,' I say, 'but I really do want to go out to the rookery.'

He holds out his hand for the taking. 'Come on then.'

I'm not a major fan of picking my way through the scrub in the dark, even with our torches and Darith holding my hand. By the time we head down the stairs there's a rough, wild feel to the pre-dawn, to the roar of the sea, and something heart-rending and magical about walking up the beach in starlight.

'Shearwaters need a runway and a launch pad,' I tell him, pointing when I can just make out the stairs up to the rookery. 'That's why they breed along the cliffs. They don't flap if they can avoid it. They glide.' I run up the sand to escape an unruly swash. 'They spend most of the year out at sea and only ever come to land to nest for breeding. David Attenborough filmed a bunch of them in Japan climbing a tree to jump from.'

'Japan? How far do they fly?'

I steer us away from the water and over the soft sand. 'Nearly all the way around the world, but these ones will be just going hunting; they'll be back tonight, or maybe tomorrow night.'

'How do they sleep out there?'

'On the water.'

'I hope we haven't missed them.'

'We haven't – listen.'

The gentle cacophony of chirping, murmuring and the occasional squabble (or maybe alarm at our approach) gets louder as we climb the stairs. I briefly click on my torch to show Darith the birds popping out of their burrows and sitting dotted over the landscape as if waking up.

'Oh, wow,' he says.

The wind has dropped and it's relatively still when we reach the rookery. The sweet funk of them is strong. We sit, and wait. From the sand below, the birds seem effortless as they wing out to sea but up here it's a different story. There's rustling in the grasses and adult birds scamper past us in numbers, scurrying to the precipice in furtive yet determined spurts. Darith hugs himself and whispers, 'They're hilarious!'

Groups of birds congregate in gaggles near the edge, looking out, like surfers discussing the weather and waves. When the time's right, they launch themselves one by one with a comical hop into the air, trusting the thermals to carry them according to a wisdom of pattern-making scientists can only dream of comprehending, to their true home – the sea. Transformed by the wind into elegance and power, they disappear against the water and the twilight sky as if they've winked into another world beyond my vision.

Shearwaters have been doing this since ancient times yet when their moment comes, the chicks will emerge for the first time, scamper to the edge and take their chances. What guides them? I wonder, watching. What gives them the courage to take off?

'They're just kinda . . . hopping off into space,' Darith whispers.

By the predawn light, they're gone. All but one, who sits on a post at the top of the stair like a sentinel before taking flight, wheeling over us, curving back over the rookery, then out to the water.

We stand and one last bird scampers past us using the pathway as a runway and flapping like mad for take-off.

'Must have slept in,' says Darith.

Then sleepy-head is gone, too, vanishing from sight no matter how hard I try to follow.

The communal chatter of the rookery has morphed into the dawn chorus and the growing sunlight reveals a criss-cross of cartoon-like footprints right to the cliff's edge. When we hit the beach to walk home, seagulls and ibis fly overhead and our footprints have been partially washed away by the incoming tide. The day's already warm enough for us to splash through the shallows.

'What do they do when there's no wind?' Darith asks, reaching out for my hand.

'They rest, I guess,' I say, taking his hand. 'And you know how when a wave breaks, there's a little puff of spray?'

'Yep.'

'That's wind generated by the sea – they surf it, shear across the face of the wave. Shearwaters.'

The sunrise is nothing showy but we sit with our backs to the granite watching until it clears to a pink blush over powder blue, impossibly fresh and pure. Sitting on the cold sand, permeated by the relentless pounding of the surf, I sense a deeper silence; the divine mastery of nature – not humanity's mastery over nature, but Earth's complete being, wholeheartedly present and undeniable. The rock at our backs has seen ages come and go and endured; it's transformed, but into something majestic, bountiful: not the crass, polluting ugliness of a Marksman casino.

A man and a boy jog past at a brisk clip, surfboards under their arms, long hair flapping. The man raises a casual hand in greeting and we wave back.

'They weren't even sweating,' Darith says.

A girl, much younger than me, stands in the swash wearing a fluorescent wetsuit, matching board under her arm, as if sizing up the ocean. She makes a ritual gesture, like some sort of acknowledgement of the gods of the sea and sets out. We watch, mesmerised, until she reaches another surfer, and cheer to ourselves when she rides her first wave.

Courage. That's what it takes to do the thing you love.

The beauty wells up in me as tears. 'They're going to—' I drag my sleeve over my face and pull myself together.

'The Foxholers were right, Darith. My father is going to turn this whole area into some kind of glitzy highrollers' hellhole.'

'Are you sure?'

'I got Dad to let me use his computer. He's some big deal property developer now – the "lynchpin" for securing Champion's interests – with investors from all over the place but mostly China. I took photos of emails between him and that Eddie Glasshouse guy talking about Shearwater and the casino thing. About retiring like gods.' I swallow. 'I think they've bribed people to change the laws – to let them build a high-rise.'

'Shit.'

'But then I broke my phone.'

Darith raises an eyebrow. 'How broken is it?'

'The screen's smashed but it turns on – I just can't see anything. I'm pretty sure I could still get the data.'

'Sounds like it's worth a shot.'

'I think we'd need more evidence, like money paid or received, that kind of thing. It's hard enough to believe my dad's involved but . . . maybe Louise knows, too? She's been acting so weird lately. And if she doesn't know, maybe I need to tell her? If anyone can hack Dad's stuff, it's Louise.'

Darith stands and brushes off the sandy grit, looks out to the horizon and back down at me. 'You have to tell someone.'

∞

When I knock, Louise snorts, loud enough for Darith and me to share a nervous grin. The light goes on and she says, 'Hell's bloody bells.' She flings open the door, tying her dressing-gown around tartan pyjamas. Her face drops. 'Who died?'

'No one's dead,' I say. 'But we have to talk to you.'

'Before coffee?' She rubs her eyes. 'What the hell time is it?'

I swallow back my tears. 'I've been out to see the shearwaters.'

'What's going on, Vanessa?'

I sit with her on the bed and hand her the photographs we've salvaged from my broken phone and printed. She puts on her glasses and looks through the evidence. 'Oh my God,' she whispers. Her face sets, grim as stone. She puts the papers aside and reaches for her laptop with one hand, thumbing her mobile with the other. 'Fiona, meet me in the office,' she says into the phone. 'No, everything is not all right.'

To us she says, 'You two go down and make us some coffee.'

'But—'

She pockets the phone, clutches the papers and her laptop, and shepherds us towards the door. 'You've done the right thing, but please don't argue with me.'

☙

It takes forever for the coffee machine to warm up and when I bring it up Mum mouths, 'I'm on the phone to the lawyers.'

They're both in their robes and Mum's hair is sticking up like straw.

I hand Louise her mug. 'I've hacked into the offshore accounts,' she tells me, cradling her coffee. 'He's in it up to his eyeballs.'

'How—?'

'I've had remote access to your father's computer for years. I suppose he thought I'd be even more suspicious if he revoked it. It's all there – payments, receipts, correspondence. His passwords are completely predictable.'

'To you, maybe,' I say. 'What did he say?'

'He fired me.'

Mum puts her hand over the phone. 'He thinks I've poisoned you both against him.'

'But—'

'Oh, no, I've accidentally hung up on her.' Mum pokes at her phone. 'Darling, it really doesn't matter. It's all going to be fine. You've done your bit and Louise is doing the rest. What *does* matter is that audition. So why don't you go and practise with Darith? It's so kind of him to offer to help you, though I suppose he's bored to death with his friend buggering off on him all the time. I'll let you know what happens.' She hands Louise the phone and reaches to me for her cup. 'Oh, thank God for coffee. Can you redial, please? And when are Ash and that girl getting back?' She takes back the phone. 'Poor Darith. I'm not sure why he hasn't taken up his parents' offer— Hello? Yes, I'm so sorry about that.' She shoos me away and puts it on speaker phone. She and Louise huddle in, giving their attention to

the call. 'Yes, I think *The Guardian* is a good place to start,'
Mum says, looking to Louise for confirmation. She glances
at me still standing there. 'Your father is *not* developing
Shearwater,' she says. 'Go on – you're just in the way, now.'

Darith's waiting in the kitchen with Roger Federer.
'How's it going?'

'I have no idea.'

He drums on the table. 'Let's go swimming.'

'You good to swing by Kelsey's?'

'Sure.'

I follow him out the back door, stepping on his foot
when he turns abruptly to say, 'And then, the Mendelssohn.'

By the time we get back it's almost dark and Eddie Glasshouse has resigned, pending criminal charges. 'The state
government has made a public promise to clamp down on
shonky investment deals – there might even be a Royal
Commission. They've vowed to ...' Mum looks down
at her notes. '... "reinstate, strengthen and extend" the
heritage listing for this stretch of the coast. In any case,
Richard's withdrawn his interest in the casino development. He's going to set up shop somewhere else and the
money has gone with him.' She takes a mouthful of water
and her hand is trembling. 'So it's done.'

'Where's Louise?'

'She's devastated. Gone to her mother's.'

I don't know why it's so shocking to me: the idea that
Louise has a mother.

'What about Dad?'

Mum takes a deep breath. 'The lawyers aren't entirely sure what's going to happen to him. If he can't pay back his debts, he might get done for fraud.'

'Why?'

'Because he's invested other people's money in land that's now almost impossible to resell, can't be built on, and certainly isn't going to offer anything remotely like the lucrative return he was gambling on.' She smiles grimly. 'If anything, he might have accidentally created a privately-owned nature reserve.'

It's as if the shearwaters are suddenly flying home all around me.

'It seems he invested a lot of his own capital, too. I'd say your father's bankrupt, I'm afraid, if he can be believed. So be prepared – he'll have to sell the house quicker than he wanted.'

My blood is like sea-swash, fizzing and crackling. 'And Shearwater?'

'Shearwater, too, but—' Mum looks a little bit proud. 'Your father bullied her out of me but now I'm buying her back.'

'You?'

'Nothing's certain until the settlement but, yes. I'm going to manage the place – home and income in one fell swoop.'

'Can you afford it?'

'I can.' She taps smugly on Dad's desk with her finger-tips. 'Thanks to Rochelle. Just.' She scrunches her hair. 'Batten your hatches, Van, because they'll be here with their lawyers in the morning.'

CHAPTER 9

Mum pokes her head into the music room and Darith and I trail off. I can't say I'm sorry; my right hand is pounding and my left arm feels like lead. She folds her hands in front of her like she's making some kind of prayer. 'Your father's downstairs. He wants to talk to you.'

'Do I have to?'

'It's entirely up to you.'

He's standing on the gravel, waiting, looking tidied up and fresh, a lot healthier than the shattered wreck that drove off to front up and explain himself to Rochelle's parents, but there's still something fragile about him which makes me feel like I'm talking to an impostor. 'Will you come out and talk?' he says. 'Let's sit on Pa-Albert's seat.'

It's dew-damp but we sit anyway.

'Things have been a bit ... topsy-turvy, since your mother and I— well, you know.'

How am I supposed to respond to this understatement of the decade? Dad gets up and paces. 'I know I've made a mess of things. I had this glimpse of what the future might be like for us. You know – effortless world travel, the best of everything for you and Ash.'

'An island.'

He stops. 'Your great-grandmother was buried in a pauper's grave with no one to make sandwiches or put flowers by her headstone.' He says it as if it's just happened and he failed to prevent it. He sits next to me again. 'The best instruments. World-renowned teachers.'

I feel like I'm floating, looking down at the red palate of blooming roses, the gnarly thorned wood of the stems, the delicate jagged foliage; but wrapped in spider web, as if I can't quite breathe. Dad tentatively touches the back of my hand with his little finger. 'Everything your mother wanted for you, too.'

'I already have a beautiful cello. Especially for a student. And Skutenko trained at the Royal Academy. Last year she flew off for a month to take masterclasses at the Juilliard school in New York. She *is* the best, for me.'

'Yes, you're right.' He pinches the bridge of his nose. 'And now I might have screwed that up as well.'

'Mum says they might be able to offer me a partial scholarship if she can't afford it – or she can pay the fees off.' There's a battle raging in me. I know it's always been my job to make him feel better and tell the little-boy part of him that everything is all right but a hard nugget of rage threatens to choke me. 'You sacked Louise,' I say.

'Yes.' He lurches over to catch his own head in his hands. 'What a cock-up. I came this close to just walking into the sea and letting the rip take me.' He shows me the life-and-death centimetre between his fingertips.

'Me too,' I say.

No I don't. I say, 'Sorry.'

He sits up to pat my forearm. 'Don't worry about me. Rochelle is helping me focus on what's important. We've got to start looking at what we have, not what we've lost.' He takes my hand. 'Don't forget you're going to have a little brother or sister.'

I may have been turned to stone. 'Have you told Mum?'

'Not yet. I thought we'd wait until . . . well, until things settle down a bit.' He lets my hand go, stretches his legs out and crosses them at the ankle. 'I've been doing a lot of soul-searching, since everything, especially after Rochelle told me about the baby. Once I'd got used to the idea . . .'

It strikes me that Dad 'getting used the idea' was what Rochelle was crying about that day in the pantry.

He shakes his head as if he can't quite believe himself. 'I'd got so caught up in the Champion dream, I hadn't even been swimming once this year – not once. No walks on the beach. No tennis, no cricket.'

This year? It's been like that for at least the last four summers. I stare at the Rose Queens wishing one of them was a psychiatrist. A baby Rochelle? What does that even mean? I hope it doesn't mean Mum running off again.

'I went surfing last night,' Dad says. 'I hadn't realised how unfit I was. But anyway, I stayed out right until dark.'

If my father is going to launch into a surfing story, I may scream. Or get up and wander off. Or die.

'I sat out there in the surf and looked back at the shoreline and at twilight felt the shearwaters raft on the water, and then a bit later they rose up and flew home – you know how they go, weaving all over the place. It was magical. And I thought about you. Admitted what I've known deep down all along.' Tears are falling from my father's eyes but I seem to be made of porcelain, or glass. 'It was wrong to jeopardise Shearwater, this stretch of coast. It *is* more important than money.' He pulls out a handkerchief and wipes his eyes. 'You're a lot wiser than your old man, Vanessa. You did the right thing.'

A rush of impatience, of *not wanting to be here* half lifts me to my feet. 'Can I go in for breakfast?'

'Hang on, please sit down.'

I sit down.

'It's not the only thing I got wrong. I know that now.' He blows his nose. 'I'm so sorry, Ness. Richard's world . . . he's very persuasive and I really did believe—' He rubs his face. 'I got a bit lost.' I feel him looking at me. 'Very lost.'

So this is it. It's not Dad's fault, it's not Richard's fault, it's not my fault: it's nobody's fault, like baldness. I plummet underground, like a shearwater chick in its burrow the moment it realises its parents are gone, flown off, driven by their own unfathomable impulses.

Dad blows his nose again, this time with his trademark foghorn honk. He's still here, I guess, and so is Mum, so maybe I am lucky. They've given me all the fat they've got to give and as I breathe in Shearwater's quiet fresh air, I have to admit it's more than most, even if right now it seems there's a goodly chance I'll drop out of the sky. 'Shearwater chicks have to head out on their own the first time they jump but then their parents meet them after replenishing themselves on Antarctic krill and they all migrate together,' I say to myself, to the bees, to the summer morning sunshine, and tears swell in my heart like a wave that doesn't break.

'Sorry...' He seems so small. 'I don't know what you mean.'

I unclench and squint at him from under my hat. 'I mean, I guess you went off the rails.'

'Ha, well, you guess right.' He takes a deep breath, as if what's coming is an effort for him to say. 'But if you want to pursue charges, I'll support you. I'll sell everything we've got left to make it happen.'

'Thanks.' I don't know what else to say and a bee buzzes through our silence to land on the crimson petals of an Imperial, crawling into its velvety heart. 'I'm going inside for breakfast now,' I say at last.

'Rochelle and I want to stick around to see Ashton before you all leave for the city tomorrow but we'll stay down at the marina again tonight – I think it's easier for...' He pushes his hair back. 'Everyone.'

The bee crawls out to buzz over the flowers. I push up from Pa-Albert's seat, letting my fingers trail over the Rose Queens. 'I'll see you later, Dad.'

'You let me know what you want to do.'

'Talk to Mum. I'm not sure there is anything *to* do.'

࠾◯

Mum and Roger Federer offer to walk the guitars over to the Lepskis with me. 'I've got a few thank yous of my own,' she says. 'As well as a proposition – I don't think Shearwater has ever taken proper advantage of having cheap beachfront accommodation right next door.'

We stop at the lookout and she breathes in deep. 'Ah, a restorative,' she says.

Her curiosity about what Dad and I said to each other is as palpable as the cirrus cloud that flicks its tails out to the horizon but I pretend I don't feel it. She rests her arm warm against mine as we lean on the splintered wood of the railing but I only look out over the sea. Eventually, she says, 'Well, come on then,' and as we wander down the path, I tell her about what Marlene has been doing for the rookeries. I don't mention her connection to the video.

'I wonder if she'd want to keep working on it?' Mum says as we turn into the park. 'Goodness, this place never changes.'

෨◯

While the boys squabble over Lachie's guitar, Kelsey unzips her soft case in her room. 'I don't think I can take this,' she says.

'Yes, you can.'

'I'm really sorry about what I said the other day.'

'No, you're not,' I say, and she laughs.

'You didn't have to do this, Van – I'm actually happy at school and everything. If you know what I mean.'

'This hasn't got anything to do with that.'

Roger winds himself into his snoozing spot on the bed

and groans and we laugh. 'Seriously, they hardly get used. And we've got two really nice ones at home anyway; and it looks like I'll be down every second weekend or so soon – you can give it back if you don't end up using it.'

She gives me a quick, tight hug and lifts out the instrument.

'You're holding it upside down.'

She turns it over. The guitar makes her look even more tiny than normal, but it suits her. Despite her trying to play it the wrong way round, I've seen her pick it up at Shearwater before and I agree with Ash that you can tell right away if someone's going to be able to play guitar before they even strum a note.

'This is a chord chart, and you can download a tuner on your phone – there are free ones. And so many how-to videos. And Lachie already nutted out how to play the St Kilda theme song when you guys came over that night to watch a movie – you should play together.'

She baulks. 'That does not sound like fun.'

'Ash and I used to fight like mad but I still miss playing duets with him.'

'Have you heard anything?'

'Yeah.' I blow my nose. 'He texted but wouldn't let me know where they are in case Mum and Dad torture it out of me.'

Kelsey strums a chord never written down. 'Look out, Justin,' she says. 'I'm on the road to rock and roll.'

'I hate to burst your bubble, but it's a classical guitar.'

She strikes another terrible chord. 'Not now it ain't.'

Amidst the goodbye-for-now hugs, Mrs Lepski gives me a card. 'Remember,' she says. 'When you judge yourself, you're judging me, too.'

'I love you, Mrs Lepski,' I say. 'Say goodbye to Old Jack for me.'

On the walk home, Mum asks, 'What was all that about?'

'Nothing.'

'Aren't you going to open it?'

'Later.'

When later comes, I find that the front of the card is a picture of the moon and Mrs Lepski's written inside with a fine black texta.

Don't expect any understanding; but believe in a love that is being stored up for you like an inheritance, and have faith that in this love there is a strength and a blessing so large that you can travel as far as you wish without having to step outside it. — Rilke

I never knew Mrs Lepski had such fine handwriting.

Everybody's leaving today. Dad and Rochelle are off to sort out the sale of the house; Mum and I are heading to the Wangs' and Darith is going to his elder sister's place until his parents get home. I fear blurting *ASH HAS RUN*

AWAY when Mum asks me if I know why he took all his gear 'to Dana's place' but she doesn't wait around for an answer, so his secret is safe – for now.

Darith watches me make tea, the coffee machine all cleaned and under its cover. 'You all right?' he says.

'Yep.'

'Do you feel weird now that we're on our own?'

'Yep.' I hand over his cup, a biscotti placed on the saucer the way Sharif does it. 'It's dodgy.'

He laughs. 'You're so romantic.' Tea splodges onto his biscuit. I think his hand is shaking. 'When I thought you might go with them, I—' He puts the tea down. 'Anyway, I'm glad you stayed.'

We nearly crack heads again when Sharif backs in through the dining room doors to tell us he's all done until February. 'I've been told business as usual,' he says with a shrug. 'So that's what I'm planning for.'

I shake the last few pieces of blue left in the jigsaw lid. 'We haven't finished it.'

Darith tuts at the irregular blotch of missing picture. 'Must be the hole in the ozone layer.'

'Let's plug it,' says Sharif but Rochelle calls for us to go. The chef shakes my hand. 'Good luck, Vanessa. Stay smart and never be afraid to wear a pretty dress.'

'You, too, Sharif.'

His laughter carries right out to his car.

∾○

I peck Rochelle and Dad on their respective cheeks. There's a tentativeness about my father which makes him seem much softer and he's prone to well up, which is entirely unnerving. Rochelle, on the other hand, seems more *present*, her hand on the small of his back. She's in charge now. Darith looks up from his phone and nods at me from the back of their Range Rover. I nod back and wander over to the dusty-looking Toyota Mum's rented to drive us back.

'Are we okay, Van?' Dad asks.

Mum interrupts by waving Mrs Lepski's Christmas present at me. 'Why are we taking this hideous thing?'

I stow it on the back seat. 'Because it's beautiful.'

'Good Lord.' She throws up her hands. 'And your brother's going to get left behind if he doesn't turn up soon,' and then she says to Darith, 'It's very rude of him to have abandoned you to your own devices like this.' She appeals to my father. 'You don't think something's happened to him, do you?'

Like clockwork our phones buzz with a collective message.

Gone travelling up North with Dana. Not sure when I'll be back. Maybe next year. Don't worry, I've got my violin. Love Ash.

He sends an extra one to me.

Stay out of my stuff and don't let them throw anything away.

Mum bursts into tears that drag my tears out too and she and Dad (and Roger Federer) regress into a parenting huddle that must make Rochelle feel like killing herself. Or them.

Darith climbs out of the car and hoicks down his bag. 'Maybe it would be better if I come back with you, Fiona?'

Mum waves him on to the hire car. 'Sure, sure.'

They try to call Ash and we watch as they become hysterical. Rochelle sizes me up. 'You don't seem very concerned.'

'It's not even the end of the holidays.' I shrug away my urge to weep again. I'm so tired of crying. 'And she might not have smelled his feet yet. He'll probably be back by the end of the week.'

Only Darith laughs.

When we're finally ready to leave, I run to Shearwater and lay my cheek against the nameplate by the front door. I kiss it.

CHAPTER 10

'February twenty-seventh: Audition Day for anyone that cares,' I say when I take my breakfast tray from Mum. 'Thank you kindly.'

'Right,' she says tightly. She's been dressed more like her pre-divorce self since we began 'camping' at the Wangs' Fitzroy 'city pad' while she finalises 'wresting Shearwater from Simon's evil clutches'. I think it's partly to appease Mrs Wang's horror that we're moments away from living on the streets, no matter how much Mum assures her that we're not even close.

My mother took the news about the baby, delivered over the telephone, pretty well.

Well, I say she took the news pretty well but what I mean is she repeatedly slammed the receiver so hard she cracked Mrs Wang's black Bakelite rotary dial 1950s wall phone right off the wall.

But she hasn't run. If anything, she seems even more determined to become a success.

'I'll leave it to you to decide what to wear. Don't forget, we're picking up Louise on the way so we have to leave early. Your friend's here,' she calls on her way out and my heart leaps but it's Suyin, still yawning.

'Good morning.' She gestures to my mother's selected wardrobe like an infomercial assistant. 'I've been instructed to recommend these. Are you nervous? Your mother's right – you want to make a good impression.'

'Jacqueline du Pré always wore a dress,' I complain. 'I wear a dress when I play at school.'

'But that's different – it's like the bikini versus undies phenomena. Clothes are a social construct.'

Suyin looks pretty much the same and maybe I do too, even with my new hairstyle, but Richard and Bodhi are stamped on me just as surely as Suyin's tattoo is stamped on her: in the skin; even if I got rid of the invisible ink of them, there'd be a scar. Maybe I *should* hide myself away under the shapeless, conservative clothes to which Suyin is gesturing with disturbing enthusiasm.

'Are you all right?' she asks, dropping her infomercial to sit next to me on the bed.

'Socrates says men like Richard find no one to guide them through the journey of the dead,' I tell her, because this idea is pleasing and appeases my ravenous thirst for violent revenge. Sometimes I dream about stabbing him.

'Good. What a creep.' Suyin leans away from me to bare her teeth to the mirror. 'At least he's been sacked from *World's Next Champion*.'

'Yeah, but he won that TV award and everyone applauded him like nothing had happened. When he said he'd had a "difficult year" I wanted to throw up.'

'But really—' She makes her most disparaging 'are you serious' face. 'Best Guest Actor in a Reality Show?'

My phone buzzes. It's Ash.

Smash the audition. Dana says Glitter like the
Pleiades on a Clear Summer Night ha ha — I say
don't talk too much and keep your eye on the
ball.

I settle myself with a bit of left nostril breathing and imagine myself under the eternal dome of that starlit sky with the shearwaters flying in. The horrible things that happened aren't the only patterns stamped into the skin of me.

It feels like an act of courage to slip on a flowered cotton dress that falls just above my knee. 'I love playing cello in this dress,' I say, pulling out my Doc Martens.

'Fine with me.' Suyin returns to the mirror and runs her tongue over her teeth. 'Just tell them I tried. What's your opinion on the tooth tattoo?'

'A fantastic idea. Not.'

'And by the way,' she warns, 'you're not Jacqueline du Pré.'

I slump but Suyin pulls me up to standing. 'You don't have to be her,' she says firmly. 'You just have to be *you*.'

When Mum opens the door to find Darith on the doorstep she sighs with an exaggerated sadness. 'I'm sorry,' she says gently. 'Ash still isn't home.'

'Hi, Fiona.' He nods past her and beams my smile right back at me. 'I'm here to see Van.'

Mum steps aside with all the wooden stiffness of Ashton in the spotlight in his Year Eleven play and I pull Darith through.

We hug and I know it's only meant to be a quick and friendly one but all the parts of me fit into all the parts of him and the electricity is like a magnet sucking us together. When we pull apart, me stepping back into Roger Federer who yips, Mum looks like she's been clubbed.

Suyin is hanging on to her hysterics by a bare thread. She grabs her own mother by the arm and manhandles her out the front door. 'We'll see you there,' she calls. 'Come on, Mum.'

'Let me go!' says Mrs Wang but Suyin doesn't and I can see them talking ten to the dozen in the front seats of their car.

'Nice plaits,' Darith says.

If Dr Skutenko thinks bare legs or me holding hands with a Year Twelve boy is inappropriate, she makes no comment. She welcomes me politely, distant, but then her sure, warm hand is on my cheek, my hair, and she says, 'Stand up straight.' She looks over my program and raises an eyebrow. 'So, you're determined to persevere with the Mendelssohn.'

'It's in me,' I say. 'Body and soul.'

'Well,' she says, affectionately banishing a stray hair from my shoulder with a twist of her elegant fingers before shooing Darith off to wait with the rest of the family. 'Let us see.'

ACKNOWLEDGEMENTS

Jodie Webster, Sophie Splatt & Matariki Williams (A&U)
Thank you, Sophie, for your fine editing.
Special thanks to Jodie for your developmental advice in the early stages
and general lovely encouragement and belief in me.

Thanks to the most excellent Melissa Keil, for your kind words.
And to the truly fabulous Cath Crowley and Readings Carlton
for launching the book.

Cultural sensitivity consultant: Hannah Presley.
Inaugural First Nations curatorial assistant at the 2017
Venice Biennale, Hannah curates the Yalingwa program at the
Australian Centre for Contemporary Art. She focusses on creative
projects with Aboriginal artists, learning about the techniques,
history and community that inform their making.
Thank you, darling Hannah, for your professionalism, keen eye, and
friendship. I cannot express how much I have valued your light touch
and courage-giving love for all the characters in the book.

Cultural sensitivity reader: Blayne Welsh; Indigenous Australian
actor and theatre creative whose ancestors come from Wailwan
Country in Central New South Wales.
Thanks for your invaluable contribution to the character of Darith,
who just happens to be Indigenous.

The Boon Wurrung Foundation, & Victorian Aboriginal Corporation for Languages (VACL).

Kate Richards and Susie Thatcher
Thank you, beautiful writers, for your sage advice in helping me to portray Van's musical process.

Teen reader: Taya Strahan ♥

Graeme Burgan (& the Phillip Island Nature Parks).
Thanks, Graeme, for taking me to the rookery and sharing your passion for shearwaters.
Thanks also to my beachy folk: Paula, Phil & James; Jenni & Sally; & Kimina Lyall.

Varuna, the National Writers' House; Jansis O'hanlon, Biff Ward, Gina Mercer & Nicole Crowe.

The writerly encouragement and friendship of the most excellent Lucy Treloar, Trish Bolton, JM Green & Dana Miltins; Leah George, Dr Jacinda Woodhead & Elizabeth Reichhardt. Thanks also to my brilliant colleagues at RMIT PWE Associate Degree for your example and inspiration: Penny Johnson, Stephanie Holt, Dr Olga Lorenzo, Elizabeth Steele, Dzintra Boyd, Dr Ania Walwicz, Yannick Thoraval, Fiona Scott-Norman, Dr Deborah Robertson, Ilka Tampke, Dr Rachel Matthews & Clare Renner; and to my lovely students from whom I've learned so much.

Love and thanks for putting up with me to my dearest friends-and-family, especially Mum and Dad (of course) and Georgia and Archer John – lights of my life; and to my brother, Peter, because he missed out last time.

ABOUT THE AUTHOR

Clare Strahan is a Melbourne writer who lives in the beautiful Upper Yarra Ranges with her dogs and cats, and sometimes her daughter and grandson too. When she's not having cups of tea with her family and friends, she writes, and teaches creative writing at RMIT in the PWE Associate Degree. Clare loves nature, having a good laugh, Shakespeare, old poets, ancient mythology, and reading novels and creative nonfiction. Her favourite place to write is Varuna, the National Writers' House in the Blue Mountains, NSW. She is currently working on another YA novel and undertaking a Master in Writing for Performance at the Victorian College of the Arts (Melbourne Uni). *The Learning Curves of Vanessa Partridge* is her second book. Her debut, *Cracked*, was shortlisted for the 2015 Ethel Turner Prize for Young People's Literature in the NSW Premier's Literary Awards and she was pretty chuffed about that.

Like Van's favourite words snag in her mind, beloved books, poetry and plays snag in Clare's. Here are a few that inspired her while writing this work: Alfred, Lord Tennyson, *Morte d'Arthur*; Plato, *The Republic*; Rainer Maria Rilke, *Letters to a Young Poet*; Virgil, *The Georgics: Book IV* 'Orpheus and Eurydice'; William Shakespeare, *Romeo and Juliet, The Tempest, Macbeth, Hamlet, King Lear*; Emily Brontë, *Wuthering Heights*; Charlotte Brontë, *Jane Eyre*; J. R. R. Tolkien, *The Hobbit, The Lord of the Rings*; Enid Blyton, *The Folk of the Faraway Tree*; C. S. Lewis, The Chronicles of Narnia; Lewis Carroll, *Alice's Adventures in Wonderland*; L. M. Montgomery, *Anne of Green Gables*.